The Old Goat and the Alien

Veo Corva

Published by Witch Key Fiction, 2024.

First published in 2024 by Witch Key Fiction
EPUB ISBN: 978-1-7394742-3-2
Print ISBN: 978-1-7394742-2-5
Veo Corva
Website: https://veocorva.xyz
Witch Key Fiction
Website: https://witchkeyfiction.xyz
Cover art by Meg James
Website: https://meg-james.com/
Proofread by Nicole Evans | Thoughts Stained With Ink
Website: https://thoughtsstainedwithink.com/
Sensitivity Read by Sarah Washington
Many thanks to the supporters of the
The Old Goat and the Alien Kickstarter campaign.

Table of Contents

For Joh. You make me believe I can do this.

Chapter One

Humans often say that they are made of stardust. Perhaps that's why we cosmorans feel a kinship with them, because cosmorans are made of star*fire*. It sits above our brows, vari-coloured balls of ever-burning flame. It is our soul, our intelligence, and it powers our world. It gives us life and shape. From the moment we hatch, it ignites, and it does not go out until we die.

Sometimes I wondered whether there was dust in my core instead of fire. If my flame was illusory, lacking in some essential way. I never wondered more so than when I was with my family.

As I was now. I tuned my family out. I focused only on the world passing through the canopy-glider's green-tinted crystal window. Four-winged musebirds darted curiously around the glider's broad solar wings. I couldn't hear them, but I knew the vibration of their long tail-feathers would sing a sweet song. Below, I caught a glimpse of the spines of a large volleybeast through the thick golden canopy, its six legs all equipped with heavy claws that let it dig burrows as easily as it climbed trees. It was early yet, and the heartstar had barely begun its ascent into the sky, the horizon tinged pink before bleeding into its customary purple. The floor of the canopy-glider hummed beneath my hooves.

'Avari?' My little brother, Lur, pawed at my natural foreleg, short claws scraping against my cloven hoof. His eyes, amber brown and sparkling with starlight, were concerned. 'We're here.'

'Huh? Oh.' I shook myself, my thick fur ruff spinning. Where my brother was a blue fox, only a head shorter than me, I was a tall, fat goat with chestnut fur and large horns that swept to the sides and up. While my brother's starfire tended to rest on a warm yellow flame, mine rested magenta-pink, and flickered anxiously at the edges.

The canopy-glider landed with a slight judder, causing me to stagger a bit, though none of my siblings had such problems. I used my starfire to adjust the positioning of my prosthetic foreleg. It was always a bit slow to react, but I couldn't help but think if I placed it slightly better, the connection might speed up. The blue lights between every joint blinked cheerfully at me, the forgetech clearly functional. Just not as functional as I'd like.

We all bustled off the canopy-glider and down the ramp. One of my mothers, Teera, inclined her head in thanks to the gull-shape pilot, who waved a friendly wing in return.

Our family were the only passengers but we'd crowded it, regardless. There were my mothers, Teera and Nova, a large blue lizard with a ponderous pace and a griffin with night-black feathers. It had been a century at least since they'd had to actually supervise any of us, and as the eldest, I'd been a mature adult for a hundred years, and all five of my siblings were adults as well. But I still noticed Teera watching the twins anxiously, as if she expected them to run off and get lost.

It wasn't an entirely unreasonable concern. Though Lur and Bloom had both long been adults, whenever they met up, they seemed to get into trouble. Teera always blamed it on them being born under The Split Tail, but most people knew that starsigns dictating personality was nonsense. Studies had proven, again and again, that the stars only affected our shapes.

Now, Bloom, a silver-grey raccoon with a resting white starfire, whispered something to Lur. They both giggled and threw a sly look at Nova, who was already marching ahead, her feather-tufted tail sweeping the leaf-litter as she walked.

The forest around us was thick. Vines climbed the trees, just starting to luminesce in the fading light. Through the clearing in the canopy we'd landed in, I could see the lesser moon, Crystallo, bright and glittering as it made its slow way toward the enormous shape of Profundus, the twin planet to our own.

Auspicious sky for a fateful night. I knew I should feel pleased—and I did, I really did—but anxiety still curled sickly in my belly. I took a last look at the canopy-glider as it folded its webbed forgetech wings and then I took off after the rest of my family.

We picked a lazy path through the trees. We didn't need any better guide than Profundus, blue and familiar in the sky. Lur and Bloom laughed and bumped shoulders, always pleased to be reunited. Teera talked animatedly to Nova, who nodded and smiled shyly, as if they hadn't been partnered for centuries beyond memory.

The families that made this journey were rarely as large as ours. Nova and Teera had been extraordinarily blessed to have four (later revealed to be six) kits. It was almost unheard of; most partners were lucky to have a single kit, if they ever did. It was a mystery of the Flowering Ancient that they'd been chosen for more. And with another on the way...

'Cheer up, Avari. Anyone would think you're going to a funeral, and not your sibling's hatching day!' The last of my siblings, Frost, nudged me with one of their heads. Frost was the eldest after me, and a chimaera besides. They were a plural system of three interdependent people—Storm, the goat head, Night, the snake head, and Illusion, the crow head. They were even taller than I was, with long necks and elegant leonine-and-deer-like legs. They had a single starfire which rested blue and hovered above Night's head.

'I am cheerful,' I told them, though even I wasn't completely convinced.

Storm flicked one ear back and raised their eyebrows, but none of Frost contested it out loud. I was sure their inner commentary spoke something else entirely.

They kept me company for the rest of the journey, pacing comfortably at my side. At times, my mothers would come to speak to me and I would tell them I was excited, and nod and bare my teeth in a smile. Lur, full of energy, raced ahead and then back to us repeatedly. It made me tired just watching him, but he showed no signs of slowing down, even though he was making the journey several times longer in pawsteps.

Something heavy landed on my back. 'Bah!' I jumped, stiff-legged, and craned my head around.

Bloom waved at me, laughing softly. 'Gets you every time.'

'Aren't you too old for rides?'

Bloom shrugged and leaned forward, resting her chin atop my head and draping her arms across my horns. 'You can take it.'

She was nearly as big as I was and heavy to boot. I grumbled under my breath but didn't try to unseat her. For one, she would absolutely try to cling on, and as she had hands, she had a pretty good chance of doing it. Lur had always been much easier to unseat. For another, I *could* take it. Goat-shapes

3

like me could take a lot of weight, and for all my forgetech leg could be a little unreactive sometimes, it was just as sturdy as the rest of me.

I flicked my tail dismissively. 'We're supposed to walk to the hatching ceremony,' I said. 'It's a whole tradition. Supposed to bring us closer together with each other and nature or something.'

Bloom tugged on my ear absently and I resisted the urge to bite her. 'I already have leaves in my fur, so I'd say I'm pretty close to nature, and it'd be hard to be any closer to you than riding you.' She yawned and slumped against my neck. 'Doesn't this remind you of when we were kits?'

Memories flashed through my mind. Bloom and Lur climbing all over me while I ran and leapt, making them shriek with glee. Bloom tying Lur to my back with a rope. Leaping up a tree to get Bloom when she climbed too high to get back down.

It was a long time ago, now. They were good memories. And they'd started with a hatching ceremony journey to the Flowering Ancient, just like this one.

'It does remind me of that,' I said. I'd been anxious during that journey as well, and look how it had turned out. Two new siblings and we'd all made it to adulthood in one piece, more or less.

We lapsed into silence. I couldn't quite stop my ears twitching nervously, and it wasn't long before Bloom slid from my back and ran off to pester Nova.

'You're anxious,' said Frost, falling in beside me. It was Illusion physically speaking to me, her sparkling crow eyes shrewd, but I could usually tell when it was all of Frost talking to me. The others threw casual looks my way but seemed content to let Illusion be their voice.

'And what else is new?' I said. 'I'll cope.'

Illusion's eyes crinkled in a grin. 'If you're well enough to snap at me, you probably will,' she teased. 'Storm wants to go play with Lur for a bit, but if you need us, we're around, okay?'

'Yeah. Thanks.' I tried and failed to smile, but at least managed to settle my ears in a more hopeful position and steady my starfire a bit. 'Have fun.'

'I will,' said Storm. They winked at me. 'You should try it sometime!'

Before I could retort, they bounded off after Lur.

I tried not to brood on that. I knew it had been jokingly meant. But it had to be said, I wasn't a very playful person. I liked to have everything in its place and know exactly what I'd be doing in a day. And while I had played with my siblings when we were younger and loved doing it, that felt like a very long time ago. Lur and Bloom might be only a decade into their adulthood, but I'd been an adult for a hundred years.

I was starting to feel it.

Instead, I focused on the world around me. The journey was about connecting with nature, wasn't it? I took in the forest. It was very different from Lost Circle, the city I called home. There, the largest of trees might have been shaped to hold a shop, or a café, or a home. There, the fireflies made the sunset sparkle, and each building glittered faintly with forgetech like jewels among the canopy.

Here, there were no buildings and no sign of civilization but the muddied forest path we walked, in the same hoofsteps as countless cosmorans before us. This was the Elder Grove, the blessed forest of the Flowering Ancient, and I could see the touch of the Ancient everywhere; from the warm golden sheen of the tree trunks and leaves, to the large roots that briefly surfaced here and there in shining arcs. It was humbling to witness, even if I'd done so a handful of times already. I wondered how long it would be until the Ancient itself came into view.

The wildlife, at least, was uncaring of the sacredness of the occasion. I heard musebirds calling to each other in long, swooping trills. Cloudmice darted across the forest floor in twos and threes, their cheeks full of nuts and fruit. And there were eyes watching us from the trees, too—three-eyed birds and six-legged squirrels and big, beautiful insects with wings like flowers, chirping to each other and swaying from branch to branch in the hopes of convincing predators they were no more than the plants they resembled. All starfire-less, of course—only cosmorans had the flames that marked us as kin of the Ancients.

And there would be a new starfire kindled today. A new member of our fire's line. Maybe a new friend, as the others had been. I felt a sudden surge of hopefulness, powerful enough to force the anxiety back just a little. Heady with it, I bleated and kicked up my hooves and plunged deeper into the Elder

Grove, just a little off the path, just enough to feel the Flowering Ancient's life-giving power all around me.

It felt surprisingly good to have the tall grass and shrubs brushing my fur. Those that bore flowers sent up clouds of glittering spores at the touch. I breathed in the smell of it, the fresh, sweet floral scent. This was good.

A small lizard skittered to a stop in front of me and up my forgetech leg. I paused, not wanting to crush its tiny toes in the machine-work. It was bright blue and had six legs and two pairs of eyes, a tiny, delicate thing.

I know I can be grumpy and set in my ways, but I was content to watch the small creature choosing to use me as a tree to cling to. I didn't mind that it was slowing me down. It was easy to become desensitised to wildlife, but at that moment, I wanted to really take it in.

The lizard shifted so that its toes were free of the joints of my leg. I smiled down at it, ears perking forward, and lifted my leg slightly to get a closer look. 'Hello.'

It blinked at me, head tilting to one side, but didn't flee. Maybe it was very brave, or maybe I didn't bear much resemblance to any of its predators. I wasn't worried that it was venomous; very little could envenom cosmorans. Our cores ran too hot and fierce.

I wondered if it would let me pick it up properly with starfire, but I didn't want to frighten it.

There was a loud crunching of undergrowth being rushed through. Nova burst from between the bushes, looking stern. The lizard fled, disappearing into the leaf mulch of the forest floor too quickly to follow. I frowned after it, my ears falling.

Nova strode over to me, shuffling her wings. Her tufted tail flicked a little too tensely for my liking. 'Avari. What are you doing off the path?'

'There was a lizard,' I said. I looked at the ground where it had disappeared, but there was no flash of blue or rustle in the leaves.

Nova came up beside me and laid a wing over my back, pulling me close. She bumped her beak against my muzzle affectionately, but her nearness was overwhelming. I tried to pull away, but her wing had me pinned. 'Are you all right, darling?' she asked.

'I'm fine.' I tried to pull away again.

She leaned close. 'You're not going to have another...episode?'

'I'm fine,' I repeated.

'Don't ruin this, darling,' she said. 'I don't think Teera could take it. Everyone's noticed you aren't smiling.'

I wasn't a smiler, truthfully. My emotions crashed within me. I didn't know how I had gone so quickly from that brief joy and sense of wonder to this painful smallness. Why did everyone think I would ruin everything? Why did my own *mother* feel the need to press me like this?

I felt tears well up at the unfairness of it. Voice thick, I said, 'Mum, I—I—'

She released me. 'I don't want to fight, darling. You should get back to the group.' She wouldn't look at me, already pretending she hadn't caused this. She disappeared back through the undergrowth and onto the path.

My heart thumped in my chest. I could feel my starfire raging and ragged. I felt the powerful urge to flee, or to scream. Tears ran down my cheeks.

I didn't do anything wrong, I wanted to say. But my mother had already left, and if I brought it up to her, if I tried to seek closure, she would cry and say I was ruining this important day.

Was I? Ruining the day? Would my sibling be hatched into tension and bitterness instead of welcoming joy, like they deserved?

I huddled in on myself, my chest tight, my pulse racing, feeling a desperate urge to run but also being completely rooted to the spot. I had been right to be anxious. This trip was as bad as I could have imagined.

There was a loud crash and a strange cry like no animal I'd ever heard. My anxiety shifted, and I tensed. There were plenty of large forest-dwelling creatures that could hurt a cosmoran. I needed to be careful. But there was something about the cry that struck me; I could sense distress in it. And I couldn't bring myself to return to the path where my mothers waited.

I went toward the sound. Cautiously, though I couldn't exactly sneak. People with hooves tend to struggle with that sort of thing, and it's only worse with leaves crunching with each step. I pushed through the bushes and peered around a tree.

A bald, brown face stared back at me. It screamed, baring flat white teeth. I screamed in return and scrambled back, the bush scratching my fur. I stumbled in my haste, landing on my rump. The animal in front of me tripped and landed on its back. It was breathing hard, clearly just as panicked

7

as I was. I got a hold of myself and stood back up, heedless of the dirt and leaves streaking my fur. It was wearing clothes. It wasn't an animal, it was—

The human sat up, pressing a hand to their chest, and met my eyes. There were no stars in their gaze, only a warm, dark brown with surprising depth, as earthy as their planet was named. They said something, but I didn't understand the words, which came through to me as static over noise.

'Keep talking,' I encouraged them, trying to keep my voice steady even as my core pulsed with leftover panic. My starfire would translate this human once we'd made a proper acquaintance. I'd just never encountered a human before.

They couldn't possibly understand me, but they swallowed hard and said something else. '—here—a portal—'

'You came through a portal?' Ahh, the visa program. There weren't so many humans on Viridus yet that it was common, but I'd heard that was going to change. 'Can you understand me?' I asked them. Her, actually. As the connection grew a little clearer, I understood that this was a human woman.

She had something clasped in her other hand. I hesitated, then nudged it with my nose, encouraging her to show me. It was a small black com-gem, the starfire inside it a faint, swirling glimmer waiting for activation.

She was watching me carefully, her eyes wide with shock or fear, but she didn't pull away.

I picked up the com-gem with starfire and inserted it gently into her ear. She flinched and cried out, but it was fixed in place now.

I cleared my throat. 'Can you understand me now?' I asked.

Her mouth popped open. 'I—yes! Oh thank god—I have no idea where I am. You're cosmoran, right?'

I thought about the unused com-gem and how far we were from the nearest settlement. What was a human doing here? Why had she taken the com-gem out? 'Where did you come from?'

She stood up and I backed up a few steps. She brushed leaves from her blue dress. She wore leggings underneath. Her dark brown hair was in a long braided tail that came down across her shoulder, and her skin was a golden brown. She was a round human—fat like me, I guessed. When I had learned about humans, all the images of them had been much leaner than she was. 'I came through...I can only describe it as a portal,' she said. 'A swirling, starry light appeared in the split trunk of an old tree, and when I touched it, it pulled me through and put me here. Maybe...I don't know. Ten minutes ago? Twenty? I didn't know where to go, but then I heard you and saw the light.' She gestured to my flame.

She was a new immigrant. I ground my teeth from side to side, working through what that meant. The first and most obvious thing was that it made her my responsibility, and that was *definitely* not something I wanted to deal with right now. No wonder she hadn't been wearing her com-gem...

'That's the current immigration protocol for Earth,' I said. 'I don't remember why, but it was decided portals were better than space travel.'

She ran a hand down her hair-tail. 'Some warning would have been nice.'

'You didn't apply for a visa?'

She shrugged. 'I did. I just...didn't expect it to work like this.' She hesitated, then stuck out her hand toward me, the other still crossing her chest. 'I'm Jenna, by the way.'

I wasn't sure what to do with the hand. I didn't know much about humans.

'It's a handshake,' she said, her hand starting to fall. 'Sorry...that's probably not how you greet people here.' She looked embarrassed. And as annoyed as I was to be saddled with a newly-arrived human, I didn't want her to feel *bad* or anything.

I extended my natural hoof and touched her hand with it. 'I'm Avari,' I said, a little gruffly because this whole situation was ridiculous.

She laughed and gave it a gentle bob up and down before releasing it. 'How do cosmorans greet each other?'

I sniffed toward her, extending my neck and bobbing my head very slightly so she could clearly tell what I was doing. She smelled of strange air and chemicals and also an oddly floral musk. It wasn't unpleasant, but was unlike any scent I'd come across before.

Well. She was an alien, I supposed.

She frowned. 'You sniff?'

I nodded. 'Just the air, toward each other.'

She bobbed her head toward me, nostrils flaring. It looked quite ridiculous. 'Like this?'

I snorted. 'Close enough.'

'So,' she said, shifting from foot to foot. 'Do you know where I'm supposed to go now, or...?'

'Avari!' Three voices called. Frost emerged from between the trees. Beside me, Jenna audibly sucked in her breath. Was she going to be surprised by every cosmoran? Were all humans like this?

'Avari, Teera's noticed you're gone and is starting to fret, so—wait.' Frost stopped. Each of their heads held a different expression: Storm looked delighted, Night wary, Illusion shocked. 'Is that a human?' asked Storm.

'Evidently,' I said, unable to keep the sarcasm from my voice.

Jenna gave a tiny wave. 'Hi.'

'Well, introduce us!' said Night. All three heads sniffed toward Jenna, who sniffed a little dramatically back.

'We only just *met*,' I grumbled. I nodded from Jenna to Frost. 'Jenna, these are my siblings, Frost. They're plural. Humans can be plural, right?'

Jenna nodded, still staring at Frost with something I was starting to think might be awe. 'It's...it's a pleasure to meet you,' she said.

Storm beamed at her. 'Likewise! Well, we're actually in the middle of something right now, so I'm afraid I must take Avari from you—'

'Frost,' I said tiredly. 'They're a new arrival.'

Frost blinked three pairs of eyes. 'How new? Like *new,* new?'

'Ten minutes lost in the Elder Grove kind of new.' I said the words a little begrudgingly, knowing it would only tie this human to me until I could get her to the proper authorities.

'Oh. Oh!' Illusion leaned forward and studied her more closely. Jenna looked a little nervous. I suppose Illusion's long, sharp beak might have made her look like a predator to something as small as a human. 'Well, you must come with us, then! This is a fortuitous meeting, don't you think, Avari? A traveller met on the road to the hatching ceremony?'

'Hatching ceremony?' Jenna asked uncertainly, but Frost curved their necks around her and ushered her back to the path.

'Don't worry,' said Storm. 'We'll sort you out very soon. Avari, come on!'

Jenna threw me a pleading look over her shoulder.

I sighed heavily and followed them back to my family.

There was a lot of fuss over the appearance of a human. Bloom immediately attached herself to Jenna, rapidly firing questions about her planet while Lur watched them raptly, his eyes alight with interest. Nova and Teera both welcomed Jenna with what I thought was genuine warmth. A boon traveller met on the road was generally seen as a good omen on a hatching day. For that traveller to be a human was, as far as I knew, completely unheard of. I could see Nova puffing herself up with pride over it. Both mothers promised Jenna she would be settled as soon as the hatching ceremony was over.

Jenna, for her part, seemed more than a little dazed but happy enough to have found herself among an excitable family.

I walked a little behind the group, watching them all talking and laughing but not feeling able to join in myself, or even sure how I would.

Frost nudged my shoulder. 'Don't abandon her,' they said.

I shrugged and flicked an ear back. 'I'm right here.'

'You're the first person she met on Geminus,' said Frost. All three pairs of eyes watched me reproachfully—even Night, who usually took my side on things like this. 'She's just had everything she knows change rapidly. She needs consistency for a little while.'

Frost was a guardian, a career that focused on legal proceedings. It was very like them to insist on responsibility and care, which was a large part of what they did.

I put both my ears back. 'I'm *right here,'* I repeated, and Storm blew air at me while Illusion rolled her eyes. They trotted ahead to walk with Teera, their tail raising a cloud in the dirt behind them.

I brooded for a bit—I didn't like people telling me what to do, and I was used to Frost taking my side—then reluctantly moved up to join Jenna and her admirers.

'Are all humans as small as you?' asked Bloom. Bloom was only a little taller than the human when standing on her hind legs, but was significantly broader. It had to be said that Jenna *did* look small. A spindly thing compared to most cosmorans, even with her healthy padding of fat.

'I'm average height,' she replied. 'So...yeah, I guess! Though some are shorter. And a lot are thinner.'

Bloom hooted her delight at this and ran a quick circle around Jenna to let out her feelings, striped tail trailing like a fluffy pennant. 'And I heard Earth has starsigns, too,' said Bloom. 'Is it true you are all the same shape, no matter what stars you're born under?'

Jenna looked a little surprised. 'Well—some people think that starsigns affect personalities, but no, it doesn't change how we look. Does it change how *you* look?'

Bloom clapped her hands together. 'Some people think that here as well!'

Lur asked quietly, 'Do you have any siblings?'

Jenna stiffened, her shoulders going tight. 'Uh, well—' She stopped, seeming to struggle to find the words. Lur and Bloom watched raptly.

I shouldered between Bloom and Jenna. 'Let me talk to Jenna for a bit. Go bother Frost or something.'

'We already *know* Frost,' said Bloom, her ears completely flat against her head. 'I want to talk to—'

Lur nudged her shoulder. 'I think maybe she wants space, Bloom.'

'But—'

'Come on.' He herded his twin away.

I looked at Jenna. Her chin was down, her mouth trembling. She was a little hard to read, without mobile ears or a tail or even any feathers, but I didn't think she was comfortable. I decided to change the subject. That usually helped me when I got caught out like that. 'So,' I said. 'You've met my siblings.'

'Cute kids,' said Jenna, giving me a faint smile. She still looked a little lost.

'Oh, they're adults,' I said. 'They're sixty years old. Bloom is just a terror, that's all.'

'Sixty?' Jenna chewed her lip and looked away. 'How old are you, then?'

'Me? I'm a hundred and fifty-ish. Eldest sibling. My mothers—Nova and Teera, over there? We're not even sure how old they are. They can't remember; the fog, you know. That happens after a certain point, for cosmorans.'

'A hundred and fifty!' said Jenna. 'So you're an old goat!' She suddenly clapped her hands over her mouth, eyes widening.

There was some meaning there that was missing me. 'Old goat? But I'm not old.'

'It's a human saying,' said Jenna. She looked...embarrassed, maybe? 'It means cantankerous. Grumpy. But old, too, I guess. I'm sorry, I didn't mean anything by it.'

Sometimes I felt old beyond my years. Especially when Bloom was pulling on my mane. Something about the idea pleased me, in spite of its technical inaccuracy.

'How old are you?' I asked.

She crossed her arms and looked thoughtful. 'I'm forty,' she said. 'You must think I'm a child.'

'Not really,' I said. 'Well, maybe a little? But different species mature at different rates, you know? It'd be unfair to call you a kit. Forty is adult for humans, too, right?'

'Some people even call it "middle-aged",' she said. The word had static around it and I couldn't quite hold onto it.

'What was that word again? What people call it?'

'Middle-aged?' she said again, but I still couldn't make sense of it. 'It means half-way through your life.'

I nodded, but I didn't know what to say to that. There was a time limit on human lives? For a sentient species with stardust in their bones? 'Humans live eighty years?'

'Well...not any more. We typically live to a hundred and twenty now, and they're developing something to stop ageing but...well, it was middle-aged for a long time so I guess it stuck.' She shrugged.

I considered this. 'You do kind of look like a kit, though,' I said. 'All bald and round like that.'

About a second after I said it, I realised it was probably a rude thing to say, but Jenna laughed, a hand going to her mouth. 'I guess I do,' she said. 'Humans don't even think we're bald if we have hair up here.' She touched her head.

It was, I had to admit, nice to make somebody laugh. Especially somebody who'd looked pretty panicked a little while ago.

She stumbled and I immediately reached out with starfire to catch her and help right her. A magenta glow suffused her and leaned her back onto her feet.

She stared at her hands as the starfire vanished. 'Woah. That was you?'

I nodded. 'Just starfire. All cosmorans can move things like that.'

Her eyes went to the flame above my head. 'It's like magic,' she said quietly, as if to herself.

'Not magic,' I said. 'Just nature.'

She still seemed a little awed. It made me feel uncomfortable, like someone was stunned to see me take a step or pick a fruit. I hadn't done anything noteworthy.

I lapsed into silence, not sure what to say from there, but Jenna didn't seem to mind. We walked in silence apart from whenever Bloom got away from her brother's watch long enough to pelt Jenna with a new question. At last, the Elder Grove opened up. Luminous butterflies fluttered past as we gazed up at a golden tree so large its canopy blotted out the sky like a vast golden crown.

Jenna inhaled so sharply I could hear it. 'What's that?' she asked.

I heard my mothers cry out in excitement. Several of my relations started running.

'That's the Flowering Ancient,' I said. 'That's where we are hatched.'

And where soon, I would meet my new sibling.

My chest felt tight with anticipation, but for once I felt more wonder than anxiety. I bleated a cry as well and kicked into a run.

Chapter Two

The Flowering Ancient. The eldest and largest tree on all of Viridus. Its bark was smooth and golden, its leaves shining and veined with light. It was almost large enough to house an entire city, but no-one had ever shaped the Flowering Ancient for such a purpose. It was entirely wild and of its own power, and every one of us owed it our lives. The vast roots that snaked out from the base to plunge into the rich soil were said to run through the core of the planet, and investigation had shown that they went far deeper than our technology could allow us to safely follow.

Seeing it, my heart filled with joy and...peace. A sense of completeness that had been lacking during the journey. Perhaps even my entire life.

I heard Jenna yell behind me. She trotted after us uncertainly. With no wings and only two legs, she couldn't keep up with our pace, and she stumbled often on the uneven ground. While my family raced ahead, I slowed to allow her to keep up with me, though my heart yearned to bound forward toward the Ancient and to bask in its light.

'You're...so fast...' Jenna panted when she caught up with me.

I shrugged, one ear flicking back. Since she already seemed to be out of energy, I matched my pace to hers, still gazing up at the Ancient. Perhaps there was solace to be found in this slow journey as well. To the anticipation of resting beneath its canopy.

'So...what is the Flowering Ancient?' she asked.

I glanced at her, too surprised to be irritated at further interruptions. 'You don't know it?'

She shook her head.

I ruminated on that for a moment, a hint of unease flickering through me. Jenna had been granted leave to travel to and settle on Geminus. That she hadn't bothered to learn anything about us didn't speak well of her. 'The

Flowering Ancient is one half of god,' I said. 'It gives life to cosmorans and nourishes the land on which we live.'

'Oh,' she said. 'And that's why you hatch here? What's the other half of your god?'

I snorted, my irritation growing. 'The Starfire Ancient, whose name is beyond knowing by cosmoran minds. The Starfire Ancient resides on Profundus, and gave us starfire and knowledge. It feeds the waters which allow us to learn, grow, and change. You really ought to know things like this.'

Jenna looked stricken. 'Oh. Sorry, I—'

'Nevermind.' I looked away from her, irritation and guilt making an unpleasant mix in my belly. *She* was the one in the wrong. I didn't see what right she had to be upset at me pointing that out.

'I tried,' Jenna said. 'It was hard to get any information. I kept trying. And this is a lot earlier than I was told I'd get here.' There was a note of frustration in her voice.

I nodded and tried to focus on the Flowering Ancient, on its light and presence. On its beautiful, relaxing scent. Jenna fell silent, and I was able to put her from my mind, though I remained at her side.

As we approached the base of the trunk, I saw my family fanned out and waiting for us. Two figures in hooded white cloaks waited with them: the Flowering Servants. Indeed, as we approached, I could see the moss and flowers that sprung from their fur and scales as if it had grown there, their cloaks not quite obscuring the changes their role had brought on them.

'Is this the last of your party?' asked the first Servant, a tiger with grey fur and silver stripes.

'These are the last,' said Teera. 'My kit, and a boon traveller met on the road.'

'A boon traveller?' The second Servant—a brilliant orange-and-black gecko—approached Jenna and sniffed politely toward her, tongue tasting the air. Jenna hesitated and sniffed back toward him.

'Uh, hi,' said Jenna.

'You are most welcome,' said the gecko Servant warmly. 'Now, come.' He turned to face the group, his thick tail sweeping the ground. 'The path is not easy, but the fruit is very sweet.'

THE OLD GOAT AND THE ALIEN

The pair set off up a narrow whorl of wood against the trunk that formed something like a path, and my parents followed, with the rest of my siblings behind. Frost hovered at the back. 'Jenna, can you climb?' they asked. 'You don't have claws that I can see, and it must be hard to balance on two legs...'

'Oh. Uh. A bit, I guess,' she said. 'How much climbing is there?'

'It's just a bit steep,' I said. 'You might have to scramble up a few ledges, depending on where exactly we're going.' To Frost, I said, 'She has hands. She'll be fine.'

'That's a big assumption,' said Frost. To Jenna, they asked gently, 'Are you tired? Will you need any help? You're quite big, but I think together we could lift you with starfire over anything too high. And if you like, you can wait at the base of the tree, but we'd love to have you at the hatching ceremony.'

'I'd like to come,' said Jenna. 'And I think I can go up this path all right.' She didn't look that confident, though. In fact, she looked really tired, and maybe a bit ill. She hadn't been so ashen and sweaty when I'd first met her. 'I'm just surprised you want me at the ceremony. Why is everyone so excited about a "boon traveller" at what seems like a family event?'

I snorted. 'It's an old superstition.'

'But a beloved one,' said Frost. Storm and Illusion shot me warning looks, though what they felt like they needed to warn me about I couldn't guess. 'Come on. We'll catch up with the others. Jenna, you follow me, and then Avari will come up behind, so you'll be quite safe. You can hold onto my fur if you need to.'

We started up the path. The others hadn't gotten very far, the Servants setting a sedate pace that even Bloom was forced to follow. The bark of the Ancient clattered beneath my hoofsteps, but Jenna's steps were surprisingly light.

The woody path spiralled up the tree. It seemed to grow smoothly from the Ancient, though none had ever shaped it. The ground fell away as we climbed but I was sure of my footing and surer still of the warm peace and belonging the Ancient radiated. As we went higher, the Ancient started to branch, vast boughs that bore heavy fruit or the gleaming flowers of cosmorans past.

Staring at the back of Jenna's head, separated from my family by a stranger, I reflected bitterly that the 'boon traveller' tradition was a useless one. Why did we want a stranger at the hatching of the newest member of our family? Someone who knew nothing of us or what we'd been through—or in Jenna's case, anything about cosmorans at all? Did she even understand what an honour it was to be present at a hatching ceremony?

'Avari?' Jenna glanced back at me. She walked with one hand on the trunk of the Flowering Ancient, trailing her hand along it like it was keeping her stable. She swayed a bit on her feet. Was she tired? Scared? Ill? 'Is there anything I should know? About the ceremony? I don't want to make an awkward mistake.'

'No,' I said, and caught the harshness of my own voice. I tried again. 'Just stand back when we get there. It'll be fine.'

Still pretty gruff, but Jenna seemed mollified. That only irritated me more. She shouldn't be part of this. It wasn't fate that we found her on the road, it was nothing more than random chance. Obviously the portal she'd taken from her planet had malfunctioned in some way or she'd gone in the wrong direction. Why did that make her *our* responsibility?

A small part of me noted that perhaps I was taking out my anxiety about the ceremony on Jenna, but I squashed that thought real quick. This was about having to kit-watch a random alien, not about me or any of *my* problems.

At least, it certainly felt better to be angry at her about it than it did to think otherwise. You might think that I shouldn't be able to hold that knowledge *and* still maintain my annoyance with Jenna, but denial and stubbornness were always two of my most powerful traits.

We started out along a branch. It was wide enough for two people at a pinch, but still significantly narrower than the path along the trunk, and with no walls to either side. The Servants guided my family along it, but when it came to Jenna, she hesitated.

Frost paused, and Illusion glanced back at her. 'Something the matter?'
'Oh. No,' she said. She flashed a smile. 'I'll be fine.'
Illusion nodded, and Frost followed the rest of the family.
I heard Jenna murmur, 'Come on, Jenna.'
I flicked one ear forward and one to the side, unsure what she meant with all of this. Annoyance still simmered, but a new anxiety had joined the mix.

She took one step, then another. Her arms were held slightly out to each side—for balance? She swayed as if caught in a strong wind.

'You okay?' I asked. I took a few tentative steps forward.

'Totally fine,' Jenna said, but her voice seemed a lot higher than usual.

I hesitated, unsure of what to make of that contradiction.

Jenna whispered, 'Come *on*, Jenna,' and took a few more awkward steps. I followed uncertainly. And then Jenna was falling forward, her legs slipping out from under her, a strangled cry ripping the air.

I lunged forward and caught her dress between my teeth and yanked back. She was heavy, but I was a goat-shape and plenty strong enough. I reached out with starfire to pull her as well, taking hold of her shoulders.

Thanks to me, she landed on her ass and not her face—or the roots of the Flowering Ancient, far below. I released her and trotted around to face her. *I* had no such trouble balancing on a sturdy bit of wood. 'Fog take it! What was that?' I demanded. I stomped a hoof. 'This isn't a tightrope but that doesn't mean you can mess around! If you slip, you haven't got anything to hold on with!' I eyed her clawless hands and flat, hoofless hindpaws.

Her eyes were watery. Her mouth trembled as she looked up at me. 'I fell,' she said. Her voice didn't sound right—was she shocked?

I took a half-step back. I felt utterly unprepared for any of this. Maybe I *was* a mean old goat. 'Look, don't—don't *cry*. I'm sorry I scolded you. You probably wouldn't have slipped off.' I wasn't sure that was true, but her mouth was still wobbling like a bar of sweetfruit jelly. Stars, why did humans have such mobile faces? I didn't think I'd ever *been* as upset as she looked.

'Jenna?' Frost's heads swivelled around to look at us and then they hurried over. 'Avari, what did you do?'

'I didn't do anything!' The accusation stung. It felt like an echo of my mother's earlier words. Did everyone in my family think I ruined everything? Even Frost? 'She slipped. She's a bit shocked, that's all.'

Illusion and Storm leaned in to get a better look at her. Storm gently nudged her shoulder with their muzzle. Illusion studied her quizzically, her movements sharp with nerves. 'She looks all right,' said Illusion.

'Hey,' said Storm gently. 'You're fine. You take as long as you need.'

Jenna nodded, her breath hitching. A tear slipped down her face.

I wanted to point out that we didn't have an infinite amount of time—the others were drawing still further ahead, unaware of our hold-up. And I knew that just like Frost, my mothers would blame me for interrupting the journey, and they would not be as gentle about it either.

But Jenna looked so small and so frightened, and her face was so wet, so I found the words wouldn't come. After a moment's hesitation, I bent my knees and settled down in front of her, to let her know that I wasn't in any rush either. It was a little awkward getting down—my forgetech leg was slow again, and rubbed a nerve unpleasantly. But nothing I wasn't used to.

Jenna's eyes seemed drawn to my movement. She stared at me for a moment, her hitching breath subsiding. I couldn't tell what she was thinking, but then I struggled to read other cosmorans at the best of times, let alone an alien. Frost continued to say soothing things, an entire support network all in themselves. Jenna nodded occasionally and eventually even managed a shaky smile. But her eyes returned to me often. As I had no soothing words, I just continued to sit with her.

When Bloom came scampering back along the path to ask us if everything was okay, Jenna took a shuddering breath and stood up. 'Sorry,' she said. 'I guess I'm not as good with heights as I thought. I won't hold you up any longer.'

Frost offered to walk beside her, but she only shook her head and said she'd be fine on her own. I thought I understood her decision, a little. I wondered if, like me, she worried about being seen as a burden. And besides which, Frost was quite broad and would make the path for her even narrower.

I let her pass me again and followed, keeping a wary eye on her. She didn't put her hands out this time, though I often saw them flex and clench as if she was thinking about it. Sometimes she would glance back at me, her jaw tight and eyes bright.

We caught up with the rest of my family, ranged out across the branch. A large fruit hung just above them. It was beautifully gold, like all the Ancient's fruit and flowers, but this particular one had a faintly pink sheen to it. My pace quickened. The fruit was maybe four feet in diameter, clearly at the height of ripeness. The skin was perfectly smooth, almost metallic, but it was segmented by the petals of the flower it would become.

THE OLD GOAT AND THE ALIEN

The tiger Servant asked, 'Are you ready?' She addressed this to my mothers. Nova put a wing around Teera, drawing her close. Teera nodded. 'We're ready,' she said. Her starfire burned a little brighter, her excitement clear.

The servants bowed to the fruit and then lowered it to our branch using starfire, their flames mixing and shifting in a rainbow of colours. The moment the fruit touched the branch, the skin split and started to crack. The shape of it bulged, as if something inside was shifting or pushing on the edges of it. In spite of my anxiety, in spite of all the strangeness of the day, I felt my own breath catch at the sight of it.

Liquid seeped from between the cracked petal segments, sticky and golden, like honey. And then the skin separated out into petals which peeled back, allowing the inside of the fruit to slough out onto the branch. The Servants released the flower, which sprang gently back, opening into a gorgeous bloom still dripping with nectar.

Beside me, Jenna breathlessly whispered, 'Oh.'

The mound of goo on the floor stirred. My mothers lurched forward and started to clear the nectar with paws and starfire. Between them, I could see flashes of a tiny figure. Narrow hooves, short brown fur. A flash of feathers.

My parents shifted enough that we got a clear view. On the floor, fur still wet with nectar, was a tiny fawn with a faintly pink sheen to her light brown fur, a paler version of my own. Her flanks were speckled with white, and two small wings—brown and white—were folded on her back. Her eyes were closed, and the smallest white candle-flame of starfire hovered above her brow.

Nova preened her ears with her beak while Teera nudged her little flank. Her eyes flickered open and she started to bleat.

'And what name do you give your newborn kit?' asked one of the Servants.

My mothers stared at the little fawn with open adoration. 'Journey,' said Teera, without looking away from her.

The Servants bowed. 'Welcome to Geminus, Journey,' said the other.

As my family crowded in to greet our newest relative, my gaze lifted to the flower shining down on them, still dripping nectar. Just one of many aspects of the Ancients.

I hoped Journey would grow up to be as loved as she was in this moment.

Chapter Three

The journey back thankfully lacked the tension of the journey out. Bloom and Lur walked beside Nova, cooing at the kit, who alternated between staring blearily at them and bleating plaintively. Frost, too, jostled for a chance to walk beside Nova, whispering sweet things to the kit and congratulating our mothers again and again. As for our mothers, they walked with obvious pride and delight, radiating joy in the set of their feathers and the proud tilt of their heads.

I wasn't sure how to manoeuvre in amongst my crowding siblings, though I did want to meet Journey properly. Unable to insert myself beside her, I found myself walking beside Jenna instead.

She was lagging more than ever, her footsteps heavy and shuffling, her gait swaying. Maybe humans found walking difficult? Even with a prosthetic leg, I could keep going for hours on land, but then I had three other legs. Jenna only had two, and no wings or lighter core to compensate.

'Congratulations,' she said breathlessly. 'On the new sibling, I mean.' She hesitated. 'It was an honour to be present.'

I inclined my head, not really sure how to deal with the awkwardness of this conversation. I had no script for discussing the hatching of my sister with an alien. I wasn't sure I had one for cosmorans, either. I suppose I probably should have said thank you or something like that, but those small niceties often evaded me when I was anxious. And I was more anxious than ever now, even without my parents judging me. I felt like an outsider among my own family, and that hit all the harder because my family were all I had.

She looked like speaking had taken a lot out of her. 'Are you...okay?' I asked her.

She smiled like the smile pained her. 'I'm not,' she said. 'I'll just have to manage, though.'

We lapsed into silence. She'd been so chatty earlier, so full of questions, but it was like a spark had gone out in her. We fell further and further behind my family. I hated to see my chance of meeting Journey get away from me, but neither could I leave a lost alien alone on the path. I wondered if I should offer to help somehow, or ask more questions about her condition, but I couldn't see how to do so politely when she'd already said she'd manage.

Eventually, Frost got closed off from our hatchling sister by our enthusiastic younger siblings and made their way back to us. At first, they were smiling, their flame a warm and content orange, but as they neared all three of their gazes fixed on Jenna and their tail started to lash. 'Is everything all right?' asked Illusion. 'You look terribly tired.'

Jenna nodded limply, then, almost as if that motion had wrung the last scrap of energy from her, she sank to the ground. 'I'm so sorry,' she said. 'I just...I need a minute.'

'Of course, take all the time you need,' said Illusion, while Night glared at me.

My ears went back. Why be angry at me? I hadn't made Jenna collapse!

'I'll let the family know to wait at the glider for us,' said Storm. Illusion added, 'Look after Jenna, okay?'

I snorted as Frost turned away, and stomped a hoof to let out my frustrated energy. My mothers hated it when I stomped but something about the motion was really soothing to me. I stomped a few more times because the repetition was nice, then considered Jenna.

If she had any feelings about me stomping, they were lost in deep exhaustion. She stared blankly at the ground from where she sat, legs crumpled, skirts askew, utterly still. She looked like she might melt into a puddle at any moment.

Frost quickly returned. 'They're waiting further up the path,' said Storm. 'Nobody's in any rush.' Illusion lowered her head to peer worriedly at Jenna. 'What would help? Should we stay here awhile? Or do you need to talk? Or healing?'

Jenna took a shuddering breath. 'Sitting here for a bit would help,' she said. Her words were a little sluggish, like she was falling asleep. 'I don't need healing. I just can't... *move*...any more.'

'Okay,' said Frost. 'You take all the time you need.'

Night flicked his tongue at me and gestured for me to step aside. I sighed and followed Frost.

'What?'

Night glanced at Jenna. 'Do you think she can hear us?'

I considered her. She still looked pretty out of it. 'No idea,' I said. 'How sensitive is human hearing?'

'She looks absolutely done in,' said Storm. 'How long has she been struggling?'

I hesitated. 'She started looking pretty tired as we got to the Flowering Ancient.'

'That long ago? Ughh.' Night hissed and shook his head.

'The canopy-glider won't be able to stop here,' said Illusion. 'There's not enough room. Avari, you should let her ride you.'

My fur stood on end. 'What? No!' I stomped a hoof.

'She's your responsibility!' said Storm.

I ground my teeth from side to side. She was a random human I'd stumbled across. A stranger, and an alien besides. 'She can't ride me.'

'Well, we don't exactly have a hoverseat for her or anything,' snapped Night.

'Then *you* let her ride you,' I said, knowing Night would hate that almost as much as I did.

Night glared at me, but Illusion shook her head at him, something silent passing between them. Storm said, 'It can't always be like this.' Then Frost turned around and strode over to her. They spoke quietly for a moment, and then Frost gently lifted Jenna with starfire and placed her on their back. She draped there like a blanket, not even enough strength to sit up.

'Come on,' said Frost, walking past me with smooth, careful steps. I snorted and followed.

We easily caught up with the others, who gave Jenna curious looks but didn't have much to say, thankfully. Jenna herself seemed to be fast asleep. I couldn't imagine falling asleep while riding on the back of someone else, not to mention someone she'd only met a matter of hours ago, but whatever had so thoroughly exhausted Jenna seemingly couldn't wait until she had a nice nest to rest in.

I still desperately wanted to meet Journey but she was also asleep, nestled between my mother's wings, and Bloom and Teera were still on either side cooing over her, so there wasn't really a good opportunity. I didn't want to bother her while she slept, anyway.

Frost didn't speak to me at all, though sometimes I caught Night's eye and he shook his head at me minutely. It was extremely unfair. Frost was usually on my side!

Though I had to admit a certain discomfort knotting my insides. I might not accept that Jenna was my personal responsibility, but she had been really ill, or tired, or something, and I hadn't helped her. But even watching Frost carry her seemingly easily—perhaps humans were not as dense as cosmorans—I couldn't imagine carrying her myself. Touching anyone made my skin crawl. I had learned to tolerate my siblings, but even that wasn't always easy for me.

At length, Jenna stirred. For a while, she still rested with her cheek pressed to Frost's back, awake but with a haze to her sight that reminded me of when people tried to remember something the fog had taken. But eventually, she asked to be let down, saying she thought she could walk a little while longer. She didn't look much better to me, but Frost knelt to let her slide off and she did walk, falling into step with me where I trailed the rest of my family.

'Sorry about that,' she said.

I shrugged. 'Can't help it if you're tired,' I said.

She smiled, and I thought maybe it looked a bit bitter. 'You have no idea,' she murmured.

Ahead, Bloom exclaimed as Journey woke up. She started covering her eyes with her hands and then suddenly moving them and squeaking at her.

Jenna watched her. 'Do you think it would be all right if I asked to meet her? Journey?'

I flicked one ear back. 'Yeah, sure.'

She nodded. 'Would you come with me?'

Dread curled in my stomach but I said, 'Okay,' because my mouth is a traitor that does nothing but get me into trouble.

We caught up with my mothers, and all the while my mind was full of static as I tried to work out how to ask permission to greet my own sister without seeming like a total weirdo or getting in the way of my siblings. It was a tie between, 'So, Journey?' and 'Mother, might I please meet my kit sister?' but I was ninety-percent sure my mouth just wouldn't work. I knew it was ridiculous; that there shouldn't be any reason I felt this way. But I did, and I couldn't help it, and I couldn't change the fact that although I very much wanted to meet Journey, my body felt like it was rusting into place.

My mothers both looked at me as we arrived, Nova's ears pricking forward, Teera's head canting to one side. My mouth felt terribly dry and I couldn't help my ears from flattening slightly. But before I could so much as open my mouth, Jenna said brightly, 'Thank you so much for allowing me to witness the bi—the hatching of your baby. Kit. I would love to say hello to her?' Any awkwardness was erased by her wide, winning smile. It was so bright I felt like I needed shades.

'Oh, of course!' said Nova, absolutely glowing with motherly pride, her starfire bright and shimmering.

Jenna thanked her and started to walk on the side. My siblings gave way to her, but she gestured for me to come stand beside her. I took my opportunity to get close.

On my mother's back, semi-obscured by her folded wings, was Journey. I had seen kits before but was still awed by how small and fragile Journey looked. Her limbs were so thin and gangly, her wings little more than twigs with pin feathers. She blinked at me, staring like she had no idea what she was looking at—and I supposed she didn't. Her eyes seemed too large for her head—dark eyes, as black as night, and studded with stars.

Shyly, I sniffed toward her. She didn't reciprocate—one of many things she would learn as she grew. And hopefully more easily than I had. 'Hello, Journey,' I said gently. Her ears twitched—over-sized ears that dwarfed her narrow face. I perked my ears toward her and smiled. 'Hey,' I said. 'We're going to be friends. I know it.'

I wasn't overwhelmed by fraternal feelings, or any rush of protectiveness or anything like that. I knew some of my siblings were—Frost had mentioned it before, and Bloom. I had fretted about that when Bloom and Lur hatched. That I was lacking the emotions required to be a good sibling to them, to make a connection. But we had become close. It was only that they were strangers when they hatched.

27

Journey was a stranger to me now, but she was also family. And if I made an effort, there was no reason we couldn't be as close one day as I was with any of my siblings.

Jenna watched our interaction with a smile. She said, 'Nice to meet you, Journey,' and sniffed toward her as well.

I leaned forward and touched my muzzle to Journey. It felt like a very forward thing to do with someone I just met, but as Journey was a hatchling kit, I couldn't see her complaining. Her muzzle was very soft; she had fruit-fur, velvety, and not yet grown coarse and protective like mine.

I didn't want her to grow up alone. She would need her siblings to show her the world, to be friends and guides in ways my mothers could not. I felt a little at a loss for how to do that now. Frost had hatched only a decade after me, and Bloom and Lur only a handful of decades after that. We had been a mature family for so long now. But I was determined to try.

I stayed with Journey for a little while, but when Bloom started hovering at the sides, clearly wanting to spend more time with her, I said goodbye and Jenna went with me.

'She seems like a lovely kit,' Jenna said. 'I don't completely understand how cosmorans relate to each other yet. Compared to humans, you all look very different. But her fur reminds me of yours.'

I felt my starfire pinken, pleased that she'd thought so as well.

When we got back to the canopy-glider, Jenna inhaled sharply. I watched her gaze sweep the ship, from the smooth, ovular body painted an earthy brown, to the webbed green wings folded at its sides. 'So you do have ships,' she said. 'I thought, when the portal appeared instead of a ship...'

'Well, that's a canopy-glider,' I said. 'They aren't equipped for space travel. That'd be a cosmo-swimmer. I think, when we first made contact with humans, it was in space.' Honestly, I probably should have paid more attention. It was a little over a century now and the fog of time made it hard to hold onto details like that. I seemed to be particularly prone to it; I knew there were some people who could remember almost everything and were very little affected by the fog.

'Does it flap its wings?' Jenna asked.

'A little,' I replied, and her obvious delight made me more excited to fly on it than I'd been in a long time. The gull-shape pilot waved a wing at us as we approached. She'd been lounging outside, feathers puffed and legs tucked beneath her.

'Hello!' she said, and sniffed toward us politely. We all returned the gesture, even Jenna. 'I see your group has grown by more than one.' She strode forward, her movements deliberate, her small talons scoring the ground. Her pilot's badge, with a silhouette of a canopy-glider stitched onto it, was worn on a buttoned collar around her neck. 'I'm Lirri,' she said, bowing to Jenna with a flourish.

Jenna giggled and made an awkward bow in return. 'Jenna.'

'And how did you become part of this trip?'

'Well—'

'She's just arrived,' said Frost. 'She was present for our Journey's hatching.'

'Journey?' Lirri looked around excitedly, feathers rising. 'Where's the new kit?' She excitedly rushed over to Nova and Teera.

Jenna blinked in surprise, then laughed. 'I'm an actual alien but a kit is still more exciting than me,' she said. 'Truly, there's no hope for me.'

I snorted and gestured inside the canopy-glider with a hoof. 'I wouldn't take it personally,' I said. 'Kits are very rare, and very loved.'

Jenna raised her eyebrows. 'You have *four* siblings! Or...maybe six? That's a lot on Earth!'

'We're...a very unusual family,' I said, a little uncomfortably. I didn't know how to explain hatching rates among cosmorans.

Inside the canopy-glider, it was exactly as we'd left it. I ushered Jenna over to a low cushioned seat and, because I didn't see how I could go sit somewhere else without being rude, took the seat beside her. Frost ambled in a moment later and took the seat on her other side, their long tail curling around to tap on the floor while they sat.

'So...where are we going?' Jenna said. 'I haven't seen an embassy, or...or greeter, or anything. I have no idea where I'm going to stay, or how to pay for it...'

I flattened my ears at that. I knew our diplomats had been advised to be close-lipped about the specifics of our worlds and their geography, but to tell a traveller *nothing at all* and expect her to start a life here seemed like a step too far. Several steps.

'You won't have to pay for anything,' said Frost. 'We don't expect trade from travellers until they become settled, and even then, all essentials are exempt from trade. We'll talk to the local Travellers' Union about getting you a house and supplies.'

'We're going to Lost Circle,' I said. 'That's the city Frost and I live in. The others will be travelling on from there, but Lost Circle is big enough that there are probably already humans living there, so it shouldn't be too awkward to get you settled.'

'Probably?' Jenna repeated.

I flicked an ear at her. 'I haven't actually met another human,' I admitted. Although it was possible that I had, and the fog had taken it. Chance encounters were some of the first memories the fog would claim.

'I have,' Frost said. 'Don't worry. We'll make sure you get the help you need. As a new arrival, you're our family's responsibility until you're established.'

Jenna looked startled. 'Oh. I'm sorry, I don't mean to be a burden, and—!'

'Not a burden, an honour,' Frost interrupted her firmly.

I dunno, she was a *bit* of a burden. She seemed nice, but all I wanted to do was go home now and curl up with my cosmorb, not take a human to the Travellers' Union.

The canopy-glider started to lift, the wings unfolding and starting to gently vibrate, the glow of them shining through the windows.

Jenna gripped her seat uncertainly. 'Will this be rough?'

'A little,' I said. 'You can activate your safety gem if you're worried.' I demonstrated by touching my hoof to the gem beneath my seat. Glowing threads of crackling energy wrapped around me, fixing me to my chair, as the canopy-glider beat its wings for the first time, sending us swooping up into the air. Jenna lurched forward so I activated her safety gem with starfire. The harness caught her and eased her back into her seat.

'Oh. Thanks,' she said.

I flicked an ear by way of response.

I didn't have much to say for the rest of the trip, so I just listened to Jenna and Frost chat. Storm talked about our family and how long it had been since the last hatching ceremony, and Illusion cut in to talk a little about the magical study of the Flowering Ancient's fruits and their connection to Cosmorans. Nothing particularly interesting, but they seemed to enjoy it.

Jenna, in turn, answered questions about Earth, and what had brought her to Geminus Viridus. She seemed sort of evasive to me—lots of talk about 'needing a change' and 'not fitting in at home', but no real explanation of any of that. Not that I blamed her; for all my family had rushed in to claim responsibility for her, we were still recent acquaintances. She did mention she was a gardener, though, which was interesting. Gardening was a very respectable skill, though I couldn't imagine what it might look like on Earth, or without the use of starfire.

It was a long flight, the canopy-glider skimming the top of the forest and then soaring above open meadows. The heartstar set, turning the sky a deep purple-black, and then the stars became visible, mimicking the flowers twinkling at us below. I took off my safety guard and went to look out the window, resting my chin on the sill. At times like this, when the world was rushing past in all its beautiful shapes and colours, I fancied I could understand what it must have been like for the cosmorans in aeons past. Nomads who hadn't yet learned to shape the trees, for whom all the land was home. It was a strange feeling; a nostalgia for something I'd never experienced.

I looked to Jenna, expecting her to be excited about her first aerial view of Geminus, only to see her slumped in her seat—not asleep, but clearly too tired to do much.

A while later, Jenna seemed to rally a bit. Teera laid out a picnic on the floor for us to enjoy. Bloom took Jenna's hand and guided her over, walking awkwardly on her hind feet like she was impersonating a human herself. 'If you're sure?' Jenna said. 'I've...never had cosmoran food before, but I'm starving.'

I knelt on the floor beside my family. They'd dragged a floral-patterned blanket across the floor to make a nice eating area, and Teera had opened up the numerous packs she'd brought and pulled out various containers of soups, salads, and even some rather exciting looking pastries, the crusts still a bright, fresh green.

'Can humans eat our food?' I asked. I addressed the question to Frost, because Frost always seemed to be the most knowledgeable one. 'Cosmorans can tolerate quite a lot of toxins compared to other organisms, and—'

'I think it should be okay,' said Jenna. 'That's one of the first things I learned about Geminus. Apparently, we have similar diets, in some ways. Humans can tolerate a lot of toxins, too.' She smiled nervously. 'And I'm a big fan of spicy food.'

Lur stuck out his tongue. 'Ugh. I hate spicy food. It makes my tongue hurt.'

'I like spicy food,' I reassured her.

Frost snorted. 'It's about all Avari eats. Our mothers bring along a pot of yellow chutney just to make sure they won't turn up their nose at the picnic.'

'I'm not as bad as that,' I said. I pulled over a little wood-worked bowl and tossed a pastry and a bunch of salad into my bowl. The flowers made the whole thing look much brighter and tastier.

'Oh, that's quite nicely presented,' said Lur. 'If I had my cosmorb, I'd try to get an image of it—'

I opened the pot of yellow chutney and dropped a big dollop on top.

'Nevermind.' Lur wrinkled his nose and turned back to his own bowl.

'So...what is all this?' Jenna asked.

I scooped up my pastry and a pinch of salad and took a bite. The yellow chutney was sweet and angry, burning my tongue in a pleasant sort of way. 'Salad, soup, pastry,' I said and took another bite. It was a little too much too soon and I coughed at the aggressiveness of it.

'Serves you right,' said Lur, sticking out his tongue at me.

'This is sweet soup,' said Bloom, picking up the pot with her hands. 'It's...ah, you won't know the ingredients. Fruit and leaves, lightly spiced. Like a hot thick juice. And this is salad, it's all flowers and leaves, I think. And this is a blissfruit pastry. It's sort of savoury...the filling is blissfruit and songflower and...sungourd seeds?' She perked an ear at Teera, who inclined her head in assent. 'The pastry is made from ground up seeds and leaves to make a sort of flour. It's nice with preserves.' She side-eyed my pastry, smeared with yellow chutney. 'But not yellow chutney unless you want your mouth to cry.'

My mouth *was* crying but I liked it. I took another bite and Bloom grimaced at me like we were kits.

32

'I'd like to try a bit of everything, if I may,' said Jenna. She looked a little worriedly at Teera, and I wondered if she was thinking about how awkward it would be if she didn't like it—which seemed almost inevitable, considering it was all flavours and textures she'd probably never encountered before. Personally, I hated trying new food. Although I hated new things in general, and since Jenna had decided to move to a new planet, we were perhaps very different in that regard.

'Is it okay if I use my hands?' she said. 'I don't have...' she gestured at Bloom's flame.

'Starfire,' I supplied.

'Starfire. Just hands.' She held them out and wiggled them demonstratively.

'Of course,' said Teera. 'Help yourself. We made plenty.'

Jenna filled two bowls, one with soup and one with salad and pastry. After consulting with Bloom again, she added a bit of the two chutneys my mother had brought—one that was blue and bland and boring, and of course the delicious option of yellow chutney.

She looked eager to get started while around us, everyone started chatting. Teera and Nova tempted Journey with some kit mush, but Journey wasn't having it, turning her head whenever they tried. Lur and Illusion started up a conversation on forgetech applications I frankly couldn't follow, but that was nothing new. While those siblings were firecrafters rather than technicians, there was a lot of overlap in the fields and it wasn't uncommon for them to talk about it.

I finished up my bowl and glanced at Jenna. She was poking at the food, looking worried, but hadn't tried any. I leaned close to her. 'Not sure about it?' I asked in a low voice. 'It's fine, Teera won't mind.' Not from the precious 'boon traveller' anyway. If I had fussed about the food, it would be quite a different story.

'It's not that,' she said. 'I just...I notice you're all using starfire to eat it. I can't pick it up like that. On earth, we have utensils for that. I can drink the soup from the bowl, I think. Would that be rude?' The word 'utensils' was a little fuzzy in my mind, but I recognised it as 'tools for eating'.

'It can't be rude if it's your only option,' I said, and meant it. 'I don't mind it. Go ahead.'

She lifted the bowl. I thought she would lap at it, as a kit might, but she put her lips to the edge of the bowl and sipped it delicately. Her eyes widened at the taste, and she continued.

'Good?' I asked.

'Different,' she said. 'It doesn't really taste of anything I've had before, it's hard to describe. But I like the sweetness.'

That seemed reasonable.

The salad and pastry, she struggled over, and I understood why. Her hands would get dirty. I'd never really thought of any of this before—all cosmorans had starfire. Not all of us could manipulate objects with it, but we had aids available for people who couldn't. Ought I to think of Jenna as disabled, in that sense? Would a starfire amplifier even help her, considering she had no starfire at all?

She ate it with her hands, though the chutney stained her fingers. She gasped aloud when she tried the yellow chutney and started breathing in and out really fast, like she was trying to cool the spice through pure airflow.

'I told you it was awful,' said Bloom, but Jenna grinned.

'It's *perfect*,' she said. All of my family members were aghast, but I chuckled.

'Want more?' I asked.

'Yes please.'

I picked up a dollop and floated it over to her and at her consent, added it to the pastry. I noticed she didn't ask for more blue chutney. It was funny to think I might share more taste with a human than with my own family, but kind of nice as well.

She made her way through the salad and pastry. 'These were all delicious, thank you,' she said to Teera, who was delighted.

'Teera's a great cook,' said Storm, while Illusion continued the conversation with Lur. 'We're always pleased to enjoy her food.'

Frost's thick tail whipped around to slap me on the rump. I startled. 'Yeah, thanks, Teera,' I said. I wasn't very good at remembering to say thanks, even though I had really enjoyed the meal. Things like that often evaded me. You might think my mothers would be used to it, but Teera could be very sensitive. I was glad I had Frost to remind me, just like they had when we were kits.

We chatted for the rest of the meal, and Lirri even had a bit as well, as there was plenty to go around and the skies were clear over the meadows.

We settled down to rest for the remainder of the journey. Nova and Teera curled around Journey, already dozing, while Bloom peeked over them and waved at a bleary but still awake Journey. Lur curled up on his seat, poking his nose under his tail. I'd always been envious of how small Lur could curl up; fox-shapes were much more flexible than goat-shapes.

Frost talked to themselves quietly and stretched out on the floor. That left only me and Jenna really awake—well, and Lirri at the controls. I expect she'd gotten her sleep while we made the journey to the Flowering Ancient.

'You can sleep, if you like,' I said. 'Do humans curl up? Or I could get you a blanket if you want to stretch out like Frost?'

She gave me a tired smile. 'We can sort of curl up, I guess? Not as well as Lur, though.' She looked at my brother where he formed a perfect little fur puddle. 'I don't think I could fit on this seat comfortably. But I never fall asleep on flights anyway.'

'Me either,' I said. They'd always made me anxious, though I didn't say that.

'Well, let's stay up together, then,' she said.

So we did. And when the heartstar rose, we went to the window to watch it, me standing, Jenna sitting on the floor with her knees drawn to her chest. The sky was red and beautiful with dawn, the horizon taking on a vari-coloured gleam. 'Wow,' she said, watching it.

Looking at her eyes in that moment, they were full of stars, just like mine.

Chapter Four

When the canopy-glider landed in Lost Circle, there were a lot of farewells and a flurry of cheek rubs and cuddles. I said goodbye, and everyone but my mothers respected my boundaries. They rubbed their cheeks against me and wrapped their claws around my neck in farewell. When I extricated myself from them, I went to Journey—currently in the arms of Bloom. 'Goodbye, little one,' I said. Gently, I reached my nose out toward her, and she didn't hesitate to bump it with hers. Only just hatched and already very sweet.

Most of my family didn't live in Lost Circle—they'd be taking another canopy-glider from here to Athelean, the little village I'd grown up in on a small lake several hours away. Only Frost and I had moved to the city, and though I'd heard Bloom talking about moving away from Athelean, she didn't seem particularly drawn by Lost Circle.

Lost Circle. I looked around at it. The city was spread out below us, the canopy-glider having landed on one of the wide branches of the transport station. At the heart of it was The Circle Tree, a huge plant with pink blossoms and silver bark which had floated above the city for longer than cosmoran memory; the earth around it bursting with flowers, a circle of floating rocks and bits of land surrounding its sky island. It was believed to be a sacred site to ancient cosmorans—and truthfully, the beauty of that naturally formed circle, the meadow, and the tree itself struck even a modern cosmoran like me as something divine.

The rest of the city was made up of pathways of trees, shaped and hollowed while still living to house various buildings. Each tree might hold four or five buildings, depending on their size, with the largest trees being used for community buildings and stations. Just below canopy-level, hard-vine ropes spiderwebbed from tree to tree, each carrying the canopy-trams with their glowing bases and barred cars that acted as public transportation around the city.

And the city itself was bustling, with pinpricks of light coming from all directions—the distant starfires of thousands of cosmorans going about the day.

Jenna came and stood beside me where I took it all in. She looked tired, with bags under her eyes and a rumpled look as if she'd slept the whole journey, though I knew she hadn't. 'This isn't a forest, is it?' she said, her eyes following a canopy-tram as it swooped along a hard-vine path.

'It is,' I said. 'It's just also a city.'

'A city.' She said the word with a mix of confusion and awe. 'This is what your cities look like?'

I shrugged. 'Some of them. What are your cities like?'

Her mouth twisted to one side. 'No trees. No grass. Lots of very tall buildings made of concrete and glass. Hundreds of people in each building.'

I struggled to envision it. How big would the buildings need to be to fit so many people? Where did they get their air, if there were no trees? 'No trees at all?'

'Mm. Well, there are *some* trees. We have them in parks for people to walk around and feel closer to nature. But most of the trees were cut down to make more buildings.'

Cut down. Well, it didn't sound very sensible to me but I didn't want to judge. Although, the thought of it itched at me like a flea. I shrugged, flicking my tail noncommittally.

'How many people live here?' she asked.

I considered. 'Maybe ten thousand people?' It was the largest city in this part of Viridus, and twenty times the size of my home village, Athelean.

She gave me a wide-eyed look, but I didn't know what it meant. Perhaps humans didn't live in such density; I would find it overwhelming as well, if it wasn't the norm for me.

Frost trotted over to us, their thick tail lashing behind them in overt agitation. 'Everyone else has left for Athelean,' said Night, their tongue flicking in and out a little too quickly. 'Avari, we'll need to take Jenna to the Travellers' Union and get her registered.'

My fur stood up. 'Sorry, what? Why do I have to go if you're going anyway?'

Illusion gave me a beady-eyed glare. 'You're the one who found Jenna. You need to be her witness.'

I shuffled my hooves. 'Then why are you going?' I muttered.

Night sighed. 'To look after you, foghead.'

I laid my ears flat but couldn't argue, or I'd risk Frost abandoning us. Especially if Night was fronting for them.

I *did* want them to come with us. I hated bureaucracy of any kind and Frost was a really steadying presence.

I sighed and let my head droop submissively. '...Fine,' I muttered. I looked to Jenna. 'Come on. There should be a canopy-tram to the Travellers' Union.'

'Oh. Uh. Thanks!'

We walked through the building entrance on the trunk of the tree, an arch that appeared to grow naturally from the tree but in fact had been expertly shaped by our gardeners, probably over many years for a tree of this size. Inside, the walls were smooth wood that was soft to touch, but which rippled along with the natural fibres of the tree. Glowlights hovered in the air—little forgetech fireflies that helped light and guide—and silk lanterns were strung along the walls and across the hall in shades of green, blue, and yellow.

The floor made a ring around a central hole, through which we could look down and see the floors below. 'There's a path down to the next floor this way,' I said, leading the way and pretending like I didn't get lost in the canopy station regularly. Frost didn't argue so I probably wasn't wrong.

I made my way down. As we did, we passed several other cosmorans, many of whom startled at the sight of Jenna, their flames switching shades curiously. I glanced at Jenna to see how she was taking it. She bobbled her head in her strange approximation of a greeting sniff at everyone she passed, but her eyes kept lifting to take in the station.

I got lost on the next level down and Frost smoothly took over, guiding us to one of the canopy-tram bays. A couple other cosmorans were waiting there. They didn't greet us, but did throw curious looks Jenna's way. We queued up behind them.

'Have you ever been on a tram before?' Frost asked.

Jenna wrung her hands. 'Well—yes. But our trams are fixed to the ground, on rails.'

My ears perked forward, trying to imagine this in the concrete city she'd described. 'Doesn't it get stuck on rocks and bushes?'

She shook her head. 'We pave the ground.'

I couldn't stop my ears from flattening. I stomped a hoof to let out the unpleasant energy. Illusion hissed at me, her throat feathers ruffling, and I sorted my ears out. I didn't want to be rude.

Jenna didn't seem to notice. 'Will it be scary?' she asked. 'Your trams aren't enclosed, and they look a bit—' she hesitated '—swoopy.'

Not enclosed? Belatedly, I remembered that humans all looked like Jenna. Probably none of them had wings, or especially long necks.

Still, the thought of there being a roof on a tram made me feel claustrophobic. I already struggled with *our* trams. I didn't want to imagine being crammed into a little box.

The tram appeared around the corner, following the hard-vine path and slowing down as it reached us. It was a standard tram: a little platform with bowed sides and wide-set rails, made of carved wood. Forgetech lights glowed on the bottom. I think the forgetech helped both propel and lift it, though I didn't know the specifics.

The tram came to a halt and the gate slid open. I carefully stepped aside so that the people coming off had enough space. There were only a few departing passengers—an elephant-shape, a mole-shape, and a rabbit-shape—and they barely glanced at Jenna in their rush.

We got on last. I let Jenna go before me, so I closed the gate behind me with a kick of my hoof. When it clicked shut, the tram rocked once and then slowly glided into motion.

Jenna exclaimed softly and grabbed a spoke of the railing with both hands.

'It does pick up speed,' Storm said. 'Feel free to grab onto us if you're feeling unsteady, but it's perfectly safe.' They gave me a look with three pairs of eyes but I didn't make the same offer. Jenna seemed nice and I wanted her to be comfortable, but Frost had already offered and I didn't like to be touched.

I heard a murmur from the other passengers and noticed them sneaking looks at Jenna, but they were too polite to pester her. I shifted slightly to conceal her from view. I didn't like people staring at me, and she was small enough that it wasn't hard to hide her if maybe she didn't like that either.

As the tram gently rose and fell along with the sweeping arcs of the hard-vine path, I reflected that maybe the trams *were* a bit 'swoopy.' But Jenna seemed to have relaxed a bit. She had one hand on the side of the tram and another resting on Frost's shoulder, her eyes wide as she took in the forest below.

It was three stops before we got off at another canopy station. Frost got us to the floor and out into the city. I looked around and breathed deep. I liked Lost Circle. Its trees and scents were familiar. The Elden Grove had been beautiful, almost spiritual, but there was something particularly calming about home.

Jenna again seemed shocked as we strode out onto the path. 'But this is just forest,' she said. She looked over her shoulder at the canopy station, as if to remind herself that it was there.

'It's both forest and city,' I said. 'Look carefully. You can see the paths made by many paws, where the grass is flat and mixed with dirt. Paths are the easiest way to get around the city without getting leaves in your fur and mud on your hooves, but there's nothing stopping you from leaving the paths.'

Illusion pointed a claw at the nearest treelding. 'And if you look, you can make out the treeldings. Most of the larger trees on any path are buildings. You can see the way they're shaped so they can be climbed, and you can see the doors and windows. Look.'

The one she was pointing to in fact had a small family already climbing the winding bark path up to the higher levels, no doubt returning home after a morning walk.

'Oh,' said Jenna. She paused. 'It's beautiful.'

'It's Lost Circle,' I said, with a touch of pride. 'Settlements in the mountains are carved into the rocks. I wouldn't mind that, but they can be quite dark and windy. Settlements in plains or meadows are burrowed into the ground or little hills and mounds.' I made a face, my ears flattening. 'It's very boring.'

Frost thumped me with their tail and I glared at them. Night stuck out their tongue at me, while Illusion said, 'It's not boring, it's just different.'

'It doesn't sound boring,' said Jenna. 'I'd love to see those other kinds of cities. But I think I'm with you, Avari.' She gave me a shy smile. 'There's something special about a forest city.'

I couldn't quite hold in a small baa of approval. Frost rolled their eyes at me.

We headed for the Travellers' Union. It wasn't a terribly long walk from here, and I enjoyed the familiar feel of the Lost Circle path beneath my hooves. I could walk for much, much longer and not really feel it. Goat-shape advantage, I supposed; cosmorans with hooves tended to have more stamina for long journeys.

I wondered how Jenna was finding the walk. She was a biped with very long and flat feet, and unlike a bird-shape, she looked like she had quite a heavy core. Was it tiring to put all that weight on just two feet? She certainly looked tired, with shadows under her eyes and a shuffle to her steps. In spite of that, she looked around with wide-eyes, her expressive human face making her bright mood quite clear, even without the aid of ears or tail.

We passed cosmorans of all kinds, some at a distance, some even stopping to say hello. A phoenix-shape flew overhead, their starfire trailing from their wings as well as their head. A capybara-shape excitedly introduced themself to Jenna, then welcomed her to Viridus upon learning she was a newly arrived traveller. A dragon-shape flew sinuously through the air as might a snake-shape through water.

'They're wearing clothes!' Jenna commented, pointing out the dragon-shape.

I put one ear forward and one back. 'So are you?'

'Oh. Well, that's true.' She tugged on the hem of her blue dress. 'But humans always wear clothes.'

'What, always?' asked Storm. 'What if you get hot or wet?'

Jenna shrugged. 'We just wear...fewer clothes. Or thinner clothes. We take them off to wash ourselves, or sometimes to sleep. It's taboo in most places to be naked, or improperly clothed.'

'Huh,' I said. 'Sounds inconvenient.'

Jenna thought about it. 'I suppose? I've never really thought about it. But I like wearing clothes. It's a way to express yourself, you know?'

'I do,' said Storm. 'We're quite partial to clothes ourselves.'

I shrugged. I wore clothes sometimes but didn't particularly rate them. Beyond a cloak or sweater if it was raining or cold, I didn't much see the point.

The Travellers' Union came into view. Another of the huge public treeldings, it was impossible to miss. Its branches dominated the canopy and mist clung to it, shrouding it in mystery. Above the door, a sign of shaped runes embossed from the tree bark itself declared its designation. I wondered if Jenna could read it; I wasn't sure of the limitations of a com-gem as opposed to natural starfire, if any. It might not translate written language.

I'd never been to the Travellers' Union. The ground floor looked to be some kind of café. There was a refreshment counter and the floor was scattered with cushions and low tables, with several people sitting together and talking, most of them with bulging packs and satchels on the ground beside them. I looked around, feeling a tinge of anxiety. Should we go up to the refreshment counter for help or were we supposed to go upstairs? Was this a walk-in situation at all, or were we supposed to have made an appointment?

But Frost caught someone's eye. A piebald pink-and-white rat-shape rushed over. He was wearing a little bandana with a nametag on it that read: 'Hi, I'm Sittla! I'm here to help.'

'Welcome to the Traveller's Union!' Sittla said brightly, his whiskers quivering as he greeted us with a sniff. His starfire was a friendly pale orange. 'How can I help...oh!' He seemed to take in Jenna for the first time. I supposed she was pretty small; Frost alone was enough to obscure her. 'New arrival?' he asked.

Jenna nodded. 'Just arrived yesterday. Frost and Avari are kindly helping me find my feet.'

Sittla beamed, touching his cheeks. His starfire flared excitedly. 'Oh, that's *exactly* the spirit,' he said. 'I hope you've been made to feel welcome?'

Jenna smiled. 'Very.'

'Good, good. Well, let me show you to the New Arrivals coordinator. They're very understanding and should be able to tend to your specific needs as a...' Sittla paused, '...long-distance traveller.'

Sittla scampered ahead, his ratty tail whipping behind him. We followed him up two ramps to a small office.

'Elm? We have a new arrival!' said Sittla. 'I trust I can leave her in your hands?'

The small human figure behind the desk looked up. 'Sure. Thanks, Sittla.'

Sittla gave Jenna a friendly pat on the shoulder and skittered out of the room. Rat-shapes made walking look so *exciting*.

Elm took us in and sighed. They gestured to the cushions across from their desk. 'Please, sit.'

We sat, not that it did much to even the height difference. The humans were just so *small...*

Elm was even smaller than Jenna, lacking Jenna's height but carrying their own comfortable padding that nearly matched Jenna's girth. They had a short, plaited goatee that made me want to plait my own, and their dark hair was long and loose with faint curls.

'Tea?' they asked. Frost nodded but I shook my head. I didn't like hot drinks. To Jenna, Elm said, 'This is a cosmoran tea blend, quite different to ours. It's called Sparkbrew and the closest I can compare it to is a sort of floral cinnamon.' The last word was hazy to me and I struggled to make it out, but Jenna said, 'I'd love to try it,' so Elm poured out two cups of steaming tea. I found the smell of it sort of overwhelming and couldn't help but wrinkle my nose, but Jenna made a sound of delight when she took a sip.

'Did you bring anything with you?' Elm asked Jenna. 'When my portal came, I was just sitting by the lake at the local park and it appeared in the water. I came through in the deeps in Profundus. Luckily, there was someone there to help me get my breather on.' They shook their head.

Jenna's eyes went round. 'That's terrifying. I...no. It appeared in a tree in a garden I was working in. I didn't have anything on me. It put me out in—' she glanced at me— 'the Elder Grove?'

Elm's eyebrows lifted. 'I'll get on the Otherworldly Travel Commission about it. The portals have been bad for years...they're supposed to put us in settlements on Viridus, you know.' Their mouth twisted.

'Honestly, I was expecting a ship when I applied,' Jenna said.

Elm nodded and shrugged. 'I think we all were. Space travel would certainly have fewer complications. Cosmoran ships are almost as fast as human ones. But there were...problems...with early travellers on both sides and the Geminus Galactic Council decided it would be best to use portals instead.'

I struck a hoof on the floor thoughtfully, trying to remember. The fog hadn't claimed that...yes, I remembered. The First Heartbreak. I almost wished I didn't.

The first cosmorans to visit Earth had gone exploring in the wilderness. Somehow one of them got separated from their escort, and a human hunter...a human hunter had...

I shuddered.

It was not without reason that travel was so restricted now.

I glanced at Jenna. She nodded, her mouth twisting downward. She looked...sad? Angry? As expressive as humans were, the nuance here was hard to grasp.

She wasn't happy about it, though.

'So...things are a little different here. There's not currency, or trade as you're used to it. You'll be given what you need when you ask. There is temporary housing available at the Union for human travellers while we get planning permission for your house but...it's generally considered better to integrate if you can. Most of the folk you'll meet here are travellers themselves, and will not stay long. Are you planning to settle in Lost Circle?'

'Oh...uh, I hadn't really thought about it. I only arrived today.'

Elm nodded, their gaze sympathetic. 'That's very understandable. Well, think on it. You can stay here if you like, or we can arrange transport to another settlement if Lost Circle doesn't feel right. And wherever you settle doesn't have to be permanent, regardless.'

Frost looked between Jenna and Elm. 'What's the housing for humans like, here?'

Elm stroked their plaited goatee, and I again felt a surge of envy. 'Small, but comfortable,' said Elm. 'Though we prefer to move human travellers into their settled location or nomadic lifestyle as soon as possible. It can be...isolating.'

I could imagine. The Travellers' Union surely didn't have the time to show around every new traveller and adjust them to life in Lost Circle, especially not for a human like Jenna who had an awful lot to learn. From what she'd said, Earth settlements were nothing at all like ours. How would she find her way around? And I worried she would be easy prey for anyone looking to take advantage of a new arrival.

Though at least Elm was also human. I couldn't imagine they'd just let her wander out into the city without any assistance. Would they?

I could feel Frost's three pairs of eyes boring into me. It was enough to make my fur itch. I flattened my ears and blew air at them.

They stood up. 'Elm, if you'll excuse us and our sibling for a moment?'

Elm waved us away and continued talking to Jenna. 'So as an otherworldly traveller, you'll always have support from the Travellers' Union, but there are other unions you—'

Frost hustled me out the door. They weren't much larger than I was but their long necks and tail really made it very easy for them to herd people around.

'We can't let Jenna live in the Travellers' Union,' said Night, his tongue flickering anxiously. 'She's kind and trusting and clearly knows nothing at all about Geminus or cosmoran life.'

'I agree, it seems bad,' I said. 'But what are we supposed to do about it? Can you take her?'

Night shook his head. 'It has to be you. We don't have room.'

I spluttered a moment. 'What? No! I'm not good with people. And I love living alone!'

'She's our responsibility,' Night said. '*Your* responsibility. You found her when she'd just arrived.'

'That's a ludicrous tradition,' I said, stomping a hoof. 'What if I was a—a villain! Or a predator!'

Night rolled his eyes. 'You aren't, so it doesn't matter. She just needs somewhere to stay until the gardeners can grow her a house. If she even decides to stay in Lost Circle.'

I jabbed a hoof at Frost and stomped again. 'Well, why can't she stay with you? You like her well enough and you *love* people.'

'We told you,' Night said testily. 'We don't have room.'

46

'What are you talking about? You have plenty of—'

Illusion fluffed up her feathers. 'Our mate is living with us, okay?' Suddenly, she cringed back. Night looked defiant. Storm wouldn't meet my eyes.

My ears went back. I took two steps back in shock. 'You have a mate?'

I felt like there were flies buzzing in my ears. My thoughts, which had been full of anxiety and defiance before, were now completely empty save for this one thought:

Frost had a mate.

Frost had a mate, and they didn't tell me.

Frost's heads drooped. 'We haven't had a chance to tell you yet,' murmured Illusion. Their tail lashed anxiously.

'He's only just moved in,' Storm added, still not meeting my eyes. 'It's...not a convenient time for a guest.'

Frost had a mate. They were a cautious enough person; they wouldn't have moved in overnight. How long had they had this mate? Why hadn't they told me?

Probably because they were embarrassed of me. Because I really did ruin everything, just like my mothers always said.

I had never even considered they would get a mate. I was asexual—and though the idea of romance appealed to me in an abstract way, in practice, I had yet to meet anyone I had felt that way about.

I never met anyone at all.

Illusion said, 'It'll be good for you to have a roommate for a while, anyway. You always say you struggle to make friends.'

I didn't say that. I said I didn't need friends. I had the best siblings in the world, why would I need friends?

Maybe because I was a burden on them. Maybe because they were so eager to separate their lives from mine they'd keep something as big as a mate from me.

Frost asked something about whether I'd take Jenna in for a while and I just nodded, feeling too numb to protest. The rest of the time in the office was a blur to me. Jenna agreed to stay with me, Elm said they'd make enquiries for Jenna to get a house, there was some form or other that Elm filled out with Jenna's answers, using a strange little button board with their cosmorb, and then we were out in the city again.

'It was nice to meet you, Jenna,' Frost said. 'I'll stop by later this week—I should be free on Mirrorsday morning. Take care of her, Avari.'

They nuzzled my neck in a friendly farewell, which I tolerated, still not quite aware, and then they were walking away.

Jenna gave me a worried look. 'Is everything okay?'

'It's fine,' I said shortly. 'Come on. We'll catch a canopy-tram to my house. It's in Antlervine Tree.'

I led the way, numbness giving way to something deep and painful.

Chapter Five

'This is it,' I told Jenna as we approached. 'Antlervine Tree. I live in the house at the top.'

In spite of the sorrow roiling in my belly, the sight of Antlervine did strike me with its warm familiarity. It had been well-named—the tree branched out wide with beautiful spokes like the prongs of an antler, each draped with vines and hanging moss. A large crop of blue-green crystal burst from the soil at the base—entirely naturally formed, and I appreciated the faint light it gave off even in darkness.

'It's lovely,' said Jenna. I glanced at her. Her eyes were full of light, her expression solemn as she took it all in. I had no idea what she was thinking.

Antlervine wasn't a particularly large treelding. It held only five houses, and the path was external rather than internal. I guided Jenna up it. It wasn't terribly different from the path we'd climbed up the Flowering Ancient, but it was much narrower and thankfully had a hard-vine railing strung along it for safety.

As we climbed we passed the other homes, their doors closed. We could hear people moving about inside. One neighbour called from inside, 'Hi Avari!', which I returned politely but didn't pause to chat.

'Your windows don't have glass,' said Jenna.

'Glass?' The word struck me strangely, for a moment. That happened sometimes, when there was a different cultural weight between languages. 'Why would we use glass?'

'Well, for safety,' Jenna said. 'It lets light in but doesn't let...let the elements in. Keeps out rain and...thieves.'

'Your glass must be very thick if it keeps out thieves,' I said.

Jenna rubbed her neck. 'I...well, it's not. It's just...the glass breaking would attract attention.'

I supposed. I tried to adjust my mental image of her concrete block city, now sparkling with glass windows. 'We don't have a huge problem with thievery,' I said. Indeed, there was little anyone would need to steal. Everyone was issued with what they needed, and was welcome to ask more. Sometimes particularly sought after crafters or artists had problems with thieves, I supposed, but everyday folk didn't have to worry about that sort of thing. The windows were too small to climb through, anyway, unless the thief was a kit.

'We close the shutters when the weather's bad,' I said. A sudden suspicion occurred to me. 'Wait...how do animals know the glass is there?'

'Oh. Um...well, that's something that came up in my gardening work, actually,' she said. 'Sometimes I'd be hired to design greenhouses—that's glass houses for growing plants regardless of the season—and birds and other flying animals would fly right into the glass. So I'd get tinted glass, or put stickers and marks on the glass so that birds could see it. But, uh, that's not the norm, I don't think.' She wrung her hands. 'My house didn't even have that on its windows, honestly. I didn't think about it.'

'Hmm,' was all I said. The more I heard about human cities, the less I liked the sound of them. They'd surely be awe-inspiring to behold, but they didn't sound like very nice places to live. And I still didn't know where they got their oxygen from, if they were cutting down all their trees. Earth was a water planet, I'd heard—perhaps their aquatic plants did the heavy lifting in holding the atmosphere together.

We made it to my house. The door was perched just beneath the canopy, where the tree started to fork into its antler prongs. It meant there was a lovely shade of leaves hanging over it. Flowers grew beneath the windows, where I'd carried up clods of earth in the hopes of seeing what might grow. They were tenacious wildflowers, some purple and some white, which hadn't much minded the faint dappled light spared by Antlervine's thick canopy. I'd left the windows unshuttered. My name was marked on the door, and the crystal handle turned at the touch of my starfire.

I politely stepped aside to let Jenna go in first, which I quickly regretted as it led to some awkward shuffling. I went in behind her and closed the door.

I shifted anxiously from hoof to hoof, taking it all in. The low table had three large cushions scattered around it, the once-bright patterns now faded and one of them was obviously stained. My baskets were overflowing, and I'd long since taken the lid off the low basket where I kept the data crystals that didn't fit in my reading room. The shelves shaped from the walls were full of trinkets and figurines—I'd always been a bit of a collector, but I was terrible at dusting and it showed. In the kitchen, dirty dishes were piled atop the rain-barrel, which I hadn't had the energy to wash before the hatching ceremony. I saw I'd left my cloak on the floor and hastily scooped it up with starfire and deposited it into a nearby basket.

'Uh. Sorry about the mess,' I said. I hoped she didn't think I was a total slob. Hopefully human houses were different enough that she wouldn't be able to compare.

'Your house is amazing,' she said. 'Is it all right if I look around.'

'Oh. Yeah, of course. You'll be staying here.' I hesitated. 'I can give you a tour?'

She nodded. 'That would be lovely.'

Awkwardness stretched between us, and I didn't think it was just me this time. Jenna had been nothing but polite and friendly since I'd met her, but she seemed subdued now.

Probably having second thoughts about living with a messy goat-shape. Well, it was probably for the best, even if it was uncomfortable now. I had no idea how to have a houseguest.

I showed her around. 'Well, this is the main room, and the kitchen. That's my nestroom—uh, it's not very tidy, maybe don't look in there right now. And this room is my workroom. You'll want to be careful in there—there are a lot of dangerous chemicals and the equipment is quite fragile. Oh and this is my reading room—see that's why there's data crystals all over the walls. I'll get it set up with a nest for you. Humans have nests, right? No? We'll work something out. And that's a storage room there, it's mostly food, I keep my chemicals separate. And...that's the privy.'

Jenna nodded politely to all of my babbling, but something mortifying had just occurred to me. I had no idea how to ask, but I *needed* to ask. So I asked, 'How do humans eliminate? Will you need special equipment?'

Jenna stared at me, wide-eyed. Her cheeks flushed, but I wasn't sure what that meant. 'Oh, I—I don't know? How does it work for Cosmorans?'

I showed her into the privy, where there was a wide cone to sit or stand over. 'We poop energy,' I said. 'So this goes to the local power processor for conversion and use in the local power grid.'

'You poop...energy,' Jenna said faintly.

I flicked one ear forward uncertainly. 'Do humans not poop energy?'

'No we poop...it's like how animals poop. It can be used as...as fertiliser, I think, but there's a health risk so...' She trailed off.

I thought of the animal poop that could be found outside sometimes. 'Well, that seems very good for the environment,' I said. 'Everything needs something to grow in.'

Jenna nodded. Her face looked very shiny. Sweaty, for some reason. 'Well, it's probably best that you don't use a cosmoran privy for now,' I said. I didn't think animal-like excrement would process well, and might break something. 'Uh...there's probably a human privy available somewhere, but until then you could poop outside, or—or in a pot, to be emptied.'

Jenna gave me a slightly ill smile. 'A pot would be good. Humans used chamberpots until we had a good waste disposal system.' She didn't look incredibly enthused by the idea.

I went into my storage room and looked around for a large pot I didn't mind sacrificing, and came out with a somewhat chipped pot of lacquered clay. 'Will this do?'

'I hope so.'

We stared at each other awkwardly for a moment, and then Jenna laughed and put a hand to her head. 'I can't believe this is happening,' she said. 'I'm on an alien planet discussing human shit, holding a chamberpot. This isn't quite how I envisioned moving to Geminus would go.'

I pricked my ears forward. 'How did you envision it?'

She spread her hands. 'With plumbing.'

I snorted. 'There'll be some kind of human privy we can get, I'm sure. You aren't the first human on Viridus.'

'Yeah. I'm starting to wish I'd ask Elm a few more questions before I left...'

I had Jenna settle in the main room while I sorted out my reading room for a guest. My data crystals on the shelves, I'd mostly leave, but I placed a bunch of them into an unused basket so that there were a few shelves free for

Jenna. I got her a few baskets as well, so that she had somewhere to store her things.

Not that she really *had* anything to store yet. Just the clothes she was wearing. She'd probably need more of those, since apparently humans never went without them.

The thought struck me oddly for a moment. Why didn't she have anything? If I moved to another planet—and stars guide me, I hoped I never would—I would want to bring my data crystals and my kits and equipment, probably some of my dishes...it was odd.

Everything about her arrival was odd.

'Jenna?' I poked my head through the door, where she had settled awkwardly on a cushion at my table. 'Why did you decide to move here?'

Her brows lifted in an expression I found difficult to parse. Some complicated emotion moved across her face, and for a moment, I wondered whether she'd answer me.

'I needed a change,' she said.

Obviously. I didn't interrupt though, and after a moment, she continued.

'I...have been fascinated by cosmorans my whole life. We...you know, we know so little about your world. But I knew it was different, and different...was what I needed.' She looked down at the table, though there was nothing to see. 'More practically, I want to learn about your plants and share gardening techniques. Maybe humans and cosmorans have lots to offer each other on that front. It's clear our approach to nature is as different as our flora is.' She smiled a little. 'As a kid, I always liked to imagine growing a garden of magical space plants. Learning things no other human has learned about caring for them. I know it won't be like that, really, but...it's still exciting to imagine.'

It was. Though I'd never been much of a gardener myself, my flame warmed at the image of a smaller, more excitable Jenna delighted by cosmoran plants. I'd never been quite so dramatic a dreamer, myself. Maybe I'd be a better cleaner, if I sought to learn from human techniques. Jenna was braver than me, not just in how she had directed her life, but in what she dreamed of doing with it.

I went back to preparing a room for Jenna. I took out my reading cushions, which while very comfortable were quite covered in my fur, and got some clean cushions and quilts from storage and laid them on the floor for her to make up however she preferred.

When I let her know it was ready, she headed for the room, only to pause in the doorway. 'Avari?'

'Hmm?'

She took a deep breath. 'Thanks for taking me in. Hopefully it won't be for long.'

Her words reminded me that I'd had no real choice in the matter. That my sibling was keeping their life secret from me, and that I'd somehow become bound to an alien just because of some ridiculous tradition.

But she also sounded genuinely grateful. I needed to remember that this was a very big change for her, for which she'd had no time at all to prepare. 'It's fine,' I said gruffly.

She gave me a fleeting smile and disappeared into the reading room—or guest room, as I supposed I now needed to think of it.

I paced the main room for a few moments. Though Jenna was in another room, I still felt her presence. Still felt like I was under scrutiny. It didn't feel like I could just grab a snack, flop down at the low table, and read something on my cosmorb as I normally would.

Eventually, I put my ears back and went into my nestroom. The blankets and cushions there were tangled up just how I liked them. I burrowed under a blanket, circled a few times, and laid down, folding my legs under me. I hoped that it wouldn't be long before Jenna's presence felt more normal. My heart was pounding and all my fur was standing up. It wasn't a feeling I wanted to keep up.

I didn't see much of Jenna the next day. Whenever I checked on her, she was either asleep or lying very still with that fogged look to her eyes, stricken by the same strange tiredness that had taken her during our journey back from the Flowering Ancient. I kept to myself; the previous day's journey had taken a lot out of me too—not so much physically as emotionally, so I read data crystals and snacked in my nest. I left some simple food for Jenna, which when I returned for the dishes, each time I discovered she'd only picked at.

I must have dozed off at some point because I startled awake at the sound of a knock on my door. I scrambled out of my nest, a blanket snagged on one of my horns, and opened the door to a nervous-looking Jenna. She looked rumpled, her hair sticking up oddly at the sides. I glanced out the window. An early-morning sun was rising. We'd slept through the rest of the day and all through the night, it seemed. Or at least, I had.

The strange lethargy of the previous day seemed to have left her. There was maybe a shadow of it in the ashen look to her skin, but her eyes were bright and focused.

Must be nice for some.

'What?' I asked, a little grumpier than I'd intended.

Jenna hesitated. 'I want to go and get supplies,' she said. 'Elm said I should be given anything I ask for at any of the shops and that they have a supply pack coming for me.'

I shrugged and used starfire to pull the blanket from my horn. 'So go do that.'

'I would,' said Jenna. 'But I don't actually know where to go.'

I sighed and stomped out of my room. A human houseguest seemed like she would take more care than a kit. 'Well, check your cosmorb. Do you have a cosmorb?'

Jenna spread her hands, fingers curling uncertainly.

I went back into my room and picked up my cosmorb and floated it out to her. 'This is a cosmorb,' I said. 'It's how you connect to Aura. We use them to message each other, read, research, take images...that sort of thing.'

She stared. It was a fairly standard cosmorb, not even an especially pretty one. It was a sphere of slightly cloudy purple crystal about ten centimetres in diameter, a little smaller than a hoof-print. 'Oh. Sort of like a phone?' The word didn't make sense to me, but she pulled a shiny flat stone out of her pocket and showed it to me. 'Although I suppose I might as well get rid of this now. I can't do anything with it. I can't even charge it...'

I sniffed the phone-stone. It smelled of Jenna and strange materials that made my nose itch. I snorted and jerked away from it. 'All right, so we need to get you a cosmorb,' I said. 'You can use mine, if you like. You just touch it with starfire and...' I trailed off, realising what I was saying.

How did humans use cosmorbs? *Could* they even use cosmorbs? Perhaps they needed a special aid, or the cosmorb had to be constructed differently...

'Avari?' Jenna prompted.

I sighed. 'Nevermind that. I'll go with you. I don't have any work today that can't wait, anyway.' I went to get my pack, which I settled so the two bags hung on either side of my back and I buckled it underneath. Then I made sure I had what I needed. I put my cosmorb in the front pocket and got some snacks from the kitchen I thought Jenna might enjoy. At a glance out the window, the weather was mild enough, so I didn't bother to pack my cloak.

'Come with me,' I said, and trotted out the door. Jenna followed me. She seemed meek, suddenly, which irritated me. I wanted to spend the day in my workroom, and maybe visit the job boards at the Cleaners' Union and see if there was any work going. I wanted my life to go back to normal, not to be stuck kit-watching some confused human.

That wasn't fair, and I was a little ashamed even to think it. Unfortunately, shame did not improve my mood.

Chapter Six

'So...where exactly are we going?' Jenna asked. We'd been walking for a while now. As early in the day as it was, I'd preferred to stretch my legs, and Jenna had agreed. I thought she was regretting it now; she needed boots, after all, so perhaps her human feet were too soft for much walking.

I had wondered if perhaps she would be too tired, but I had kept that to myself. It wasn't my place to decide what Jenna could or couldn't do.

'At midday, there'll be a market outside the Purple Garden,' I said. 'We'll probably get most of what you need there, though it's hard to say what stalls it'll have. But there are some shops and workshops in Spiral Tree I think might have some things you need.'

Not to mention that Jenna would probably need some custom orders, which were much harder to arrange at the market.

'Purple Garden? Like...like a cosmoran garden?'

I hesitated. Once again, there was a strange kind of fuzz to her words and I knew there was some context I was missing. 'I guess,' I said. 'It's like...a conservation site. The Gardener's Union have special gardeners for it or something. The market takes place right next to it.'

'Do you think...we could go in?' She sounded so wistful and so...hesitant. Like she expected to be shut down.

'Sure,' I said, and she flashed me such a bright smile that my core warmed.

When we came to Spiral Tree, I let Jenna pause a moment to take it in. Like Antlervine, Spiral contained several treeldings. But where Antlervine was housing and largely understated, Spiral contained shops and was bright and welcoming, with flowers growing on the branches and glowlights hovering outside the doors. Many of the doors were shaped and coloured to make intricate designs, each one unique. Even so early in the day, there were already folk climbing the path and going in and out of the shops.

'This is where you do your shopping?'

'Some of it,' I said with a non-committal flick of my tail. 'I suppose it might take getting used to, after your big concrete buildings.'

'Not at all,' she said, and clapped her hands together. 'Okay! Do we just start at the bottom?' She was already moving, bouncing like a young goat-shape and not the subdued human woman I was used to. I grumbled under my breath and followed her.

The first door at the base of Spiral was marked with a beautiful watercolour-and-woodshape sign of a needle and thread creating a vast and intricate spider web. It read: 'Ever's Tailoring: Many Legs Make Quick Work'

Jenna put a hand to the door and then paused, her brow furrowing. 'Uh. Are there...spider cosmorans?'

'Of course.' I tilted my head to one side, not sure where she was going with this.

'So is this...? Sorry, I'd just like to be warned if I'm about to meet a giant spider person.'

'Oh...no. Ever's not a spider.'

We walked in and Jenna froze and made a sound like a startled mouse.

'Xe's a millipede!' I said. I looked at Jenna, who had turned a very strange colour. 'Uh...Jenna?'

Ever twitched xyr antenna and set aside the roll of fabric xe'd been examining to flow over to us on xyr many, many legs. Xe was very large for a Cosmoran, xyr great length adding to xyr mass. Xyr carapace was a lovely iridescent blue-green. Xyr starfire shifted colours in clear curiosity, and xe rose up when xe reached us and sniffed politely toward us, mostly displayed through xyr antenna wiggling.

'Avari, you have a guest! A human guest, if I'm not mistaken.' Xe clicked xyr legs together excitedly. Xyr voice was low and gentle.

I sniffed back politely and nudged Jenna, who still seemed frozen. She bobbled her head uncertainly.

'Jenna's a new arrival. I'm helping her get settled,' I said. 'I don't suppose you have anything for humans about?'

'It's a pleasure to meet you, Jenna,' said Ever. 'I believe humans "shake hands"?'

I looked at Jenna, who looked almost green and stared at Ever like xe was preparing to eat her rather than greet her.

Maybe she had social anxiety? I could relate to that. I said, 'I don't think that's—' but then cut off as Jenna suddenly roused and gently shook the offered appendage.

'It's a pleasure to meet you as well,' she said. Her voice still sounded a little...strained? But she offered Ever a small smile.

'I'm afraid I don't have anything to human proportions,' Ever said. 'But I'd be delighted to make something custom for you! A human! In my shop!' Xe circled Jenna and herded her over to shelves bursting with fabric. 'We'll start with fabric. What sort of colours and textures do you like? Then we can take measurements and plan the shape...'

Jenna reached out and tentatively touched a bolt of lichen-lace. 'Oh, this is so soft,' she said. 'I don't think we have any fabrics like this on Earth...'

She seemed to have lost whatever shyness or anxiety was holding her back, so I browsed a rack of pre-made clothes and accessories. There weren't many of them and it was mostly things that didn't require custom orders—hats, leg warmers, cloaks, scarves. There were even some rather nice looking bags. Unlike some of my siblings, I'd never been big into clothes, but it was nice to have something to do rather than hover awkwardly while Jenna shopped.

I wondered whether Frost would like any of this. Night loved anything black, and Storm was very fond of hats. Illusion preferred cloaks and robes and flowy things, but there wasn't a lot here I thought would appeal to her. I smiled to myself a bit, imagining how hard it must have been for them to adhere to the tradition of taking nothing with you to a hatching ceremony, then grimaced as all the events of that day came back to me.

Frost insisting I take Jenna. Frost admitting they had a mate serious enough that they'd moved in together.

'Something against knitted caps?' asked Ever, scuttling over to me and watching me with dozens of forelegs steepled.

I blinked, realising I'd been glaring at the rack. I shifted my starfire back to its resting colour. 'Just lost in thought,' I said. Though I frowned as I took in the knitted caps. 'Would something like this fit a human, do you think?'

Ever considered the hats, picking up five and turning them this way and that. 'Well, these both have ear holes,' xe said. 'But this one was made for a phoenix-shape, and these two for monkey-shapes. They would be a little big,

I think, but...' Xe trailed off thoughtfully. 'Yes, I think it could work. She has thick hair.'

Xe held out the hats for me to consider. The two for monkey-shapes did look a little large to me, and they were almost garishly bright. One was a purple and yellow fairisle, the other with harsh stripes of black and green. But the phoenix-shape one...maybe it was a slightly awkward shape. Humans had very round heads. But the colours seemed nice. It had been knitted from striping yarn, which gave it the effect of fading from a pastel blue to a lovely pastel pink. I thought it would go well with her blue dress, so she would probably like it.

'Could I have this one?' I asked. 'Would you like anything in trade for it?' While one never *needed* to pay for things to survive, some things were considered luxuries or favours and it was polite to offer to do something in return for someone else's hard work.

Ever's antennae twitched. Xyr head canted to one side as xe considered me. 'No, I don't think that'll be necessary,' xe said. 'Do you want me to wrap it or anything?'

'No, that's fine. Thank you.'

Xe passed the hat to me, which I picked up with starfire and tucked into my pack. I made a mental note to myself to drop off some of my best cleaning solution to Ever anyway, in thanks.

We remained in Ever's for longer than I anticipated. Jenna had all sorts of questions about the fabrics—apparently human clothing was made from either animal bones or animal fur?—and it took Ever a while to take her measurements because xe needed to ask about the kind of fit humans expected from clothing.

While we were there, Jenna asked about the plants growing outside the shop. I hadn't even noticed them, but there were some large ferns with purple leaves and shrivelled, tube-like flowers. They didn't look amazing.

'Oh!' said Ever. 'Those are pallyferns. Do you have something similar on Earth?'

'I think so,' said Jenna. 'I was wondering...are they perhaps—' she hesitated '—unwell?'

Ever sighed and clicked xyr mandibles. 'They're practically drowning,' said Ever. 'I want them to survive, but the soil here is too dense or something.

They're surviving, so I haven't wanted to bother the Gardeners' Union about it.'

'Well...' Jenna took a deep breath. She looked nervous, to me. 'Maybe I could look at them? I'm a gardener—an Earth gardener—and I know some good drainage techniques. Maybe it wouldn't work, but—'

'Oh, please do!' said Ever. The pair immediately launched into a discussion of pallyferns and their care, Jenna nodding and listening carefully.

Eventually, Jenna peeled away. On our way out, Ever said, 'Be sure to tell other humans about my work!'

'I will!' Jenna waved as we left.

'Xe was very kind,' Jenna said as we started the climb up to the next level of Spiral Tree. 'Xe said xe'll prioritise my clothes, since I don't have anything else. Xe should have the first outfit ready in a few days.'

I nodded. 'Ever's nice,' I agreed. 'A bit chatty, but I suppose xe can't help it.'

Jenna snorted a laugh and shook her head. I didn't know at what.

'Why did you offer about the plants?'

Jenna raised her eyebrows. 'Isn't that how it works? We don't pay for things, but we help each other when we can?'

'I—' I stopped. It was. It was how it worked. I guess I hadn't expected her to adjust so quickly. I'd thought...I don't know, that I'd be carrying her debts for a while.

I studied Jenna. She stared back at me, something determined about the set of her jaw and shoulders.

Not like someone who needed a new acquaintance to carry her debts.

'So what's next?' she asked.

'Well...a cosmorb seems important,' I said. 'And I thought we could browse the market later and get some food there, as well. What else do you need?'

Jenna tapped her lips. 'Washing supplies to keep myself clean. A hairbrush would be good, too. Ever's going to make me a bag, so that'll be helpful. And...' She hesitated. 'Would a cosmorb let me contact home?'

'Home? You mean Earth?' I snorted, uncertain. 'I really doubt it. Aura signal only goes so far; I don't think they even have it on cosmo-gliders. Do you even have Aura on Earth?'

'Aura being your...I don't know, communication, information thing?' Jenna asked.

I nodded.

'No, but we have the internet,' she said. 'That's...gotta be similar, right?'

I pricked an ear. 'Does internet work on the harmonic resonance of crystals?'

'It...does not.' She slumped. 'God, I know nothing about technology but I'm still *pretty* sure on that one.'

We stopped in a few other shops, getting her washing supplies and other self-maintenance things she thought would be useful. Humans were very strange. She needed some kind of filing device for her nails, since they didn't naturally wear down, and she asked about cosmetic paints and lotions to make her skin healthy, which confused the shopkeepers we spoke to. Nonetheless, by the time we were done, she had a basket of supplies including some very gentle soaps, as we'd agreed it would be best not to use anything too strong until we had some idea of what human skin could withstand.

We made our way to the Purple Garden Market. Jenna was flagging a bit, so I stopped. 'Tired?'

She stared at me with wide eyes, and then laughed, a little weirdly. 'No, no, I'm fine,' she said. 'I'll keep up, don't worry.'

My ears twitched as I considered this. My brow furrowed. The two statements didn't quite match up. 'Well, if you're fine,' I said, and carried on with a dismissive flick of my tail.

She flagged further, though. I tried to match my pace to hers but it was definitely getting very slow. She kept shifting the basket from arm to arm as if she wasn't sure how to hold it, and her skin glistened with sweat.

'Why don't we take a break?' I said. I walked off the path and settled on a boulder with a nice padding of thick moss.

'Oh good!' Jenna dropped her basket and collapsed beside me.

I frowned and put my ears back. 'Why did you do that?'

'Hmm?'

'Why did you say you weren't tired, when you were? We could have taken a break earlier.'

'Oh.' Jenna tucked her hair behind her ear. 'I didn't want to be a burden, you know.' Her mouth did an odd wobble I thought might be discomfort.

I struck the boulder with a hoof. 'Why would I ask if I didn't want to know the answer? You could have told me.'

She blinked at me. 'I'm sorry. I didn't realise it was a big deal.'

'It isn't!' I growled.

Jenna raised her eyebrow at me, which made my temper rise a bit. But that wasn't reasonable. I took a deep breath. 'Look,' I said. 'I find communicating difficult. So I like it when people are honest with me and I try to be honest with them. And it would help if, when you want to ask me something or if you have a need, you just tell me. I'm not always good about noticing what other people need, especially if they don't tell me.' I shook my head and my mane spun a bit. 'I don't want to be a bad host. If you get tired, you can tell me. If I ask you something, you can answer honestly. I won't be mad.'

Jenna nodded and fell silent. I got the sense she was digesting it, which was good, but also maybe she was unhappy? It was hard to say, human faces were so exaggerated...

She said, 'I feel like I'm a burden on you already. I know it's an inconvenience to have me staying with you, and that you'd rather I was somewhere else. So I was just trying to be...a good guest, I suppose.' She stared at her hands, open in her lap.

Fog take it. Humans had better hearing than I'd thought. 'You're a good guest,' I said. 'I'm just not used to hosting. Frankly, having someone else living in my house is terrifying. Other than Frost, I never thought—' I stopped, then tried again. 'But you've been good. And I'll get used to it.'

She didn't look much reassured, which always seemed to be a problem when I tried to reassure people. 'Look, do you know verian? I'm verian. I'm not good at...this.' I gestured with a hoof between the two of us and sighed.

'Verian.' She mulled over the word. I wondered if her com-gem was trying to find an equivalent. 'Like autistic?'

The word was a little fuzzy to me but I got a meaning very similar. A mind that didn't naturally grasp social cues and ambiguity but had exceptional focus. 'Yes,' I said, relieved. 'Like that, I think.' It had some connotations of disability rather than pure difference that I found troubling, but human culture was so different from ours that that could easily account for it.

And I supposed...being verian did feel like a disability, sometimes. I was only different, but I was often punished for that even though I couldn't help it. And I found being around other people so much more difficult than my non-verian siblings did, even though we'd all been raised the same.

'Okay,' said Jenna. 'I...I think I understand, then. I'll try to be more clear and open with you.'

'Thank you.'

She raised her eyebrows at me. 'And you...?'

'And I...?' I had no idea where she was going with this. Was this a reciprocal situation? I'd explained my communication needs and she'd agreed to them. What else was there to say?

She shook her head. 'Nevermind. It doesn't matter.'

After a while, I ventured, 'Do all humans get tired as much as you? Are you usually this tired? I think maybe I'm pushing you too hard.'

Jenna rubbed her face with her hands. It was a long moment before she responded. 'No,' she said at length. 'Not all humans, but some humans. I have a disability called ME. I got sick once and then...I just started getting tired all the time. Worse and worse. I get tired easily and sometimes it makes my head feel woolly or...or foggy, I guess. Confused. And I get really tired, painful, and even sick after activity.'

The word was new to me, but I knew cosmorans who had chronic fatigue that sounded very similar. 'So all this walking was bad for you,' I said, with a sinking feeling. I needed to make sure Jenna didn't just go along with what I suggested out of obligation.

She shook her head. 'It's...complicated. Walking makes me happy but it also makes me sick. But sometimes even getting out of bed—nest—makes me sick. I just have to manage it, is all.' She stared out across the forest, where animals and cosmorans alike were going about their days, crunching through the leaves. 'Today is an important day, so I decided I wanted to go out and take the consequences. But probably it'll be a while before I can go out again.'

'Oh,' I said. I contemplated this. 'Is it hard, being a gardener and having ME?'

'Yes,' she said shortly, and there was such a heaviness to her words that my ears drooped in sympathy.

We sat for a while until Jenna said she felt like walking again. I picked up her basket handle in my mouth and carried it. I could probably starfire it if I needed to, but I had a strong neck and it wasn't *that* heavy.

'You don't have to do that—' Jenna started.

'Obviously.' I said, a little muffled around the basket.

Jenna hesitated then gave me a small smile. 'Thanks.'

We took a canopy-tram to the market, since I didn't want to exhaust Jenna before we even got there. She still seemed nervous of the tram, particularly when it was on a downward swoop, so I let her hold onto my fur like Frost had. I didn't like the sensation of being touched but I liked her being nervous even less, and I had meant what I said about being a good host.

When we got off at the stop, Jenna froze in the middle of the path for a moment while the other passengers streamed around us. I thought maybe she'd seen another millipede-shape. Instead, she said, 'This is incredible.'

I followed her gaze. Far above us, the Circle Tree—a vast tree with beautiful pink leaves—stood atop a floating crop of rock and earth that was latticed with roots. It was the central floating island of Lost Circle, a ring of smaller rock islands hovering around it. Below the ring was a meadow of mostly tall purple flowers: the Purple Garden. During the day, they seemed inert enough, but at night their hearts lit up like crystals. They swayed gently in the breeze, their heads barely taller than the long grass.

It *was* beautiful. I'd always liked the Purple Garden. And it was considered a sacred site, a wonder of nature. But it had never struck me with awe the way it seemed to affect Jenna right now. Her eyes looked...wet. Was she crying?

'Could we go look at it?' Jenna asked me suddenly, still staring at the garden. 'Is that allowed?'

'Of course it's allowed,' I said. 'We'd better do the market first though. It's only open for a few hours.'

Jenna nodded and swiped at her face. 'That would be wonderful.'

I had questions. Wasn't Jenna a gardener? Why was she struck speechless by the sight of a tree and some flowers? But then she'd talked about human settlements being places of concrete and glass...I couldn't reconcile her job with the world she'd described. I'd have to ask her about it later.

The market, too, seemed to fill her with delight, though not the teary awe of the garden. Various stalls had been set up. Tables laden with woven baskets and carved stands and racks. Some were farmers and gardeners selling fruits, flowers, and even the rare vegetable. I filled my pack with a delicious selection including a bundle of lazyroot, which was hard to grow in forest environments and I'd been missing from home. Jenna picked things as well and chatted with every shopkeeper, asking for suggestions and cooking tips. Her shyness and exhaustion had faded, somewhat. She seemed bright and full of laughter now.

As for everyone else, they were delighted by her presence. I couldn't tell how much was the excitement of a human and how much was just the long-seated tradition of welcoming travellers, but Jenna was encouraged to take something from nearly every stall, and she walked away with a string of beads, a nested stack of beautifully woven baskets in shades of pink, purple, and green, a data crystal about the history of Lost Circle, and all sorts of other small things.

But while the people greeting her were full of kindness, I couldn't help but notice less friendly eyes in the crowd, watching from a distance or carefully giving her a wide berth. A wolf-shape with tail and ears low. A dragon-shape with starfire shifting toward shadow-edged red. A sphinx-shape with fur raised and a hint of fang. I returned their mistrustful looks by pawing at the ground and levelling my stare at them. If they were going to be rude, I was more than willing to match them. When they looked away, I shielded Jenna from sight.

Their dislike...it struck something in me.

I put the thought aside. I could look into it later.

We didn't end up leaving the market until closing. Jenna waved goodbye to several of the shopkeepers as they closed down their stalls, still aglow with socialising, though the glow was fading more back to her usual levels. I led her into the Purple Garden.

Unlike the main paths of Lost Circle, the Circle Tree and the Purple Garden had not been formally gardened and were largely allowed to grow free of cosmoran interference, excluding specialist gardeners. The grass was so tall it reached my chest and tickled Jenna's chin. The flowers were about Jenna-height, and she stopped to examine them with gentle hands, feeling the texture of the stem, leaves, and petals, and peppering me with questions I didn't really know the answer to.

'They just...grow here,' I told her. 'They always have. One of the conservation gardeners might be able to help you more.' Conservation gardeners being the folk who maintained sites of natural heritage like this, though I had no idea how to find one other than stumbling across them in the garden. 'There might be stuff about them in that data crystal you got. The Purple Garden is a big part of Lost Circle.'

We found a rocky place to sit. It had a nice view over the grass. I tucked my legs under me a little awkwardly; my prosthetic was acting up and didn't want to fold. After my third attempt to fold it, Jenna said, 'Would you like my help?'

I stared at her for a moment. 'Uh...yeah, actually. I can't quite poke the knee joint in.' I held out my leg to her. I couldn't even use starfire to shift it. The back of my knee was just out of sight and it was difficult to manipulate things with starfire you couldn't see.

Jenna had hands, though. She felt along the knee until she found the joint, then put her hands to either side and folded it in. I adjusted the fit against my upper leg and then settled down, relieved to have it sorted.

'I was always a bit jealous of my sister for having hands,' I told her. 'Not that I'd give up my hooves for them, but they do seem really useful. It's like having a second starfire.'

'I dunno,' said Jenna. She leaned back against the rock, staring up at the sky. 'I'd give up hands for starfire.'

I looked up as well. Wispy clouds drifted across the purple sky, pushed by a gentle breeze. The heartstar was red and beautiful, mid-way through its descent. The moon Crystallo glittered above it; the moon Umbra was a shadow to the west. All around us, the grass rustled gently as it swayed.

For a while, we just sat in silence. I liked that. It reminded me of hanging out with Frost, who was always happy to talk internally with themselves when they could sense I wanted quiet.

Jenna whispered, 'I'm really on an alien world.'

I looked at her where she lay with her arms behind her head, staring up at the sky like it was new and beautiful—which for her, I suppose it was. What must it be like to gaze up and see a sky so different from the one you knew?

I'd heard that on earth the sky was blue, and that their sun was big and yellow, unlike our heartstar. A brighter, harsher sky with a brighter, harsher star.

'Do you miss it?' I asked her.

Her mouth shifted to one side, considering. 'Not yet,' she said. 'But I can tell I will. When the shock wears off, I think.'

My ears twitched, one forward, one back. 'This is you in shock?'

She glanced at me and smiled. 'It is, a bit.'

She was very resilient. More resilient than me, probably. When I was shocked, I froze or fled or cried.

'Do you want to go back?' she asked me.

I realised I didn't. I was happy here. I watched a small oozemouse, trailing slime, climb up three blades of grass pulled together. Several birds flew overhead. I'd heard most birds on earth only had two wings, instead of four or six. Like a bird-shape cosmoran rather than the animals we knew. 'I'm happy to stay as long as you are,' I said. Something occurred to me. 'Oh! By the way, I...I got something for you.'

She sat up a little, propped up on her elbows. I suddenly felt self-conscious about it. I had never given a gift to anyone who wasn't in my family. But it was too late to take it back now that I'd told her about it.

I opened my pack and floated the hat over to her. 'Ever said it should fit,' I said.

She accepted it gently, running the knit beneath her fingers the way she had with the fabric. Like she'd never felt it before. She smiled. 'I like these colours,' she said. 'You know, on Earth, these are the colours of a flag that's very important to me.'

I tilted my head.

'Pastel blue and pink are part of the trans flag,' she said. 'It's a symbol of pride.'

Trans. The word was a little fuzzy to me, but not without meaning. Gender different to what was assigned to you. I supposed that word fitted me as well, though there was a cultural weight to it that I couldn't quite parse. It meant something a little different on Earth. Carried a different history that starfire alone could not translate.

She pressed it to her chest for a moment and closed her eyes. 'I love it,' she said. She opened her eyes and smiled at me. 'Thank you.' She rubbed her thumbs across the fabric. 'Maybe I should get one in aro-ace colours, as well.'

I flicked my tail dismissively, but couldn't suppress the warm feeling that gave me. I shifted a little and rested my chin on the rock. We stayed there, among the grass and flowers, for a long time.

Chapter Seven

The next few weeks passed strangely. I liked Jenna, but it still felt wrong having to edge around someone in my own house. I did my best not to show her that, but I'd always been terrible at hiding my feelings.

Jenna often went out, though it would take her a day or more to recover. Sometimes she asked me to go with her, making good on her promise for clarity and openness. Sometimes she went alone, shopping and exploring. She got her first two outfits from Ever, and it was strange to see her wearing normal fabrics instead of those strange Earth materials. One was a knitted dress over simple trousers, and shoes with woven soles that looked very different from her Earth ones. The other was another pair of trousers but this time paired with a loose short-sleeved top. Both outfits were in gentle pastel colours: greens and pinks.

She was still waiting on a cosmorb; the cosmorb crafter, Urath, thought she was getting close to a solution. Jenna got hold of a human-appropriate privy that had some kind of hidden compost bin in it and was much less smelly and messy than a chamberpot.

Except for when Jenna asked me for company, I stayed home, throwing myself into my work. I was on the verge of a breakthrough in my experiments to create a more effective, environmentally-friendly cleaning solution, and the Cleaners' Union Convention was only a few months away. I had a few brief excursions to do jobs for the Union, including a restaurant that needed a deep clean and a house job for someone who'd been struggling to keep it up themselves.

Though I didn't often like leaving the house, I did like doing cleaning jobs. It was difficult and sometimes unpleasant, but it gave me a deep sense of satisfaction to turn mess into order, and people were always grateful for the help. I was one of the more experienced cleaners in Lost Circle, too—many people only held the same job for a decade or so, and less for more physically taxing jobs like cleaning. But I'd been a cleaner for a hundred years and couldn't imagine doing anything else. It was important work that made people happy, and I could do it well. Many folk had to settle for much less in life.

I was at home in my workshop when I felt my cosmorb resonate across the room, creating an answering shiver in my starfire. I carefully turned down the heat on the solution I'd been simmering and floated the cosmorb over to me. I activated it and focused my mind, sending it the runes for communication. Soon enough, the message appeared within the crystal, each rune sketching into place as if by fiery ink.

It was from Frost. It said, 'Do you want to meet up at the lesser lake at sundown tomorrow?'

I could feel the emotions attached to the message: cautious, yet hopeful. They knew I'd been hurt by the knowledge they'd been keeping such a big part of their life secret from me. I sighed and set aside the cosmorb. I needed time to process this. I could feel a knot of anxiety in my chest over the need to respond, but I reminded myself that Frost knew me very well and was used to delayed responses from me. It didn't ease the anxiety, but it helped me resolve not to reply until I was ready.

I picked up a dollop of the solution—a great benefit of starfire over hands is that there's no physical touch, so cosmorans can move very hot things without concern—and spread it across a clay plate I'd smeared with dirt. The solution did lift the dirt very smoothly, but it seemed oddly thick and wasn't evaporating as I'd wanted it to. I investigated a bit further.

Jenna poked her head around the door. 'I'm just heading out,' she said. 'Elm said there are some supplies at the Travellers' Union for me to pick up today.'

I nodded, scanning my notes. Had I simmered the solution for too long, or had I gotten the ingredient balance wrong?

Jenna hovered a moment. 'Well. Bye.'

'Bye,' I replied distractedly and continued with my work.

When I decided to give my cleaning experiments a rest for the day, I trotted out of the room and stretched, leaning on my forelegs and stretching my hindlegs out behind me. 'Jenna?' I shook out my mane, ears flapping.

'Jenna, are you about?' The door to her room was ajar so I poked my snout in, but she wasn't there. Odd.

Oh right. The Travellers' Union.

Well. It seemed I had the day to myself. I cleaned up a bit at first, collecting up my scattered clothes and possessions and returning them to the appropriate baskets. Then I did a wipe-down of all the surfaces and scrubbed the floor, though it was already pretty clean. I was careful not to disturb any cobwebs in the corners—the little spinnerbugs and spidermoths that had settled here did a good job of cleaning up pests and I didn't want them to feel unwelcome.

I was surprisingly tired at the end. In spite of being a career cleaner, I wasn't very tidy at home, and I had a weird emotional block about it sometimes. But seeing it looking clear and clean was satisfying, and I hoped Jenna would appreciate its new state.

I went to the kitchen and chopped up a bunch of flowers and savoury fruits and threw them into a pot on the cooker. I still had some fresh rolls Jenna had picked up at the Purple Garden Market the other day that would go nicely with it. It wouldn't be a particularly impressive home-cooked meal, but by now Jenna was surely used to the fact that I did very little cooking.

While it was boiling, I got one of my data crystals down from a shelf and settled at the low table to read. I set the cosmorb hovering over the table and then tapped the data crystal against it. At the ring of crystal-hitting-crystal, the data crystal lit up and began to orbit the cosmorb like a tiny satellite. I settled down to read, projecting a screen out from the cosmorb. The cosmorb gave me not just the words but the emotional sensations embedded in the story and sometimes even a hint of smell or distant sound. Sometimes, I liked to disable sensory additions, but other times, it was soothing. I could lose myself in the story more completely and temporarily forget the anxiety knotting in my chest.

I particularly liked fantasy stories. This one played on a common theme—set in a mythical past where cosmorans were still shapeshifters and could thereby accomplish amazing things in spite of the lack of technology. It was a world more dangerous than the one I knew. In fantasy stories like this, cosmorans were war-like, some even predatory, hunting and killing other cosmorans in search of power and possessions, and killing and eating animals for sustenance. As brutal as the world was, the main characters never stopped trying to do the right thing, never stopped being kind. I found the idea comforting.

I was so engrossed in my data crystal that I didn't notice Jenna come in. 'That smells great,' she said, and I was so startled that I jumped a little.

'Oh, uh, hi,' I said. 'It's just a meatgourd stew. It should be ready in an hour or so.'

'Meatgourd?'

I shook myself a little and stood up and stretched my hindlegs out behind me. 'There's another one in the cold store,' I said. 'It's the long pink gourd with the golden markings.'

Jenna picked it up and examined it. 'I didn't think markings like this existed in the wild. I wonder what the difference is, that lets it do that...' She trailed off a moment, then asked, 'So it tastes like meat?'

I made a face. 'How should I know? Nobody's eaten meat in thousands of years.' Jenna nodded and retired to her room. I checked the stew, added some seasoning, and returned to my story. I tried not to think about the fact that humans ate meat regularly. As I understood it, most humans ate artificial meat grown in a lab now, but it was hard not to shudder at the thought.

And there were certainly still humans that ate other living creatures. But I *definitely* didn't want to remember that. The fog could have it.

The stew was really good. Or at least, very good for *my* cooking, which was notoriously bland. My flame tinged pink when Jenna took a bite and then enthused about the taste. She had three servings! I thought I would carry the praise with me forever. Perhaps the next time my mothers visited, I could cook them this stew.

'It doesn't really taste of meat,' she told me. 'Not Earth meat, anyway. I think maybe the texture is similar, though.'

How strange to be sitting across from a carnivore. Especially one with a gentle, flat-toothed smile and clawless hands. She didn't even have fangs. Even *I* had fangs.

Although she hadn't complained of the vegetarian-only diet, so... 'Do you eat meat?' I asked her.

'I eat the lab-grown stuff,' she said. 'But I've never been that into it. Never had meat from an animal.' She hesitated, uncomfortable. 'Is that okay?'

I blinked. 'I...yeah. Yeah, it's okay.' I picked up another mouthful of stew and sipped it a moment. 'Actually, our government is in disarray over the issue. Humans are willing to share the knowledge of harm-free synthetic meat, which some think would be a good addition to a cosmoran diet and could even help with the treatment of like...people with protein deficiencies, stuff like that. But some think eating any meat at all is abominable.'

'And you?'

I shrugged. 'I don't want to try meat. The thought of it makes me uncomfortable. But I don't think it's evil, if you aren't hurting anything to eat it.'

Jenna nodded. I couldn't quite read her expression, but I didn't think she was upset so I let it be and the conversation moved on to other things.

A few days later, Jenna's cosmorb arrived. I helped her navigate its use as best as I could, though her method of accessing it was utterly alien. She had a little foldable plank with buttons on it which she used to create inputs. It looked incredibly awkward, but her pace picked up the longer she used it. 'It's a keyboard,' she said. 'We have something similar at home to access our devices. That's all fine. My real struggle is that this is an operating system unlike anything on Earth.'

The words 'operating system' were a little fuzzy for me. I could understand their literal meaning, which made sense, but there seemed to be additional weight I couldn't quite fathom.

As she tapped away at the 'keys', I could see things pop up on the projected screen the same way they would if navigating by starfire, though it certainly seemed slower. 'What exactly are you trying to do?'

She tapped her lips. 'Well, a map of the city would be good. And I'd definitely like to learn to use data crystals the way you do. And Lisster at the market said we can message each other, once I got a working cosmorb, and I think that'd be fun.'

'Lisster?' I perked my ears. I didn't know Lisster.

'Oh, she runs the bead stall. That's where I got this.' She raised her wrist, showing me a lovely band of polished beads. It had probably been custom-made—not many cosmorans had wrists as narrow as Jenna's. She bit her lip. 'But what I'd really like...I don't know. You probably can't help. Elm said it's difficult.'

75

I snorted. 'Spit it out. I won't know if you don't ask.'

Jenna rang her fingers lightly across the keyboard, not looking at me. 'I want a way to contact home. There are people on Earth who'll be wondering what happened to me, and I have to go through the TU to send messages. I wondered...it seems like Aura is very similar to the internet...'

'Oh.' I frowned and swished my tail. 'Well, they don't use any of the same infrastructure. But...well, there's somewhere you could try.'

Jenna looked up, eyes wide with hope.

I sighed. 'It's hard to explain. And it's weird. I'll take you tomorrow.'

So I did. We got off the canopy-tram and I led Jenna to Lush Tree. The ground floor dwelling had a sign over the door. 'INTERNET CAFÉ', it read, and there was a sign of a steaming mug and a little box and keyboard. The windows were decorated with hanging beads and strips of fabric, and the door was open and filled with the same.

'I figure they'll probably know what to do,' I said, pointing with a hoof. 'I've never gone in myself, but—' I stopped. Jenna stared at the café with wide eyes.

'Oh my god,' she said, which seemed like a weird thing to say when confronted with a small café.

'Uh.'

'I just...there used to be cafés like this on Earth like...a hundred years ago or something.' She shook her head. 'It's even weirder to see one here than it would be on Earth.'

'I'll take your word for it,' I said. I led the way inside, pushing aside the beads and fabric with starfire so they didn't catch on my horns.

Inside it looked like a normal enough café. It had low tables and a counter in front of the kitchen at the back. Most of the tables were normal enough, but I couldn't help but notice a crowd of people around a table, each with their cosmorbs hooked up to...some kind of large, shiny black stones, like big versions of Jenna's phone. They also had keyboards, though anyone could see their starfire was plenty functional.

As we walked in, everyone looked up. The cat-shape behind the counter actually gasped. 'A human customer!' She pressed her paws to her cheeks and then bounded over the counter to run up to Jenna.

I interposed myself between them, puffing up my chest. She tried to peer around me. Her fur was a calico pattern of greys, blues, and purples. Her starfire was sparkling pink and her eyes were mismatched lilac-and-blue. Her three tails whipped the air behind her in obvious excitement.

'Welcome, welcome!' she said. She didn't even sniff toward Jenna. 'I'm Cloud, and this is the Internet Café!'

I relented and stood aside, since she was just going to crane her neck to stare past me anyway.

Jenna, for her part, showed none of the shock she'd exhibited when meeting Ever. She'd really adjusted to cosmorans. She offered Cloud a bright smile. 'I'm Jenna,' she said. 'And this is my friend, Avari. We're hoping you might know something about contacting Earth?'

'Oh, do I!' Cloud said happily. She had an unbearably smug expression even for a cat-shape. 'Well, let's get you comfortable and with something nice to eat and then we'll see about sorting you out with an internet connection. Do you want to shake hands? I've always wanted to shake hands.'

Jenna laughed and dutifully reached out with her tiny soft human hand and touched it to Cloud's enormous padded paws, and they bobbed them up and down.

Cloud led us to a low table and took our orders. Jenna ordered a fruit smoothie and a sandwich. I ordered a glass of water and some soup and rolls. She practically skipped back to the kitchen.

Jenna put her elbows on the table and leaned across it toward me. 'This is great!' she said, her voice squeaky with excitement. 'I had no idea it would be this easy to get an internet connection. Elm made it sound so difficult!'

'I dunno,' I said. 'Didn't Cloud strike you as...a little intense?'

Jenna made a little snorting sound and said, 'No more so than some people I've met here.'

I put my ears back. 'You're teasing me.'

I thought she would apologise, but instead she smiled very gently. 'Only because I like you very much.'

I was too shocked to know what to make of that, but it made me feel very warm inside. Better than an apology, I decided.

'Ahem,' said someone. I looked up and flinched. Somehow every cosmoran at that crowded table was now standing over us and sniffing excitedly at Jenna, their flames all a-sparkle. A crow-shape, a hyena-shape, a jackalope-shape, and a chimaera-shape with four dragon heads.

'It's an honour to meet a human traveller,' said the hyena-shape earnestly. 'No, really.'

'Can I shake your hand too?' asked the crow-shape.

'Oh. Uh, of course,' said Jenna. She tried to get up but it was awkward to extract herself when they were hovering so close.

'Give her some space!' I growled, and they jumped back as one unit.

Jenna 'shook hands' with each of them and they seemed delighted as they introduced themselves. I didn't see how I could remember their names when they were given all at once yet, but then they didn't seem too interested in me. This was a Jenna problem.

'We use the internet nearly every day,' said the chimaera-shape, whose system name was Mers. 'We're really happy to show you how it works.'

'That'd be great, tha—'

'Do you know anyone who would want to be a "pen pal"?' asked the hyena-shape, whose name was Nila. 'I know it doesn't involve any pens! I just find the concept fascinating...'

'Uh, I'm not sure—'

'Do you have a fursona?' asked the crow-shape.

Jenna blinked at that one. 'I'm sorry, did you just say "fursona"?'

That was a word I absolutely didn't know but I didn't want to hang around for a better definition. The café weirdos had all crowded closer again and I was getting a tight, panicked feeling in my chest I knew could grow into something worse. I stood up and shouldered through the group. They made way because their options were to move or get stomped on and headbutted, but they closed ranks again the moment I passed.

I paused a moment. Jenna was hidden from view, but I could hear her laughing so she was probably all right. I made my way to the counter.

Cloud was there, assembling food and drink on a tray. She brightened when she saw me, nose quivering in a polite greeting. 'I'm just about to bring your order over,' she said. 'Just trying to make it nice.' She took three dried flower heads from a ceramic jar and arranged them artfully on the surface of my soup.

'Oh,' I said. 'Yeah, thanks.'

She hummed to herself a moment, a sweet tune I didn't recognise. 'I haven't seen you around here before,' she said. 'Are you just here because of your human friend?'

I nodded. 'She's a new arrival.'

'Really? Wow. How did you meet?'

'In the Elder Grove,' I said. Somehow, Cloud's earnest attention drew it out of me. 'She says her portal spat her out there alone. I was going to my sibling's hatching day ceremony.'

Cloud picked up the tray and froze. 'Sibling?'

I nodded. 'My fourth sibling, actually. Well, sixth, depending on how Frost is counting themselves...'

Cloud's ears perked forward. She grinned at me. 'You're funny.'

I laid my ears flat and drew back a bit. 'It's not a joke. I have six younger siblings.'

Cloud laughed and carried the trays around the counter, shaking her head. 'Good one.'

I couldn't completely keep down the irritated bleat that grew in my belly. I stomped once and followed Cloud to the table.

I hated it when people didn't believe me. I wasn't in the habit of lying to people, and claiming I had six siblings was a ridiculous lie to make anyway. I knew having lots of siblings was highly unusual—having two kits was uncommon, let alone seven—but it wasn't *impossible*. We were the proof, and I knew there had to be other families like ours out there. I'd read plenty of data crystals about it. Statistically, there were probably many other families with multiple kits in Lost Circle.

Still, her disbelief irked me. Reminded me of how everyone treated us as either blessed or freakish when we were kits—one of many reasons I'd been excited to leave Athelean, the village I'd grown up in, behind.

When I got back to the table, the jackalope-shape, Keera, had already taken my seat and was seriously directing Jenna. 'Right...pairing to the café's computers is difficult, but if you enter the right rune sequence...that's right, the harmonics need to be translated into human numbers...'

I cleared my throat and stomped once. Everyone except Keera looked at me. She continued her monologue. Jenna looked between her and me and gave me what I thought must be a pleading expression. I'd definitely want to be rescued in her position. I tried to think of an easy way to get the jackalope out of my seat without offending her, since she was clearly Jenna's best bet for getting connected to her human Aura.

Cloud used her paws to make room on the table and then set down the trays of food. 'That's enough for now,' said Cloud. 'Let's give them some space. And give Avari their seat back.'

I stared at her, one ear forward and one back. I hadn't realised she'd even caught my name, as focused as she'd been on Jenna.

There were various murmured agreements, farewells, and apologies. Keera blinked and hopped up and out of the way without a word.

Cloud narrowed her eyes at me in a friendly smile and trotted back into the kitchen, her tails swishing.

I hesitated, as stunned by the abrupt absence of Jenna's admirers as I'd been by their sudden appearance, then settled across from Jenna. I studied my tray; the soup looked spectacular. Cloud's control of her starfire was so precise that not a drop of soup or drink was spilled.

'You okay?' I asked Jenna. I noticed she still had one of those big black slates—computers—connected to her cosmorb via a thin, crackling line of energy. And one of those strange keyboards as well, with runes I didn't recognise. She'd set it aside to dig into her sandwich.

'I'm good, thanks,' she said. 'A little overwhelmed, I guess. But those people are really kind and seem to know a lot about communicating with Earth. I think I'll be able to send a message by the end of the day.' She took a bite of her sandwich and made a little happy sound.

'Tasty?'

'Very,' she said. 'It's also great that I can just use my hands for it, as I forgot to pack my cutlery today.' She patted the bag beside her, but without the support of her other hand, some of the filling from her sandwich fell out. 'Shit.'

Seemed like a weird thing to say about your food falling apart, but she said it a lot so I let it pass. 'They might even have cutlery here,' I said. 'They seem...enthusiastic...about humans.'

Jenna snorted. 'Just a bit.' She glanced at the table of her fans, some of whom immediately waved.

Jenna's cheeks flushed and she looked down at her plate. 'I wonder why there aren't any other humans here, though? I ought to tell Elm about it, they could get some help sending messages to Earth...'

I didn't know what to say to that because it seemed painfully obvious why Internet Café didn't get human customers. I took a gulp of my soup instead, lifting a solid dollop of it with one of the dried flowers floating on top. It was absolutely delicious, a touch of spice and a pleasant crunch added by the flower. 'Wow. Cloud really knows how to cook.'

Jenna raised her eyebrows. 'Why the surprised tone?'

I snorted and took another sip instead of answering.

'Oh...Avari, you've got some soup in your beard...are there napkins here or anything?'

'Hmm? Oh, I have a cloth.' I took a cloth from my pack and wiped my beard as best as I could, a little embarrassed.

'Better,' said Jenna. I folded up the cloth so the mess was on the inside and put it back into my pack.

I left Jenna to her admirers and headed to a cleaning job I'd picked up from the union the other day. Someone who lived north of the Purple Garden wanted help with their house, but didn't provide any further details. I stopped home to collect my cleaner's kit, prepared for something absolutely wild: slime, flooding, mould. It was always the people who gave as few details as possible who had the most outrageous mess.

But when I arrived, a tired-eyed rat-shape with a dwindling dark starfire and pearlescent black fur peered out at me. They took in my kit, which had all sorts of bottles and rolled up cloths poking out of the external pockets. They vaguely sniffed toward me. 'You're the cleaner?' Their voice was raspy and barely above a whisper.

Misgiving stirred in my belly. Something wasn't right. 'I'm Avari, Cleaner's Union,' I said. I took my accreditation badge out of my bag and showed it to them.

They got up on their hind legs and wrung their hands nervously. 'Come in, come in,' they said, stepping aside. 'I'm—I'm really sorry about the mess.'

I walked in cautiously, expecting disaster. The floor was cluttered with objects, as were all the surfaces. The kitchen was overflowing with dirty dishes which looked like they'd been left for some time. I had to pick my way into the room, glad I had hooves rather than large flat feet like a gorilla-shape. It was a big job, but not unpleasantly so.

The rat-shape shuffled after me, their claws clicking on the floor. 'I know it's—I know it's really bad,' they whispered. I looked at them. Their whiskers and ears drooped, and they stared at the floor. 'I just didn't know what else to do. I kept saying I would get to it later, but later never came, and then...and then it was too big.'

My ears went back. It was a perfectly ordinary mess. A little out of hand, maybe, but I'd seen far, far worse. But this rat-shape...with their tired eyes and tiny flame. The sparkle in their eyes reduced to the faintest shimmer.

'What's your name?' I asked them.

They smoothed their whiskers nervously. 'I'm Needle.'

I nodded. 'There's no need to apologise,' I said. 'This is my job.'

They seemed to shrink on on themself. 'I wanted to clean up a bit before you arrived but—'

I shook my head. 'Then what would be the point of calling for a cleaner? What do you need cleaned—just this room?'

'Oh, whatever you think,' Needle said hurriedly. 'Just this room would be a huge blessing.'

I checked the other rooms. Bedroom and privy both needed work. Storage room was mounded with clutter to the point it would be difficult to get in. I wasn't sure I'd be able to do it all in one day, but I was happy to come back as often as needed to finish the job.

'For now,' I said, 'You go into the bedroom or go out for a bit and I'll clean in here. Is there anything you don't want me to handle?'

Needle shrugged a little helplessly. 'I just want help. Any help.'

I sent Needle off and got to work. The first job was picking up everything on the floor so that I'd have more room to work. I found several baskets that were either empty or jumbled and decided to use them for sorting. In spite of the mounds of stuff, it didn't take that long. My goal was less to get everything perfectly organised and more to get things off the floor and vaguely in order.

Once that was done, I realised there was a rug on the floor which had become horribly stained and a little mouldy, so I found a wash basin and took it outside to give it a good scrub. With the help of a fabric detergent I'd picked up from another cleaner at the CU, and with a large amount of dragging it against a washboard, I got it nearly as good as new, the pattern bright and fresh-looking.

While I hung that up to dry, I tackled the kitchen. I won't go into the details—the dishes had certainly turned—but the magical thing about cleaning is that if you have a strong enough stomach, you can make anything good again.

At first glance, I'd thought the kitchen hadn't needed much cleaning. But once the dishes were gone, I could see there was more grime than expected and I was well aware it needed thorough disinfecting. I used an older, stable version of my cleaning solution, which didn't evaporate like I wanted but had excellent lift. I dusted surfaces and mopped the floor while I let it dry, then came back for more applications. Sometimes you needed a few attempts to really get something clean.

On a hunch, I checked the cold storage and cooker and could see that they were badly in need of attention as well, so I started on them, taking any gone-off food outside to Needle's composter.

I took a break outside for a quick snack and sip of cold rainwater from my pack, but otherwise I focused wholly on the cleaning. I knew that if I needed to, I could stretch out the cleaning over a few weeks to pace myself, but every time I considered that I thought of Needle, tired and apologetic as they stared at the floor, and I worked harder. I wanted them to come home to a transformation.

When they returned, their nose quivered and their eyes filled with tears. 'This is—you did all this for me? Thank you. Thank you so much.' They covered their eyes with their hands and started to sob.

I didn't know how to comfort a near stranger. I didn't like to touch even my family. But I settled down beside them while they cried, folding my legs under me and projected patience as best as I could. When their tears subsided a little, I said, a little gruffly, 'I'll be back tomorrow to work on the other rooms.'

I left with Needle's profuse thanks still following me. I felt both warm inside and a little...sad. I had been in Needle's position before. I'd been in a black place where doing anything at all seemed impossible, and then doing a little became inconsequential in the face of the size of work I had left. Frost had come and cleaned everything up for me so that I could start from fresh and it had changed my life.

When I returned to the Internet Café, Jenna was sitting alone. She projected out an image from her cosmorb which depicted a white screen covered in unfamiliar black runes that matched those of her new keyboard. 'I've done it,' she said. 'I've got a way to contact home.'

She didn't seem happy.

Chapter Eight

I decided to help Needle clean every week. When I returned from the latest session, I found Jenna poking at her cosmorb. She stood up as I came in and leaned against the wall. 'Frost came by,' she said, watching me as I moved. 'They want you to come visit.'

I flicked my ears back and said nothing, instead shucking my cloak and pack and shaking out my fur.

Jenna flinched as the water hit her.

'Sorry,' I said, though I didn't completely mean it. 'Raining.' I went to the kitchen to see if there was a snack in the cold storage. I'd picked up some mushroom rolls from the market just the other day.

Jenna followed me in. 'Well?' she asked. 'Are you going to go?'

I glared at her. 'Are you going to message your family on Earth?'

Her mouth pressed into a thin line and she looked at the floor. She scuffed at the floor with one foot.

I snorted. 'Maybe mind your own problems before you come poking at mine.'

I got out a roll and a plate and carried them to the low table. Jenna had tidied up, it looked like. My cushions were all fluffed and arranged, so I settled comfortably on them. I took a bite; it was a really good mushroom roll. The bread had been wrapped around a seasoned mushroom mix with just a touch of sauce and it had enough bite to it that I didn't feel the need to get out the yellow chutney my mother had posted to me.

Jenna crossed her arms, her shoulders high and tense. 'It's not the same, you know.' She didn't look at me.

I flicked an ear and continued eating.

'Your siblings love you,' she said. 'My family...well. It isn't like that.'

I set down my roll. 'You don't know anything about my family.'

'No? I know Frost made a mistake and they're trying to make up for it. Are you really never going to speak to them again?'

I glared at her. 'No. I don't know. What business is it of yours?'

'None!' She threw up her hands. 'Just...nevermind.' She strode into her room and closed the door.

I got up and stomped hard a few times, just letting the feelings out. Then I shook out my mane, again and again, until it felt like I'd burned up all the restless energy Jenna had put into me. She didn't know what she was talking about, and it was none of her business anyway.

I went into my room to read on my cosmorb, but before I activated the data orb, I checked my messages. There was an unread message from Frost still shimmering at me.

I bleated once and left the house, the angry beat of my hooves on Antlervine Tree's path driving out the unwelcome emotions. I left the paths and trudged toward the lake near my house, rustling through bushes and ferns, small animals fleeing my loud movements. The rain had stopped and everything now was wet and muddy.

When at last I found my hooves at the edge of the lake I stopped, breathing hard through my nose. The waters stretched out before me, the surface given gentle current by the wind. A lizardfox lapped at the water on the other side, two of its four legs in the water. Several birds swam on the surface, their wings riotous in colour with diaphanous feathers that caught the light, the hind wings folded, the forewings lifted like sails.

There was hardly anyone here, leaving the quiet undisturbed. Across the lake, I saw a glimmer of starfire behind a shrub, and another disappearing between the trees. I liked that this lake—my lake, as I thought of it—was so often quiet. It didn't have the wide appeal of the larger lake, Prenthea, which sat at the north of Lost Circle and was fed by a small waterfall. People went there to bathe and play and socialise, and I had always found it unbearably loud. As far as I knew, this lake, with its little island in the middle, was not even noteworthy enough to be named.

I found a mossy patch of grass beside the lake and settled down, folding my legs under me. The fur on my legs and belly was wet with mud but I didn't care. The breeze and the moist moss seeped into my fur, the chill of it clarifying. I lowered my chin, resting it at the edge of the lake.

THE OLD GOAT AND THE ALIEN

Was I really never going to speak to Frost again? Frost, who had spent time with me nearly every week since we'd moved to Lost Circle. Frost, who'd played with me when we were kits, and who stood up for me when my mothers got into a lecturing mood. Frost, who visited me when I was in the deepest, darkest hole of emotions and knew only how to snap and sleep; whose patience with me had been a much-needed lifeline.

For as long as I could remember, it had always been me and Frost. A pair, taken together almost as naturally as people paired the twins. Not many were lucky enough to have siblings, and even fewer were fortunate enough to have siblings that were their friends. And Frost and I...we had been friends since we still had fruit-fur. Since before I knew I was verian. Since before they knew they were plural.

I remembered Night's frustration as we stood outside Elm's office. *'Our mate is living with us, okay?'*

Like I had dragged it out of them. Like they were fed up with explaining themselves to me. Everything about that moment still made me miserable and squirmy and...shocked. Why had they hidden something so big from me?

Because I was a ruiner, like Nova had said. Because I was awkward and bad at making friends and they were embarrassed of me. Because they didn't really see me as a friend, but as an obligation. There was no end to the reasons, and each one rang painfully, sickeningly true.

I snorted, my breath causing the tiniest ripple on the surface of the lake. They were better off without me.

I recognised this pattern of thinking. I knew it was no good—that I was playing into my own insecurities, letting myself spiral—but I couldn't seem to stop myself. Because those insecurities weren't based on nothing.

A waterbird drifted over to me and started to preen their wing. They fell asleep mid-preen with their beak tucked between their wings. Gently, careful not to disturb the bird, I reached out with starfire and shifted a feather out of their eye. They didn't stir.

Eventually, I got up and went home. I picked up my cosmorb from where it had rolled when I left. I looked at the unread message, still blinking at me.

I opened the message. *'I miss you.'* was all it said. I could feel the rush of regret included with it.

I stayed there a long time, trying to think of what to say.

I didn't reply.

When I emerged from my room, I was surprised to find Jenna sitting at the low table.

She stood up, taking me in with soft eyes. 'Do you want to talk about it?'

Something about her gentleness made my fur stand up and my ears go back. 'No!' I stomped past her. 'Just give it a rest, all right?'

'All right! Sorry!' Jenna threw up her hands. 'I didn't—I don't mean to push you.' She sighed, her breath ragged. 'I just...we're friends, aren't we? And I don't like to see a friend hurting.'

I stilled in the doorway to my room as I took that in. I felt like she'd struck me. Of course, people had been referring to Jenna as my friend ever since she arrived, but that had meant nothing—just a shorthand for acquaintance, for the person staying in my home. But Jenna's earnest concern struck an entirely different note.

And I was angry at her. I was really, really angry at her. For pushing me. For trying to make me do things I *knew* I should be doing. For being in my home so that I couldn't have these angry, hurt feelings in peace and solitude.

Exactly the kinds of things my siblings did, in fact.

I sighed and pressed my forehead against the doorframe. 'Of course we're...we're friends.' The word came out slightly strangled. 'I can't deal with Frost right now. I just...I can't.'

Jenna took a few steps toward me, wringing her hands. 'I shouldn't have pushed.'

I blew air. 'It's fine.' And weirdly...it almost was. 'Maybe we could go somewhere and try to forget this?'

She smiled. 'I'd like that.'

And we went out. If it wasn't happy, it was at least comfortable. I wasn't so angry at Jenna after that.

Chapter Nine

I walked into the Internet Café and instantly noticed the lack of Jenna. I tried to back out and my back thumped into someone else. I leapt away and spun to face them, horrified. It was Cloud, already laughing a snorting laugh more reminiscent of a pig-shape. She was carrying a stack of empty plates.

'I'm so sorry!' I said. 'I'll just...I should leave...'

Cloud's ears perked forward. 'You just arrived?'

I hesitated, distressed by the lack of Jenna.

'Sit down,' said Cloud. 'I'll bring you something to drink. You like fluff-fruit juice best, right?'

I murmured my thanks and went and sat down at Jenna's usual table, all too aware of my flame's embarrassed dance and pink tinge.

I didn't have anything to do so I took my cosmorb out of its pouch and started poking around on Aura. Lur had sent me several images of artfully arranged meals and of various close-ups of flowers. I didn't understand their love of documenting their life, but it made me smile to see it, and I felt a little less anxious.

Cloud placed a cup of juice in front of me. Something small and colourful bounced around inside it. I picked it out: a small stick with a carved figure on top of it that was sort of humanoid but had cat ears and two tails. It was holding its hand with two fingers out, like I had sometimes seen Jenna do when she was counting.

I was going to set it aside when Cloud flopped down onto the seat across from me. She put her forepaws on the table, her tails twitching in excitement. 'Do you like it?' she asked. 'I've been waiting for the order to come in.'

'Uh.' I studied it more closely. The humanoid had one eye closed. Was it winking at me? 'Yeah. What...uh, what is it?'

'It's me as a human!' she said. She pressed her paws to her cheeks again, a pose I still found extremely odd on a cosmoran. 'My humansona!'

I tried to parse that word. 'Your human...persona?'

She nodded excitedly. 'Yes! I'm friends with a lot of humans on Earth that have the same thing but for animals, called 'fursonas'. Some of them have even made cosmoran versions! So I wanted one but for humans.'

I stared at the little carving. 'It has cat ears,' I said.

'Yes!' She stared at me with bright eyes.

I tried again. 'It has two tails. Humans don't...humans don't have tails.'

She rolled her eyes. 'Well, obviously humans don't have *tails*. It's the essence of a human, not the reality, you know? It's about what it would *feel* like to be a human.' She paused. 'Besides, it's not real. Why shouldn't I make it however I like?'

I honestly didn't know what to say to that. Cloud's pupils contracted and her ears went back. 'Nevermind,' she said. 'I shouldn't have expected someone like you to get it.' She plucked the little stick right out of my starfire and bounded behind the bar to disappear into the kitchen.

I stared at my cup of juice, my own ears flat. When I took a sip and it was delicious, it only made me more irritated.

'Hey.'

I startled, choking on my juice. Jenna slapped my back a few times. 'Sorry! Are you okay?'

'Why did you *hit* me?' I glared at her.

She raised her hands palm-out, which I was learning to read as apologetic surrender. 'To help clear your throat so you wouldn't choke!'

'That's ridiculous,' I said. I stomped a hoof to drive it home.

Jenna cringed and I realised I was glaring at her. She wasn't the reason I was irritated. I opened my mouth to say as much when Cloud bounced back over. 'Jenna!' she said. 'Can I get you anything?' She excitedly took Jenna's order and then bounced away without looking at me.

Jenna raised her eyebrow at me.

I leaned forward. 'She's got some carved stick she's excited about,' I murmured. 'It's meant to be a human but it doesn't look like a human.'

'Oh, she has a humansona?' Jenna said.

I nodded.

'That's fine. Some humans have fursonas and it's the same thing—they aren't really animals most of the time, because they're built like humans and have colours not found in nature.'

It sounded very silly to me. 'Do you have one?'

'No, but I've known people who do. It's important to them, and fun as well.'

I considered this. 'I don't really understand it,' I said.

Jenna shrugged and nodded. 'Well, me either. But you don't need to understand it to be polite and supportive, right?'

My ears went back. '...I suppose...' I said. On reflection, I had been neither of those things.

'Jenna!' I looked up. Mers, the chimaera-shape, and Nila, the hyena-shape, were hovering at the side of the table, looking at Jenna with obvious hope. 'Do you need any help today? Is Keera's internet connection still holding up?'

'I don't need any help,' Jenna said. 'I'm just here to grab a quick drink and a snack before I head out with Avari today. And later, I'm heading off to sign up to the Gardeners' Union.' Her eyes shone. 'I'm hoping to shadow a cosmoran gardener and learn something new.'

Mers and Nila both seemed to shrink with disappointment.

Jenna caught my eye and gave me a pleading look. I shook my head but she mouthed 'sorry' and said brightly, 'Avari and I are going to visit Prenthea Lake as I haven't been yet. You're welcome to join us.'

Mers and Nila looked delighted, but before they could say anything, Cloud piped up, 'I *love* Prenthea Lake!' She set Jenna's small sandwich and smoothie on the table. I hadn't even noticed her walk over.

'I think I actually have other plans,' I said hurriedly. 'There's still a lot of cleaning contracts on the go at the CU, so—'

'Nonsense,' said Jenna. 'You just finished a three day contract yesterday. Surely you're entitled to a break.'

I snorted, lowering my brow. I didn't appreciate being boxed in like this, and I was going to say as much.

And yet, somehow, by the time Jenna had finished her sandwich, I hadn't said anything at all and found myself walking north with the Internet Café regulars, Cloud having handed over control to her co-workers who usually—very sensibly—hid away in the kitchen.

I thought they'd spend the whole journey talking about humans, but to my surprise the conversation was quite varied. Mers was a kit-carer and had just finished an educational trip to the Circle Tree with a handful of kits. Nila was a guardian and an artist but his usual paint supplier had retired and he was deciding whether to find a new supplier or to learn to mix paints himself, as he was still quite new to the skill. Cloud talked non-stop about some data crystal she'd been reading, though after a while I realised it was a translation of a human book. To my surprise, it actually sounded interesting—a story about someone who had the ability to walk through other people's dreams and end their nightmares, but was pursued by their own nightmare creatures in the waking world.

It felt odd to be walking in a group that wasn't my family. I saw other people walking places with friends or clubs or such, of course, but outside the CU convention, I'd rarely had more than a passing conversation with other people. At times, it felt sort of lonely. I had Frost, of course, but Frost could hardly spend all of their time with me, and split their social hours between family and friends. With Frost being my only family in Lost Circle and having no idea how to make friends, I'd done my best to make my peace with spending all my time alone. But as nerve-wracking as it was to be travelling with Jenna's friends, I had to admit, it was nice. It was nice to be included in conversations, and asked my opinion, and to learn more about other people's lives.

'So what's it like being a cleaner?' Mers asked me. They had all four of their heads fixed on me, swaying with serpentine focus.

I shrugged, not really sure how to explain. 'It's like any other job, I suppose,' I said. 'I take contracts from the union and head out to clean. Sometimes it's something public, like cleaning a canopy station or pavillion. Sometimes it's more personal, like helping someone clean their house or shop.'

Mers's heads bobbed one at a time. 'Isn't it like...dirty?'

'A bit,' I agreed. 'I usually need to wash after. You get better at avoiding getting dirty the longer you've been at the job, but you can't avoid it all, and sometimes you get splashed by cleaning chemicals as well. But it's not so bad.'

Mers shook their heads. 'We hate cleaning. We've had to ask the Cleaners' Union for help before, when the kits make a mess in our house and it feels like too much to sort out.'

'I'd be terrible at looking after other people's kits,' I offered. 'So it's good that we can all do jobs that suit us.' It felt like a nothing statement but I wasn't sure what else to say and I wanted to be encouraging.

Mers nodded. 'We did try cleaner's work before. We really wanted a job that gives back to the community. But kit-caring suits us much better. Although now that I think of it, kit-caring can be quite dirty as well...'

'Humans should stick to their nasty little planet,' someone said loudly as they passed. It was a wolf-shape, speaking to a coyote-shape, but they glared at Jenna as they passed. I immediately trotted ahead to stand next to Jenna. Her eyes were wide and she looked shocked, one hand resting on her collarbone.

'They don't know what they're talking about,' I said. I bumped her with my shoulder. 'We're all happy you're—'

'Hey!' Cloud pounced toward them, fur all on end. Her voice was almost spitting. 'Maybe you should stick to your nasty little friends! The rest of us don't have a taste for your shit!'

The wolf and coyote hurried away. I didn't blame them. Cloud was not small. She was tall and fat and a cat-shape besides, and everyone knew that you didn't walk away from a fight with a cat-shape.

Cloud glared after them a moment, tails lashing, then trotted over to join us. She paused to run a paw across her face, smoothing the fur and whiskers there. 'Sorry about that. I cannot abide pests; hazard of working in the food business, I suppose.'

Nila laughed, a loud, yipping laugh, but Cloud only stared at him and slowly his laughter died.

'Jenna?' I prompted.

'It's fine,' she said. She waved her hands as if swatting flies. 'It's nothing, really.' She started walking, so the rest of us followed. Conversation resumed and largely, it seemed the moment was put behind us. But I watched Jenna closely and wondered if her smiles seemed a little forced, if she seemed a little more subdued than her usually cheerful self.

When we got to Prenthea Lake, Nila whooped and raced forward with Cloud on his tail. Mers asked Jenna, 'Do you swim? We're used to giving swimming instruction if that would be helpful.'

'Oh, uh. I didn't bring a swimming costume,' she said.

'A what?' asked Mers.

'A swimming costume. You know, like a bikini or swimming trunks or a swimsuit?'

Mers and I exchanged a look. 'Is this part of the human nudity taboo?' I asked.

'Uh—'

Mers said, 'We thought bikinis were a sexual thing?'

'Well, I guess they kind of can be, but—'

'You can wear your normal clothes,' I said. 'The weather's warm—they'll dry out by the time we get home.'

Jenna wrung her hands. 'Won't...won't people think I look strange?'

Always so concerned about appearances. I'd lived with her for weeks now and every day I felt like stomping whoever put all this nonsense into her head under my hooves. 'They'll think you look wet,' I said. 'Which you will be. It's not uncommon after a swim.'

'You don't have to swim if you don't want to,' Mers said. 'It was just a thought.'

Jenna took a deep breath. 'No, I would really like to, actually. On Earth, fat people like me, we can't—it doesn't matter.' She crossed her arms over her stomach, something I'd seen her do before when she got like this. 'I'll keep my clothes on though, if that's okay.'

'Of course,' said Mers. They turned to me. 'Would you like to join us as well?'

I stiffened and took a step back. 'Oh, haha...no. I prefer to be dry.' My heart pounded far too quickly and I could feel my starfire turn jagged.

Mers bobbed their heads. 'Suit yourself.'

I watched as Jenna and Mers strode into the lake, Mers keeping a careful eye on not just Jenna but on the other swimmers and wildlife as well. I found a springy patch of grass threaded with moss and settled down, folding my legs under me. Prenthea wasn't too crowded today—our group made up nearly half of the people in sight—but it still made me long for the solitude of the nameless lake near Antlervine Tree.

Hardly anyone ever swam in *that* lake.

Jenna made a tentative swimmer, but under Mers' direction, she was soon paddling away like everyone else, her clothes dragging behind her in the water. Water fountained up beside her as Cloud burst from the water, laughing and pulling faces.

Jenna used her hand to splash water at the cat-shape; Cloud laughed and used starfire to splash her back.

It did look sort of fun—in a wet, crowded, busy sort of way. I felt the gentlest tug of loneliness; unfamiliar to me, in such company. I supposed I'd gotten used to being included in the Internet Café group's antics.

But the thought of splashing around in there, with the water weighing down my fur and a vast emptiness beneath my hooves...no. Even knowing a lake wasn't as bad as an ocean, even then. A koi-shape breached the surface then dove joyfully back down, no longer relying on a water-aid to generate a bubble for them to move and breathe as they needed to on land.

I sat there a long while, watching the others and enjoying the gentle breeze rippling my fur. When bugs climbed on me, I gently lifted them and placed them elsewhere to continue their journey.

'Gah! Hrrk!' Cloud burst from the water near the shore and dragged herself onto land, coughing and spluttering. Out of the water, her normally plush fur hung lank and dripping from her body, highlighting her round middle and bony face.

She rolled over onto her back and pressed a paw to her forehead, dramatic as a human.

'I hear it helps if you don't swallow the water,' I said, ever helpful.

Cloud turned her head to glare at me, her ears flattening. 'Thanks for the tip,' she said. She got to her paws and shook out her fur, sending a spray of water over me. I grumbled and tried to flick some of it off with starfire while she trotted over to me. 'Ahh, that's better.' She plopped down beside me. 'So do you not swim because you're a miserable old goat or because you don't like swimming?'

I wondered briefly at her use of the human idiom. Had she learned it from Jenna, or was she just that immersed in human culture?

I considered. 'A bit of both.'

'Heh.' She stretched out her forepaws in front of her and rested her chin on her forelegs. 'I love swimming,' she told me. 'I'm wondering if Ever or Tonalia would make me a "swimming costume", like Jenna said.'

I snorted. 'What do *you* need with a swimming costume?'

She flicked an ear at me. 'I don't need one, I *want* one. It'd be fun.' She flicked her tails at me, sprinkling me with more water. 'I know fun is a foreign concept to you.'

I glared at her, laying my ears flat. 'I'm fun.'

'Oh?' She canted her head to one side. 'And what does that look like?'

'I read,' I said. 'I hike. I play.'

'What do you play?'

I shrugged. 'I play kethero and lily-pad,' I said, naming two of my favourite board games. 'And I used to play chase and hide-and-seek with my siblings until they grew out of it. I'll probably play it again with my kit sibling who just hatched.'

She gave me an appraising look. 'You really have siblings? Like...multiple siblings?'

I resisted the urge to chomp my teeth at her. 'Yes, I have siblings,' I said. 'I'm not in the habit of casually lying.'

Her tails lashed once. 'Sorry, I thought it was a joke. How many?'

'I'm the eldest of seven,' I said. 'The youngest, Journey, hatched last month. The rest are adults.'

'Six siblings...' Cloud trailed off, looking thoughtful. 'That must have been strange for you, growing up.'

I thought about it. 'I think it was stranger for other people,' I said. 'And they tried to make it strange for me.'

She paused. 'I see.' She rallied. 'So you play board games? Have you ever played Monopoly?'

'No?'

'It's this ancient human game where everyone is cruel to each other for material gain and then they all get angry at each other. I can't work out whether it's satirical or not.' She sighed happily. 'Either way, it's art.'

'It sounds miserable,' I said honestly.

'Oh, it is. Art doesn't have to be *easy.*' She grinned at me, baring her sharp teeth. 'You should play with me sometime.'

I wanted to snort and tell her, 'Not likely', but something about her smile caught me off-guard. 'Maybe.'

Cloud left me not long after that. I watched her continue her game of popping up beside people to startle them, like a kit that had just learned how to swim. Jenna raced Nila, surprisingly fast in the water for such an ungainly build. I was surprised to find that I wished I could join them.

I headed home alone. When Jenna walked through the door, I immediately set aside my cosmorb even though I'd just gotten to a really good bit of the story in my data crystal. 'How'd it go? Are you in the Gardeners' Union?'

'It went great,' Jenna said. She smiled, but it looked more like baring her teeth. My ears flattened in concern, but Jenna pushed on, 'I had a long chat with their onboarding team. I'm the first human gardener in Lost Circle, and the first human professional gardener the GU is aware of on Geminus. I've been assigned a few gardeners to shadow but I was surprised that they want to set me up with my own plot and have some of their gardeners shadow *me*. We had a long discussion about techniques and it turns out greenhouses aren't used here at all, and they think it might help cultivate some endangered species. I may even get to run classes on it!' Something about her tone sounded forced. I couldn't parse it.

'Jenna? Something is wrong but I don't understand what,' I said.

Jenna rubbed her face tiredly and collapsed onto the cushions across from me. 'It's not the GU,' she said.

I perked my ears forward. 'What?'

'It's—ugh, it's those people who Cloud scared off earlier,' she said. She didn't look at me, just stared at the wall with her lips pressed into a thin line. 'I wish I had said something but I was just so...I don't know. Not surprised, I guess. Tired. Just so tired.'

'From Pem?' I asked, referencing the word she used for when her disability made her sick.

'No. From...from life. From people. From...I don't know. I thought it was supposed to be better here. And I guess it is better! But it's not...not perfect. What they said to me...I got enough of that shit on Earth.' She shook her head. 'And then there's all the mess around my immigration and...I'm tired.' She looked at me and smiled a little at my expression, though I wasn't sure what face I was making. 'I can deal with it, okay? I will deal with it. But I don't want to talk about it right now. And...yeah. I think PEM is starting to hit, too. I'll see you later.'

She stood up and went into her nestroom. I didn't see much of her for the week, but when she emerged she was smiling and making plans as if nothing had happened.

I knew Jenna had made a lot of effort to be honest with me about her needs. So I didn't push about it. But I tried to remember that day, and what she'd been through, and resolved that if she *did* ask for my help, I would be there.

Chapter Ten

'Jenna!' I called as I bustled around the house. I got a pot of soup from cold storage, which I carefully sealed and wrapped and put in my pack, then checked through my cleaning supplies. 'There's a contract to clean up an old market stall I'm taking this morning,' I said. 'But I'll be back later to go to the housing meeting with you...' I trailed off. It didn't look like Jenna had gotten up yet. The cushions on her side of the low table were still stacked neatly, as she preferred to leave them.

I went to the door to her room and kicked it gently. 'Jenna?'

I thought I heard a mumbled response. Oh no. She'd been dealing with something she called Pem for days, the tiredness and pain that followed activity.

I sniffed; there was a strong smell of sweat and some other acrid scent I couldn't name. That wasn't normal.

'I'm coming in, okay?' I said cautiously. I opened the door.

Jenna lay tangled in her nest blankets, legs sticking out. Her skin glistened with sweat and she seemed unusually wan. Her hair was matted and sticking out strangely, as if she'd been tossing and turning all night. She blinked blearily at me and mumbled something.

I approached cautiously, my heart sinking. 'What was that?'

'M'ill,' she said. Her voice was raspy. 'Feel hot.'

This wasn't just Pem, this was something different. I didn't know anything about looking after sick humans. I touched my nose to her forehead. It felt mildly warm, but she didn't *look* like she was mildly warm. Maybe for a human, this was burning up. Weren't humans made of dust and not fire, or some such?

I got a temperature gem from one of the baskets in the room and laid it on her forehead. The gem shifted from clear to a sort of pastel pink. That wasn't hot for a cosmoran, but I felt no more reassured.

'M'gonna be sick...' Jenna said. She suddenly lurched upright and wretched. I ran and got a ceramic pot and thrust it into her arms just in time for her to loudly vomit into it. The smell was horrendous: powerfully, acidically alien. It was a sort of lumpy orange-pink liquid. Jenna groaned and slumped back into her nest.

I pulled my cosmorb from my pack and called Frost.

They answered immediately. 'What is it? Are you okay?'

I never called them. They must have known it was an emergency. 'Something's wrong with Jenna,' I said. 'I think she's really sick. I don't know what to do. I don't even know what temperature she's supposed to be.'

'Let me see her,' said Frost.

I spun my cosmorb and took an image. There was a pause as Frost looked at it. 'Take her to a healer,' they said. I could hear Night saying something in the background, but he didn't seem to be looking at me and his voice was muffled. 'To Glister. Do you want me to come with you?'

I nodded, then remembered it was a call. 'Yeah.'

'Okay. I'll meet you there. I think it's better not to wait.'

I nodded again and ended the call. Jenna still sprawled in the nest, like she couldn't bear for any of her limbs to touch. I felt both better and worse about the situation since calling Frost. I was glad to have their help, but terrified of how seriously they took the situation as well.

'We're going to a healer,' I told Jenna. 'Can you stand up?'

Jenna murmured something incoherent. I nudged her with my nose. 'Jenna? Can you stand up?'

Her eyes fluttered open. She propped herself up into a sitting position, panting hard, the strain of it clear in her expression. It seemed impossible that she would be able to walk.

I used starfire to steady her and prop her up. 'Hey,' I said. 'It's okay. We'll take it slowly.'

My thoughts spun and my gut knotted with anxiety. Surely she was in no state to get to a healer? Did I need to call someone to come here? But that could take a lot longer and all the while, she'd be getting worse. Glister's healing rooms weren't that far away, but...

It struck me like a shard of glass in my core that I couldn't bear for anything bad to happen to Jenna. This felt no different to when Lur had wasting sickness when he was small, or when Frost had broken their legs falling from a large boulder. The same tight panic laced with pain. The same sense of the world falling away from my hooves.

'Lean against my back,' I said to Jenna. With difficulty, I bent my forelegs. My forgetech leg pinged painfully and got stuck mid-way down, but I'd deal with that in a moment. 'Climb up,' I told her. 'I won't let you fall.'

Jenna leaned against my back but it was clear that even the lift necessary to get her up the next few inches was too much for her. I used starfire to lift her, but it was a huge strain and I started to pant heavily. I could just feel her fold across my back, her legs were lifting...there! I pushed her the last bit and turned her, so that she was draped across my back with her head padded on my mane. She'd crushed my pack but that was fine, that hardly mattered at all. It might even give her something to hang onto. She was a very round human but her weight was similar to Lur or Bloom, so I could carry her easily on my back, even if she was too heavy for starfire alone to lift. I used my starfire to steady her and carefully left the house. She radiated warmth on my back—I was certain now that she was running a fever, as we'd sat close before and she'd always seemed quite cold to me.

I picked my way down the curving path of Antlervine Tree—for all her weight was manageable, I was terribly frightened of dropping her. I planned the route in my mind. Glister lived twenty minutes away. Taking a canopy-tram was out of the question; it was nearly ten minutes in the opposite direction. I'd just have to hoof it. Several times, I felt Jenna begin to slip and had to adjust her on my back. Her sweat started to soak into my fur, but I had no headspace to spare for disgust. I only wanted to keep her safe. The strain of using my starfire for such a large weight for so long started to wear on me; even holding her in place was an uncommon effort and difficult to sustain. I reminded myself again and again that it was only a short walk. I talked to Jenna but she didn't answer and fear pecked at me.

'Not long,' I told her, wondering whether she even understood me in her addled state. Wondering whether she was even conscious. 'We're almost there.'

Glister's healing rooms were part of a larger healer's collective in Dancing Tree. There was a queue at the bottom but thankfully not a long one. I looked ahead at those waiting; nobody bleeding, nobody obviously suffering. It was possible Glister'd call Jenna and me first, given how unwell she looked.

The hawk-shape in front of me glanced back at us. 'Is...that a human?'

I nodded. I didn't state the obvious; that she was horribly unwell, that I had no idea what I was doing here.

The hawk-shape gave us a sympathetic look. 'I'm just waiting for a twisted talon. I'll suggest they see you first.'

'Thank you,' I said. Tears stung my eyes. I blinked them away.

It felt like an age before we were seen. Though the shadows hardly moved, I could feel the breeze chill across my fur, feel Jenna begin to shiver on my back.

'Are you awake?' I asked her. I turned my head, trying to get a look at her. Her eyelids fluttered, her cheek still pillowed against my mane. 'Feel cold,' she croaked, and then shivered more.

I cursed myself for not bringing a blanket. She'd seemed to be *overheating* when we left...

The queue moved on and we weren't called forward yet. I did my best to hold still and not shift Jenna too much, though normally I constantly moved my weight from hoof to hoof. My chest was so tight with panic that it was hard to draw breath. I reminded myself that Jenna wasn't dying, she was just ill. *Really* ill. And Glister would look at her and give her an antiviral harmonic treatment or something and everything would be fine.

'Avari!'

I turned carefully as Frost galloped over, their claws digging into the dirt. Illusion immediately leaned down to Jenna. 'Hey there, human friend,' she said. 'Everything's gonna be all right.'

'Cold,' Jenna murmured.

'What's going on?' asked Storm. 'Will Glister see you?'

'I don't know,' I said. 'They haven't spoken to us yet. I guess we don't look like an emergency.'

Night took a crocheted blanket out of his pack and draped it over Jenna. 'Hope this helps,' he said gruffly, tongue flicking nervously.

Storm and Illusion looked at each other. 'We'll be right back,' they said. Frost strode ahead, disappearing into the queue ahead. I could hear their voices but not what they were saying.

I felt a wave of relief wash over me. Frost was here. They knew what to do. They were a guardian and it was their job to advocate for people. Jenna didn't have to rely on my lacklustre assistance.

What felt like an age later, Frost returned with a sheepish Glister behind them. The scarlet-furred gibbon-shape rubbed the back of their head as they considered me and Jenna. They sniffed politely toward us. 'You'd best come in,' they said. My ears twitched; did they seem...apologetic?

I followed them into their consultation room. It was a broad room with unusually smooth walls and no windows. My hooves clicked on a crystal-washed floor—all the better for cleaning, though I supposed it might also help with harmonics. Instead of cushions, there were low seats in a hard enamel. The walls were covered in shelves which held various data crystals and sealed boxes which I assumed contained temperature-controlled treatments, as well as various vials and bottles. A long, padded table rested along one wall.

Glister took a seat to one side of a table and nodded to me. 'Lay her out there,' they said. 'She'll be more comfortable.'

With Frost's help, it was easy to gently move Jenna to the padded table. She continued to shiver under the blanket, and she didn't open her eyes.

'So,' Glister said. 'What seems to be the problem?'

'My friend is sick,' I said. 'She seemed fine yesterday, but today she was...vomiting. And weak. And I think she's running a fever.'

Glister nodded. 'Hmm, hmm. And what colour temperature was she running?'

I flicked one ear forward and one back. 'It was pink,' I said. 'But she felt much warmer than usual.'

'Hmm.' Glister walked over to Jenna. They reached for her forehead, hesitated, reached for the blanket, hesitated, and then folded their hands behind their back. 'And do humans respond to harmonic therapy?'

I paused. The question stumped me. 'I—I don't know. Don't you?'

Glister's starfire pinked. 'I have never treated a human before.' Before I could express my shock, they hurried on, 'But, I will do my best! Human—'

'Jenna,' Frost supplied, frowning.

'—have you eaten anything unusual, in the last day? Been bitten by anything, perhaps?'

103

I walked over to Jenna and nudged her with my nose. 'Well?'

Jenna's eyelids cracked open. She gazed blearily first at me, then at Glister. 'I don't...think so,' she said.

'And what were you doing yesterday?' Glister asked.

'Uhh...nothing,' she said.

'It was a normal day,' I said. 'Jenna was tired after the market a few days ago.' I wracked my brain for any useful information—hadn't she been hoping to find a conservation gardener on the market day? I didn't know—I hadn't gone with her. Wait, hadn't she gone to the Travellers' Union, too? Or had that been the day before?

'Do you consent to harmonic therapy?' asked Glister.

Jenna blinked a few times. She seemed to be struggling to make sense of it. 'What's that?'

'Hmm. Well, it's a fairly standard procedure. We use an energy pulse refracted through crystals to cause the crystalline structure within the body to vibrate in harmony, cleansing it of invasive illness and injury and stimulating healing.'

'I don't...I don't have that. Crystalline structure.'

Glister stared at her a moment, then motioned to me and Frost, drawing us aside to the other side of the room. 'Here's the thing,' they said. 'I can't treat her. No crystalline structure? What do they have, meat and blood like an animal? I don't know a thing about animals! Do they even have resonance?' They wrung their long, leathery fingers. 'Anyone can see she's not well. She does *need* treatment. But I'm afraid you'll need to find a human healer to see to her. I wish I could help, but...' They spread their hands apologetically. 'I really have no idea what to do.'

Frost frantically searched on their cosmorb. 'There aren't any human healers in Lost Circle registered with the Healers' Union,' Storm said. Illusion nudged Jenna. 'Did the Travellers' Union put you in contact with a human healer?'

Jenna shook her head. '...no.' That seemed to exhaust her words.

I thought about it. 'I've got Elm's contact details. I'll check with them. They're human; they'll know what to do.'

'Meat and blood like an animal ...' Night's tongue flicked out twice, and he hissed softly. 'We might have an idea.'

'You can't be serious,' said Storm. 'He isn't qualified!'

'It's the best option we have,' said Illusion.

I looked up from the message I was hastily composing. 'What?'

Frost looked at themselves. 'I have a friend who might be able to help,' they said.

I knew Frost. They had a strange, tense energy about them. There was something they were dancing around telling me. 'Who?'

Storm looked sheepish. Illusion ducked away. Only Night would solidly meet my gaze. 'Our mate.'

Chapter Eleven

We took Jenna home. Frost helped me settle her in her nest. She became more alert when we got home and requested something to drink, so I got her a cup of water and set a carafe beside her nest so she could get more. Frost insisted she remained in her nest even if she was feeling more alert, and sure enough before Frost's mate arrived, she was sweating and weak again.

While she was resting, Frost and I settled at the low table. It was funny to sit across from Frost, in what I had once considered Frost's seat and was now firmly Jenna's. Somehow, over the last few months, my world had tilted on its axis, so slowly I hadn't even noticed it happening.

Frost said, 'It's good to see you. We missed you.'

I ducked my head, embarrassed by what they left unsaid. 'I did mean to come see you,' I said. 'I just...didn't know how.' The hurt I'd felt at learning they'd kept their life secret from me had faded, but the wall it had created between us seemed impenetrable. Every time I'd thought about seeing them, there had been such a confusing mix of shame, guilt, and fear that it had been easier to tell myself I'd do it later, even though later never came.

Frost seemed to think carefully before replying. 'We wish you had,' they said. 'We...it hurt. But we understood that it was partially our fault. Night wanted to come kicking down your door, but we decided to wait until you felt comfortable.'

The thought of my siblings at home and upset because of me was painful to imagine. 'I'm sorry,' I said, because I didn't know what else to say.

'We're sorry, too.'

We lapsed into silence. I could hear Jenna shifting in her nest, unable to get comfortable in her feverish state.

'So your mate is a healer?' I asked. I didn't want this new connection between us to fail. I didn't want the wall to rebuild.

Frost smiled. 'His name is Vya, and yeah, he's a healer. He used to be an animal healer—heals cosmorans now—and has a big interest in human healing, too. I think you'll like him. He's not one for small talk and he's always talking about whatever he just learned about animal behaviour or human biology.'

I tried to fight down my innate urge to retort. I did hate small talk, and I did love learning new things. And if Frost liked Vya, perhaps he was worth getting to know.

My cosmorb warmed as I received a message. I checked it. 'It's from Elm!' It was quite short. Simply, it read: 'There's a doctor living just outside Lost Circle to the west in Silverfold. In a pinch you can try an animal healer instead—Lorea at the Willow Dome helped me when I broke my arm.' Like a message from Jenna, there was no emotion communicated with the message, but I imagined it in Elm's clipped tone.

The Willow Dome was a large animal healer's treelding that had been grown out of several young trees on the forest floor, an old-fashioned treelding. 'Elm says animal healers will do in an emergency,' I said. 'Though the Willow Dome wasn't so far away, the idea didn't sit well with me. Jenna didn't bear much resemblance to an animal.

Frost nodded, relieved. 'Vya's been reading and attending classes on human biology and they mentioned there's a lot of cross-over.' They paused. 'Just another strange thing binding Geminus and Earth, I suppose.'

I shrugged. Sometimes, I amused myself by pondering the ties between Earth and Geminus, cosmorans and humans. It was a mystery our scholars had been working on since we'd made first contact with humankind. Right now, I had no room to think about anything but Jenna.

There was a knock at the door. I stood up and opened it with starfire. A large aardvark-shape came in, soft nose quivering, his black fur shining with a blue-green iridescence. He wore a blue shawl around his shoulders, spectacles on his nose, and carried a large case under one arm, gripped with long, flexible claws. 'I'm here about a sick human? Jenna, wasn't it? Oh.' He sniffed toward me politely, as if only just remembering. 'I'm Vya.'

I sniffed back, and hated how much I instantly liked him. 'I'm Avari. She's through here,' I said. There was a retching sound followed by a wet splat and a groan. 'I...think she might have just been sick again.' I showed him to Jenna's room, where Jenna was just now slumping back into her nest.

Jenna gave Vya a beady-eyed look. She forgot to sniff and waved a hand instead, which I knew to be another human greeting and not just a means of gaining attention—mostly because Cloud had taken up waving at me whenever I came in. 'You're an aardvark,' she croaked. As exhausted as she was, she still sounded delighted.

'I'm a healer,' said Vya. 'How long have you been sick?' Vya got out a cosmorb and peppered Jenna with questions, taking notes as he did. 'What is a normal human body temperature? Excellent. And does this anatomy seem familiar to you—acidic digestive sack, fleshy heart, long hairy intestine? Good, good...' After a bit, they got out some quite horrible-looking tools—a needle and syringe with some kind of forgetech sensor. 'Hold out your arm, if you please.' He jabbed her with the needle and the syringe filled with red. The sensor projected runes I couldn't make sense of. 'Hmm. You have a high viral load. How long have you been on Geminus?'

'A few months,' she said.

'Since the 3rd of The Queens,' I said. The date was lodged in my brain, since it had been Journey's hatching day.

'Ah. Not long. You'll be experiencing an entirely different viral ecosystem,' said Vya. 'Cosmoran viruses are rarely transmissible to creatures with your sort of physiology, but there is some evidence of humans being more susceptible. We aren't sure why, yet.'

'What does that mean?' I asked, feeling my panic rising. Vya's quick, competent manner had set me at ease but I was feeling worried again. 'A different viral ecosystem?'

'It means Jenna won't have any protection from Geminus viruses. It can be fatal. But it isn't likely to be,' he said quickly as all my fur stood up in alarm. 'Jenna, you're very sick but your body *is* mounting an immune response. An effective one, from the readings here. You should be fine in a few days. Honestly, I'm surprised; I wouldn't have thought your immune system would adapt so quickly.'

'Vaccinated,' Jenna said. She cleared her throat and tried again, but her voice was no less croaky. 'I was vaccinated at the TU. When I first arrived. And three days ago.'

'This is a vaccine reaction?'

She shrugged and closed her eyes, seeming to have exhausted her words.

'What's your rough weight? Hold on.' He picked up a forgetech device and pointed it at Jenna. It surrounded her in a bright yellow glow, and then faded. Vya looked at the device, and then at me. 'Does about twenty stones sound right?'

'It does,' I said nervously. Bloom was about that weight, too.

'I think she'll be all right to take these,' Vya said. He took a vial of strange little pellets from his pack and handed it to me. 'Those should suppress viral symptoms. She can have two a day. They've been approved for use on humans. That should give her enough of a break from her symptoms that she can start to get her strength back—eat, drink, etc. But it's essential that she rests. In nest for two days.'

'Two a day,' I said. 'Thank you.'

Vya reached up with a claw to straighten his spectacles. 'It's no problem. It was nice to finally have a human patient. I hadn't realised the situation was so dire in Lost Circle for humans. I'll see about getting listed for human healing, as well as cosmoran.'

We left Jenna to her rest. As I closed the door, Frost bounced to their feet. 'Is she okay?'

'She'll be fine,' said Vya. 'More bad policy for travelling humans, from the looks of it. She should have been monitored if there was a chance the vaccination would cause such a strong reaction.'

'I'll let Elm know,' I said. As the first stop for humans in Lost Circle, it was information they might be able to put to good use.

'Well, there's nothing else for it but for Jenna to rest. If you need my help again, please feel free to contact me and I'll come as soon as I can.' He paused. 'It was nice meeting you. Even if under unpleasant circumstances.'

'It was nice meeting you, too,' I said, and meant it. 'Thank you again.'

Vya nodded and ambled out the door.

Frost looked at me. 'Would you like me to go? I can stay, if you like.'

'Stay,' I said.

They smiled at me, even a rare smile from Night. 'So? What did you think of Vya?'

'They seem a little suspicious to me,' I said.

Frost's smile faltered. 'Oh?'

'Yeah. I just can't work out what someone so great is doing with you?'

Storm gasped and Night stuck out their tongue at me. Illusion said, delightedly, 'You like them!'

'I don't really know them,' I said. 'But yeah, I like them.'

My siblings' glowed at me, their starfire warm with happiness, and it hit me all over again how good it was to see them. I felt like some void in my chest had been filled.

We talked a while and they cooked dinner for us all, and helped me look after Jenna. Gradually, they didn't seem out of place in Jenna's seat any more. I made a mental note to get more cushions for my table, and dared to hope that this might become normal again.

Chapter Twelve

Elm and a hedgehog-shape with flame-coloured spines and cheerful turquoise starfire sat chatting in the Travellers' Union café over steaming cups of tea. Elm's beard was again gloriously plaited, this time with small blue flowers woven in, which matched a small crown of the same upon their head. A wave of jealousy overtook me, and I resolved to ask Jenna to do the same to my beard. I would suffer through physical touch if it meant my beard would look that magnificent.

Jenna and the hedgehog sniffed politely toward each other and then Jenna and Elm shook hands. 'Thanks for setting this up,' Jenna said.

Elm inclined their head. 'Of course.'

I greeted Elm and the hedgehog as well and then we joined them at the table. My leg got stuck while I was lowering. Jenna quickly used her hands to help me bend it—she'd become used to the problem and her human hands were more effective at fixing it than my starfire, particularly because she had a better angle for viewing it.

I settled on a large cushion, wiggling a bit as I tried to get it comfortable.

Elm said, 'Jenna, meet Tempest. Tempest is a housing planner for the Gardeners' Union. He'll help you choose a plot for your home, design its shape, and walk you through the timeline for it.' They paused. 'Tempest helped me get my house planted and grown. He did a wonderful job of it.'

Tempest smiled at Jenna, his flame flaring warmly. 'What sort of home did you have in mind? Would you prefer to live in a large treelding with others, or would you rather a more traditional home grown from longwillow? Do you prefer to be higher up or lower down?'

Jenna tapped her lips thoughtfully. 'I hadn't given it much thought. I thought a house like Avari's was the only option.'

Tempest turned to me. 'And you live in...?'

'Antlervine Tree,' I said. 'Modern treelding.'

'Ah. Of course, of course. Well, perhaps we should go for a walk and get a look at your options? And then we can discuss location.'

Jenna agreed, and we headed out. I was surprised to find Elm accompanying us. I'd assumed the TU administrator was too busy to spend time on us. While Jenna and Tempest chatted, Elm caught my eye. 'Jenna's a friend,' they said stiffly, and I *had* heard Jenna talk about them. 'I want to make sure she has all the support she needs.'

I nodded. 'She's not had a very easy time of it so far.'

'No, no.' Elm frowned. 'I'd hoped the otherworldly traveller system would be smoother since my own immigration. I made a lot of complaints, and helped others to do the same. I don't know what the Otherworldly Travel Commission is getting at, bringing humans here with no knowledge, no prep, and no support.'

I said nothing. I'd considered bringing complaints to the Otherworldly Travel Commission myself. I'd have to talk to Frost about it—guardians knew about that sort of thing. If Jenna hadn't been found by my family, who knew what might have happened to her?

I felt out-of-place, trailing Jenna around the city. I wondered several times whether it would be better if I excused myself. But every now and then Jenna would turn a nervous look my way, catch my eye, and smile in relief, so I decided to stick around. If my presence was a comfort to her, then it was worth a little awkwardness.

'So how are you finding living with a human houseguest?' Elm asked.

Honestly, I was surprised they wanted to talk to me. We'd been travelling in companionable silence for a while now. 'I hated it at first. I've always chosen to live alone, and Jenna needed a lot of support to begin with, given she's so far from home. But I'm used to it now.' I hesitated, my stomach sinking with realisation, and added, 'I'll be sorry when she moves out.'

Elm nodded. 'I stayed at the TU, you know. There wasn't anyone to help me when I first arrived. Because I was dropped on Profundus and headed straight to Viridus, there wasn't really anyone placed to help me. Nobody took responsibility for me until I found my way to the TU. I...sometimes wish that hadn't been the case.' They smiled sadly. 'It would have been nice to have had a friend. No, don't look at me like that—I feel quite settled now, and take much satisfaction in my work.'

I hadn't realised I was looking at Elm any sort of way, and quickly averted my gaze. But I did feel sorry for them. I knew what it was like to be lonely, but to be alone on another planet...

'I like your beard,' I said, because I didn't know what else to say.

Elm smiled. 'I like your beard too.'

'Avari!' Jenna bounced over to me, shining with excitement. It never failed to surprise me just how bright humans could look, even with no starfire or natural luminescence. 'What do you think of somewhere like this?' She gestured to a willow house in front of us. It was a very traditional style of house, from before we had the gardening knowledge and forgetech necessary to hollow and shape trees. Instead, it was made by growing coppiced longwillow for the walls and then braiding them together to create a roof. The trees continued growing happily in their knotted shape, and the top of the willow house was layered in mud and clay, as was done in meadow settlements to stop the rain getting in. This particular house was thickly coated in moss, giving it a quaint, homey feel.

'It's fine, I guess,' I said. 'Wouldn't you rather live in a nice big treelding?'

'Treeldings are nice,' she said. 'But they feel a bit like human apartments. This reminds me of a country cottage or something. And I like that it's on the ground. I still don't completely trust my balance on treelding paths.'

Some of the words she mentioned didn't have clear meanings to me—multi-homes and old houses, I supposed, but I had no inkling of what that would look like on Jenna's concrete homeworld.

'You seem fine on Antlervine Tree,' I said. I felt the urge to defend our home—hadn't she been happy there?

'I am fine on Antlervine Tree. I'm just saying what I would prefer for myself.' Her smile didn't ameliorate the sting of her words.

I blew air and looked away, my mood growing dark. Jenna didn't seem to notice. She continued to talk longwillow cheerfully with Tempest.

When we got home, before I could disappear back to my nest, Jenna asked, 'Are you feeling all right? You seemed quiet today.'

'I'm fine,' I said shortly.

Later that night, I messaged Illusion. *Do you think Antlervine Tree is a good place to live?*

She replied, *I think it's perfect for you. You like the climb, and the lake, and the beautiful antler-like branches. ~ Illusion.*

But do you think it's good enough for anyone?

I think everyone is different. ~ Illusion.

I scowled and tossed aside my cosmorb. I knew she was right. It wasn't the answer I wanted.

A few weeks later, I shifted uncomfortably in my seat at the Internet Café. It was after hours, which made the whole situation feel forbidden, even though Cloud had arranged everything. She'd pushed all the tables together to form two large tables. I sat at this one with Cloud, Frost, and Mers, while Jenna sat with Nila, Shade, and Keera at the other. Cloud put her paws on the table, knocking over a stack of paper rectangles.

'I'm so glad you could all make it!' she said loudly to the room. 'We have one experienced player at each table, and refreshments have been laid out on the counter and are self-serve. So with that, it is time to experience true human *art!* Let the Monopoly begin!' Cloud cackled at the same time that Jenna groaned loudly. Both tables began talking quickly at once as pieces were dealt out and rules were explained. I found it to be a near impenetrable wall of noise, so I excused myself to get some snacks.

I snorted when I saw them. Of course Cloud had made custom monopoly-themed food for her big board game party. There were little cakes decorated to look like the paper rectangles—which I think Cloud had described as 'money'. There were savoury bread rolls with the shapes of the player pieces burnt into them. Though honestly, I wasn't completely clear on what any of the pieces were supposed to *be*. I filled my plate with two rolls: one marked with a long wheeled thing, another with...I guessed it was a patterned bucket, perhaps? And grabbed a scoop's worth of fruit jerky as well.

When I returned to the table, there was a stack of Monopoly money in front of me as well as a little piece of a human riding a horse. Frost nudged me. 'We thought you'd prefer a piece where you can tell what it is,' they said.

They weren't wrong. The other pieces around the table were largely unintelligible and it *would* have irritated me. I wished Jenna was on our table; I could have asked her what everything was meant to be.

'All right,' said Cloud. There was a bit of black fabric stuck below her nose and sweeping out in each direction. It wobbled as she spoke. 'The aim of the game is to make the most money and put everyone else out of business. You do that by—'

'What's on your face?' I interrupted.

Cloud drew herself up proudly. 'This is my moustache, in honour of the Monopoly mascot, Rich Uncle Pennybags,' she gestured to the centre of the board, where a cartoon human in a monocle winked at the players.

'Oh dear,' said Frost.

'That can't be the actual name,' said Mers.

'I assure you, it is. I have a hat as well, one moment!' She ducked under the table and rustled around a moment before popping back up with a large cylindrical black hat, the twin of the one Rich Uncle Pennybags was wearing. She beamed at us.

'So...onto the rules...'

Thus commenced the most aggressive evening of board gaming I'd ever experienced. The rules of the game were painfully simple and yet the emotions were high. Your only job in every trade was to get the better of your opponent while convincing them they were getting the better of you. When Frost couldn't afford to pay Mers without selling off their properties, Mers offered to let them go free.

'No!' Cloud stood up, ears going flat. 'No free passes!'

Mers' heads bobbed uncertainly. 'But Frost isn't doing very well and we have more than enough—'

'That's the point of the game!' said Cloud. 'Just...lean into the concept. That's the only way to get the full experience.'

So we did. Frost extorted all the rest of my properties in exchange for the final property for my set. Mers and Cloud got into a shouting match over a particularly difficult trade. I slipped Frost some money under the table when it looked like they were about to go out. I had never cheated at a game in my life, but this game was just so *unfair*. And so dreadfully, miserably long...

Cloud started hiding her money so that people wouldn't know how much she had when it came to trading. Frost and Mers made an arrangement where Frost could travel for free on Mers' public transport for the rest of the game in exchange for forgiving Mers' immediate debt.

Somehow at the end it was just me and Cloud. The others sat miserably around the table. Frost's fur and feathers were all askew, and Mers rested their heads on their own shoulders in silent self-support. I had no idea how much money Cloud had left, but I knew I had plenty. But plenty still wasn't enough. If I landed on Cloud's hotel properties twice, I would lose everything.

Cloud rolled the dice...a seven!

She moved her piece seven spaces, her expression impassive. It landed on my largest property: Mayfair.

'That would be 2000 money, please,' I said.

Cloud stared at the board a moment. Then she got her money out from under the table. 'I only have 500 money,' she said.

I'd thought that meant it was finally over, but it wasn't. Cloud refused to give up until the bitter end, mortgaging and selling off all her properties until she had nothing left. She couldn't recoup enough money from what she had left and at last, she had nothing else to sell and finally had to accept her defeat.

'Is it over?' Mers asked sleepily.

Cloud sighed. 'It's over,' she said. Her false moustache drooped. She looked very little like Rich Uncle Pennybags now. Her flame was a tragic blue-grey.

Jenna came over from the other table. 'Who won?'

Cloud waved a paw in my direction. 'Who won your game?'

Jenna looked sheepish. 'Ah. Well...'

'We formed a union!' Shade fluffed her feathers excitedly. 'Jenna was so far in the lead and we didn't want anyone to go out. So we formed a union against Jenna and then when we were stronger than Jenna we let Jenna join our union!'

Cloud blinked. Her ears laid flat. 'That's not how it's meant to be played!'

'You were right, Monopoly *is* fun!' said Nila. He yipped delightedly.

'It wasn't supposed to be fun,' Cloud said defiantly. 'It was supposed to be *art!*'

Everyone at our table groaned.

Frost looked to Jenna. 'Are all human games this brutal?'

Jenna looked surprised. 'No, actually. There are some really lovely ones. Most are competitive, but they don't necessarily make you miserable. Like I really enjoy—'

'Risk!' said Cloud, slamming a paw down on the table.

Jenna blanched. 'No! I was going to say Forest Garden. Isn't that another really old game?'

Cloud frowned. 'Do you get to crush your enemies in Forest Garden?'

'Not really,' said Jenna.

Cloud pouted, her tails thrashing in irritation, while the group excitedly made plans for another game night. I thought about all the effort she'd made for this night: the themed snacks, her costume, her rearranging the café. I had no idea how she'd even gotten her paws on a human board game in the first place but it couldn't have been simple. It was true that the game had been miserable, but I'd had a good evening anyway. Surprisingly good. I'd never actually had an evening out with friends before.

'I thought Monopoly was interesting,' I told her. My tail twitched nervously. I was glad it was short enough that the motion would be difficult to pick up. 'And I really liked the themed snacks. Thank you for inviting me, and letting me bring Frost.'

Cloud's ears perked forward. She tilted her head to one side and smiled, eyes narrowing. 'It was my pleasure,' she said. There was a hint of a purr in her voice, barely audible. I ducked my head and looked away, heating with a mix of embarrassment and something else I couldn't name.

I realised all of Frost was watching me with a bemused expression. I laid my ears flat. 'What?' I demanded.

Storm chuckled and didn't reply. Night stuck his tongue out at me, and Illusion winked and turned to speak to Mers.

When I got home later that night, my mind spun as it ran over everything that had happened again and again, picking apart my every interaction. Much of it made me cringe or even gasp aloud at my own foolishness. Tears stung at the corners of my eyes.

But it also made me feel warm as well. My first night out with friends. And I'd even been invited back for another one.

When I thought of Cloud in her moustache and top hat, I couldn't help but smile.

Chapter Thirteen

There was a knock at the door.

'Just come in. We're almost ready!' I glanced at Jenna. 'We're almost ready, right?'

Jenna looked at our bags, open on the floor. 'Cosmorbs, clothes, food for the trip?'

'Yes,' I said.

'Washing supplies?'

'Yep.'

'Gift for Journey?'

I snorted, my ears flicking back. 'No! Ahh, wait, I just had it!' I ran into my room and dug the gift out of a basket. When I came back and deposited it into the least-stuffed bag, the house was looking significantly fuller. Frost grinned at me. Vya sniffed politely toward me with his ridiculously soft-looking snoot.

'All good?' asked Frost.

I picked up my bags. 'All *ready*, at least.'

'Good enough.' Illusion cawed a laugh. 'Time to go home!'

Home. My stomach churned as I followed my siblings out the door.

It was thankfully a short trip to the canopy station. There was a regular canopy-glider to Athelean and we got there with half an hour to spare. Jenna, Vya, and Frost chatted excitedly about what to expect from Athelean—Jenna's invitation from my mothers gave her a reason to see more of Viridus. I hovered beside them, shifting from hoof to hoof, unsure what awaited us in Athelean. I tried to distract myself by watching the other passengers arrive, or watching the pilot go about her safety checks, but my mind was drawn again and again back to my family.

I avoided Athelean when I could. As many good memories as I had there, they were all stained by the oppressive atmosphere I had grown up in.

Always too loud or too quiet. Always doing the wrong thing. Always seeking praise and approval from parents that had little time for me. Nova was always friendly but distant, absorbed in her own projects, disinterested in parenting beyond what was easy—and I was never easy. Teera had rarely been around, busy with work that took her away from the home and snappish with me when she was around, forever finding me lacking.

In many ways, Frost and I had parented ourselves—though I knew Frost had never seen it that way. We had entertained each other, educated each other, and looked out for each other—and for Lur and Bloom, once they hatched. But while us kits had felt like a unit, I had often felt like a loose part within that unit. Lur and Bloom had each other. Frost had themselves—and lots of friends besides. And then there was me. Always in trouble, always upset, and always, *always* alone.

'Lost in thought?'

I looked up and around in surprise. I hadn't noticed Vya come to stand beside me. He sat on his hind feet, rubbing his paws together, long hooked claws scraping over long hooked claws. 'Oh. Hi.' I tried to adopt a less tense stance and my forgetech leg got stuck, causing my shoulder to twinge in pain. While I leaned down to fix it, I cast around for something to say. 'It's just weird going home, is all. Have you met our family yet?'

'No, no,' said Vya. His long ears drooped. 'I'm quite worried about it, truth be told.'

'What do you have to be worried about?' I flexed my forgetech leg, which seemed to be working again, and glanced up at Vya.

His nose twitched. 'How long has it been since you've been to Athelean? Frost says you didn't go with them on their last visit.'

I flicked my ears. 'A handful of years. It's not such a big deal. I see my parents when they come to Lost Circle to visit, and see the twins more often still.'

Vya nodded and looked away. 'I expect it'll be nice to see your newest sibling again. I still find it incredible that your family is so large. Your parents must have been blessed by the Flowering Ancient.'

'Something like that.' I let the conversation drop. People were always saying things like that—like my mothers were in some way chosen, or special, to have received so many kits when many mated pairs or groups were fortunate to receive even one kit. It was said admiringly. Like Nova and Teera had done something to deserve it. Like they were incredible parents, to manage such a large household, when in fact we had largely managed ourselves.

All they had done was drink the nectar from the Ancient's flowers, like any other hopeful parents. There was nothing special about it.

I realised Vya was watching me, his nose quivering like he was on the verge of a question. I held in a snort and tried to think of a way to gracefully excuse myself from this conversation.

'I'm sorry,' he said, before I could turn away. 'You're probably sick of talking about how large your family is. I'm just nervous, and when I get nervous like this, the words just come out and keep coming out and I get myself into all sorts of trouble.' His claws clicked as he rubbed his paws together again.

I sighed. 'I know that feeling.' I'd done it a lot as a kit, before I'd been scolded until silence was the norm. 'What're you nervous about?'

'Well. Frost is...really important to me.' His tail swished behind him, striking up a cloud of dust. 'And their family is really important to them. And I'm just...not good at making first impressions.' They paused. 'Or second impressions, for that matter.'

I had no idea how to comfort people but I felt the urge nonetheless. 'You made a good first impression on me,' I said honestly. 'And Jenna...though I suppose she was half-delirious at the time. And Frost seems to like you.'

Vya snorted, his starfire pinking. 'They didn't at first,' he said, with a touch of nostalgia.

Frost hadn't told me how they'd met. I was curious, but Vya didn't say anything else on the matter and I didn't want to pry. 'Well,' I said. 'Any time you feel awkward or don't know what to do, you can come find me and we can be awkward together.'

'That's what Frost always says.'

I nodded. 'To me as well.'

The border of the canopy-glider door lit up with green light, then opened with a hiss, slowly lowering to create a ramp for our entry. I found Jenna and strode reluctantly on-board, my hooves knocking hollowly against the ramp.

123

We found seats on one side of the glider; Jenna pressed the gem for safety restraints with barely any hesitation.

I watched Frost introducing themselves to the other passengers—a handful of folk just incidentally travelling to Athelean today. I didn't recognise any of them, thankfully. I wasn't looking forward to seeing any of my former neighbours. I had never known them that well and I knew it would be painfully awkward—for me, at least. Most of Frost seemed to relish meeting old acquaintances. Only Night could really relate.

Jenna gently bumped her shoulder against my flank. 'You okay? You look...tense.' Her eyes went up to my flame, which I could feel dancing even more jaggedly than normal.

'I'm fine,' I said, but my ears went back before I could stop them. I saw Jenna's eyes follow them; she frowned but didn't say anything. Perhaps she didn't recognise what it meant. After all, it had taken me the majority of my life to get a tentative grasp on body language, and human body language was often very different.

The journey was much shorter than the one to the Elder Grove. Athelean was only a few hours away by glider. We had a picnic on the floor, joined by the other passengers, exchanging fruit, bread, stews, and pasties. I let Frost do most of the talking and nodded and put my ears forward when addressed, even managing to smile sometimes. My face didn't want to make the motion so it almost hurt, but that was nothing new.

After lunch, Jenna joined me at the window. She didn't say anything, just leaning against the glass and gazing out across the rolling hills in all their riot of flowers and purple grasses. I watched her sidelong. She was so friendly and talkative, but she was often happy to sit in silence with me. I didn't know whether that was because she was more comfortable with me after living together, or whether she did it specifically for me, but I really appreciated it. It gave me time to gather my thoughts, if nothing else.

At length, I said, 'I thought I was better at this now.'

'This?'

'People.' I shuffled my hooves, my ears laying flat. 'I talk to Cloud and the others every week without any problems worse than someone getting on my nerves, but for some reason a glider ride with strangers has me jumping like a kit in a dark cave.'

Jenna smiled to one side. 'Well. You're friends with Cloud. You aren't friends with these people.'

The word 'friend' hit me like a kick in the guts. It was a word I'd never had use for. There were my siblings, and there was Jenna, who felt more and more like a sibling. I knew, intellectually, that Cloud and the Internet Café crew were friends. That what it meant was that we chose to spend time together so often. But it was hard to reconcile that with my mental image of myself—which, if I was honest, was still of a lonely goat-shape kit watching from the edge of the room while Frost talked to *their* friends.

Stars, going 'home' was making me maudlin. 'You must think I'm a fool,' I said bitterly.

Jenna leaned briefly against my shoulder, just a small amount of pressure that was more reassuring than oppressive. 'I think you're wonderful,' Jenna said. 'And I think your friends think you're wonderful, too.'

I snorted and shook my head.

'It's true! Cloud thinks you're really funny, and only last week Keera was saying how much she finds your cleaning alchemy interesting.'

Interesting. Funny. I wanted to shake my head again and keep shaking it until the words flew out of my head. Nobody could really think those things about me. I *bored* people. I *ruined* things. I was the worst of all my siblings, the imperfect practice of the Flowering Ancient before it got the fruit formula right with Frost, like an alchemist experimenting in a lab. Jenna's words had opened up some vast and terrible void inside me and I couldn't stop myself from stomping just to feel the force of the strike travelling up my leg.

'Avari—'

'I don't walk to talk,' I said shortly. Flower meadows rolled on beneath my angry gaze. There was a hesitant air about Jenna, a hovering moment that made me want to snap at her, but I squared my shoulders and stared resolutely out the window. I heard her exhale a long breath and move away.

Good.

I stayed at the window a long time, only returning to my seat when the hill-homes of Athelean bloomed in the distance.

The canopy-glider set down and the other passengers left in a chattering crowd, eager to get on with their journeys. Our group was the last to get off, because Frost was thanking the pilot and I had no desire to lead the way to my family's hill-home alone.

We walked down the ramp, hooves, claws, and paws clattering hollowly against the metal. As we got to the bottom, Jenna actually gasped, staring around with wide eyes.

'It's beautiful,' she said.

I snorted. 'I guess.'

Athelean *was* beautiful, loathe though I was to admit it. A rainbow of long grass speckled with flowers spread in all directions, shorter grass being the only marking of roads and paths. Swelling above the grass were little hilly humps that made up the hill-homes, recognisable as buildings only because of the windows and doors that marked their faces. Most of them were gardens themselves, covered in cultivated flowers or even planted with fruiting shrubs or vegetables. The paths here were beautiful and meandering, winding between the hill-homes and hilldings but with none of the height and bustle of Lost Circle. Indeed, it was hard not to feel lost beneath the enormous purple sky and cotton-fluff clouds, so wide and open was it all.

'Come on,' said Frost. 'Our mothers live on the other side of the village. It's not a long walk, but we can always take a beetle-bus.'

'Beetle-bus?' Jenna threw Frost a curious look.

Frost's faces split into three devious grins. 'Oh, you're going to *love* this.'

Sure enough, Jenna was beaming when we boarded the hovering trams pulled by an enormous beetle covered in moss and flowers. The squirrel-shape riding it stared at Jenna with the same open awe Jenna had for the beetle, but managed to shake off their shock and set the bus rolling.

Jenna gripped the edge of the bus, watching the hilldings and fields roll by. Every now and then we could see a flash of a creature in the rustling long grasses—the tip of a feathered tail or four pointed ears, or the scaley curve of a snake.

I couldn't help the way her wonder blunted my misery. 'There's a glimbeetle migration due to pass us while we're here,' I told her. 'I think you'll like it.'

'Glimbeetles,' she repeated, and for a moment her eyes seemed almost as starry as a cosmoran's.

Eventually, the rocking motion of the beetle-bus came to a halt and we all hopped out of the tram and onto the grassy road. At the end of the road, just curling off to one side, I could see it. I felt a lump in my throat at the sight of it—windows and door set into a small hill, the shutters thrown open, flowers and grass swaying in the breeze upon the earthen roof. A small garden patch lined both sides of the door, where even now a small strikerabbit was digging up a vegetable, two pairs of paws digging quite successfully while their long hind-paws thumped excitedly on the ground.

Home. Or it had been once, anyway.

The strikerabbit started to scoot backwards, the crown of some kind of root vegetable clenched between its teeth. It jerked its head hard, trying to free the root.

'Should we...shoo it off?' Jenna asked uncertainly.

'It has as much right to anything growing from the ground as we do,' said Vya. I glanced at him; it was the first time I'd heard him say more than 'yes' or 'no' in a few hours. He watched the strikerabbit with a soft expression.

'All right,' said Frost. 'It's time.' They strode forward and knocked on the door, not pausing before they strode inside. Delighted cries erupted. Vya hesitated, then followed.

Jenna paused in the doorway, looking back at me. 'Avari?'

I reached out with starfire and freed the vegetable—a saltroot, by the looks of it—and watched the strikerabbit triumphantly flee with it dragging behind it. 'Coming,' I said. Jenna regarded me with an expression I struggled to read, full as my mind was with worry over this visit.

I followed her inside, my ears flattening as the door closed behind me.

Chapter Fourteen

Inside it was a lot of fuss and happy cries and pressing cheeks to cheeks. I stiffened as Nova greeted me with a cheek-press and a quick preen of my ears. 'Lovely to see you,' she said. It sounded genuine. I put my ears forward and nodded, trying to project happiness.

Teera came up on my other side. As she pressed her scaly cheek against mine, she whispered, 'Glad you've finally stopped avoiding us.'

My stomach plummeted. I flinched away from my mother, but she'd already moved on.

'Jenna!' She and Nova converged on Jenna. 'So good that you were able to make it! Avari didn't scare you away, then?'

'Oh!' Jenna blinked and took a half-step back toward the door, then smiled uncertainly. 'No, not at all. I'm really looking forward to exploring Athelean with them.' She looked around and gestured, as if to take the room in. 'You have a lovely home.'

I took it in as well. Warm earthy walls coated in resin that kept the worst moisture out. Shelves bursting with small carved figures or ceramics or jars of paintbrushes or pigment—the tell-tale sign that Nova had spent a significant time anywhere. Rugs woven in bright colours and bold floral patterns—some of them made by Teera, who had been a weaver once and still dipped a paw into the craft now and again. Everything smelled of earth and spice. It simultaneously made me feel nostalgic for Athelean and homesick for my treelding in Antlervine Tree.

'Rooms?' I asked, because I didn't want to sort through that.

'We've put you and Jenna together in your old room,' said Nova. 'But you don't need to—'

I squeezed past my family and fled into my old room, closing the door behind me. It didn't look very different to how it had when I had lived here—tidier, certainly. It was depressing to think that this was less due to my family choosing to preserve my room and more due to my room having nothing to preserve. I hadn't decorated the walls or filled it with trinkets. I hadn't known enough of who I was then to feel comfortable expressing myself. For years, I had felt like there was nothing to express. Like I was a ghost and not a person.

There were two nests, one against each wall. I took the larger one without remorse as I was easily three times as large as Jenna. I plopped my bag down beside it and climbed into the cushions, shunting them here and there with my nose and then circling twice before settling down. The sound of my family was muffled through the door. I could make out the faint murmur of their voices, but not what they were saying. It was a relief. I wasn't sure I wanted to know what they were talking about.

After a while, the door opened a crack. I opened my eyes and frowned at it. 'Go away, Frost. I'm fine.'

The door opened a little more, a small, soft nose appearing in the gap. A little deer-shape kit with a tiny pink flame stood there on trembling legs, her small, downy wings folded on her back. She shook her head, over-sized ears flopping and wobbled away.

'Wait!' I tried to launch to my feet but my forgetech leg got stuck and I tripped. I hit the floor hard, cursing, as Journey vanished from the doorway. 'Shit,' I said. There was something soothing about using one of Jenna's ridiculous human curses. I untangled my legs and took off my forgetech one, leaning it against the wall in irritation. It had been acting up more and more recently—I probably needed to take it for maintenance. I hadn't taken it in at least a year now. Somehow it just seemed like too much trouble, recently. Ridiculous.

I could do without it for now. It actually felt really nice to have it off. My shoulder always got so sore where it was connected, a pain so normal it had faded into the background of life even though its absence was a sweet relief. I looked back to the door, only to watch Journey creep in, her eyes fixed on my forgetech leg. She sniffed toward it, stretching out her neck in a clear example of curiosity overcoming hesitance. Her hind legs trembled with the strain.

'That's my leg,' I told her. Her ears moved to me first, followed by her head. She transferred her sniffing to me, more out of instinct than politeness, I thought. I sniffed back at her, because it was important to model manners for kits. 'It goes here, look.' I picked up my leg and attached it back to my upper leg, wincing a little at the pinch of the nerves connecting to the forgetech. I did it slowly, so that she could watch me using starfire to move it around. She was only a handful of months old, so she was unlikely to be skilled with starfire yet. She crept closer, her little hooves making tiny ticks against the ground, then sniffed it where it was attached to my leg. I took a few steps with it so she could see how it moved, then I took it off again. 'It helps me walk,' I told her. 'But I don't always need it.'

She stared up at me solemnly with wide, star-filled eyes. Her eyes were black, I noticed. Dark and sparkling with curiosity. Her fur was still that fine, soft fruit-fur of a recently-hatched kit.

'Do you remember me?' I asked her. 'I'm your biggest sibling. Well—your eldest sibling. Frost is biggest.' She wouldn't pick up the nuance of that. Likely she didn't understand most of what I was saying. Cosmoran kits were quick to walk but she'd likely be a year old or older before she started speaking.

She stretched up to sniff at my face, so I leaned down and let her. She sneezed, shuffled her wings, and ambled out of the room.

I watched her go, a lump in my throat. She was already so much bigger. The last time I'd seen her, she'd been a tangle of legs and pin-feathers curled up on my mother's back.

Maybe it was good to be back after all.

The door creaked open further. Frost poked two heads into the room. 'Are you done sulking?' asked Night, flicking his tongue at me cheekily.

I flicked one ear forward and one back. 'For now,' I said, and followed them out of the room.

Lunch was a loud affair, as was often the case when my family got together. Food was passed around, preserves were dolloped and smeared, Lur got up frequently to follow Journey around and make sure she didn't get into too much trouble, Bloom and Night argued loudly about a data crystal they'd both read recently, and Nova and Teera grilled Jenna about her stay so far on Viridus.

'And the Travellers' Union is looking after you, are they?' asked Teera. 'I was a traveller myself in my youth. They're meant to have special care of otherworldly travellers.'

131

'Well...yes and no,' said Jenna. She shifted awkwardly. 'The TU specifically looks after human travellers but there's so few of us that...well, it isn't perfect.' Her mouth twisted for a moment, and I wondered what she might be holding in. 'Actually, the TU official handling my case is a human as well, so they know what I'm going through and have had all sorts of advice. They've advocated hard for me, and I know it would have been much worse without them. But they're overworked, so...well. There's a lot I have to do and learn by myself.'

Nova nodded. 'It must be difficult.'

'A human in the TU?' Teera frowned. 'Well, I suppose that makes sense.'

Jenna's smile became strained.

I resisted the urge to scold my mother. I wasn't sure Jenna would appreciate it. I couldn't quite stop myself from glaring at her though. 'Elm is great,' I said. 'They've been a good friend to Jenna.'

Nova nodded. 'And how have you been getting on, living with Avari?'

'Oh, it's been great,' said Jenna. 'Avari's a wonderful host. I'm really going to miss them when I move out.'

She smiled at me and I gave her a shaky smile back, staggered, as I always was, by the idea that she would be gone soon.

Nova brightened, her ears and crest perking. 'Avari is a good host! Oh that's so good to hear,' she said, a little too heartily and with an obvious note of surprise. She turned a warm and approving gaze on me, but I found I didn't want it.

A few minutes later, I excused myself from lunch and went for a walk, my hooves treading the familiar paths without any conscious direction, winding between hill-homes and past beetle-buses as I took a short circuit that would end back at the front door.

'Avari!' I turned to see Bloom chasing after me, her tail a striped pennant behind her. She caught up to me, huffing and puffing. 'Stars, you're quick!'

'Well, rage really puts a kick in your step,' I said dryly.

Bloom's ear's quirked. She considered me a moment, eyes unusually serious behind her mask of dark fur. 'You don't look angry.'

I sighed. 'Well.' I wasn't full of rage, not really. I was hurt and frustrated and maybe a little sad. But I couldn't bring myself to retract my words, because so much of me *wanted* to rage. It would be justified, wouldn't it?

It would make everything worse.

Bloom rubbed her ear with one hand. 'Our parents can be, you know, pretty mean sometimes.'

Hearing it acknowledged loosened something in me. Tears stung at my eyes. I stomped, trying to burn off that energy elsewhere. 'Yeah.'

Bloom rubbed her hands uncertainly. 'Would you like a hug right now?'

I nodded. 'Yeah, actually.' It surprised me how true it was.

Bloom wrapped her arms around my neck, burying her muzzle in my mane. 'I'm glad you came,' she said. 'I've really missed you.'

I'd missed her too. I couldn't stop the tears leaking from my eyes and this time I didn't try to stop them. After a moment, I shifted my hooves to signal I was done, and Bloom released me.

'Is it okay if I walk with you?' Bloom asked. 'We don't have to talk.'

'I'd like that,' I said. So we walked. And we caught up—about Bloom's plan to move to Lightning Valley, and her worry that Lur was isolating himself. About my new friends at the Internet Café and Jenna's odd reaction to meeting a millipede-shape. And as we talked, I felt a knot come loose in my chest.

Maybe Athelean would never be home to me in the way it was for the others. But that didn't mean it couldn't carry a piece of my home inside it.

When we looped back and could see my parent's hill-home in the distance, Bloom winked at me. 'Race you!' she said, and scampered ahead on all fours. I galloped after her, the grass and wind whipping past, my heart as light as my hooves.

Chapter Fifteen

'Have you got your coat?' I asked Journey. The little kit blinked up at me with solemn incomprehension, so I leaned down and tugged at her coat with my teeth. It was yellow and had little wooden toggles. 'Coat,' I said. 'Yes, coat. Do you have your hat?' I tweaked the broad-brimmed hat on her head, and she wiggled her ears. 'Yes, hat. I think we're ready to go!'

Whether she understood me or not, she didn't need much encouragement. The moment she saw me heading for the door she scrambled after me, her little hooves slipping on the floor tiles in her excitement. I let her fall, since it didn't look serious, and helped her stand back up.

'You're like a different person around kits,' Lur said quietly as I led Journey to the door.

'Not really,' I said, shrugging. 'There's just less to complain about right now.'

Lur chortled and strode away, flicking their long fluffy tail at me in amusement.

As I opened the door, I noticed Vya with Teera. 'Is there anything I can help with?' he asked. 'I know it's a lot of work, cooking for all of us, and I'd be happy to—'

'No, that won't be necessary,' said Teera. 'I'll call in Frost if I need help.'

'...right.' I watched Vya's head and ears droop as I closed the door behind me.

Journey started bouncing and kicking, full of excitement. I tried to put the miserable sight of Vya behind me. For now, anyway. 'Which way do you normally go?' I asked Journey. 'You can lead.'

Journey continued to buck and bounce for a moment before putting her head down and charging off down the grassy path. I smiled and followed her, keeping pace easily even without my forgetech leg.

We wound through the village and out onto a broad flat meadow that had been thoroughly grazed by the nearby herd of lightningsnails, their shells gleaming colourfully in the afternoon sun. Journey bounced up to a snail and sniffed it excitedly, fearless in spite of it being even larger than she was. It goggled at her with its antenna and an electric pulse of light went crackling through its translucent shell. Journey squealed delightedly and ran in circles a moment before racing back to my side.

It wasn't long before she ran herself out. We spent some time sitting in the grass, watching the flowers dance in the breeze. She cuddled up close to me and rested her chin on my knee. Her eyelids fluttered tiredly.

'It's good to get out sometimes, isn't it?' I said. I wasn't sure whether she was still awake, but I didn't mind either way as long as she was comfortable. 'I used to take your siblings out for walks like this. Bloom would always run ahead, like you did at the start, but Lur was always glued to my side, like you are now.'

Her ear flicked once; her eyes closed. The beautiful pink sky above was clouded with swirls of dark grey. It would likely start raining soon. But Journey had her coat and hat, and I had my cloak. A little rain was fine, even healthy. Especially if she could go home after and get warm and dry.

I looked down at Journey's head, where her ears poked out of her hat. 'You're going to grow up so fast we all hardly realise it's happened,' I told her. 'You're going to have opinions and we'll probably fight sometimes. Maybe you'll grow up bright and cheerful and have lots of friends. Maybe you'll grow up lonely, like I did. Maybe you'll do something unthinkable, like hating spicy food. You might be someone completely different than I'm imagining right now. Maybe different than *you* are imagining right now.'

I looked up at the sky, where the clouds were gathering. 'But I'm going to love you anyway. I'm your older sibling. So you can always come to me or to the others and we'll help you. No matter what.'

I wondered who she'd become. I certainly hadn't turned into the person my parents had expected me to be. Frost and Lur and Bloom—they had all changed so much, as well. I hoped that whoever she grew into, we'd be friends.

Thunder boomed in the distance and with a sudden hiss and roar, the skies opened, drenching us. Journey yelped and staggered to her hooves, looking briefly panicked.

'It's okay,' I said, as soothingly as I could. 'It's only rain. Rain is fun.'

She trembled a little as I got to my feet. I jumped and kicked a few times, staggering on the landing, which was a lot harder without my forgetech leg. The grass squelched beneath my hooves.

Journey stared at me with wide eyes, frozen, water running in streams from the brim of her hat, and then all at once, she started kicking and bucking as well, stomping around beside me. It was raining so hard that we quickly both got splattered in mud.

We ran home together, Journey squeaking and dancing the whole way. I shook out my fur on the doorstep before we went inside and Journey did the same, falling into me when she lost her balance.

'Had a good time, I take it?' asked Storm as we walked in. Night and Illusion were in earnest conversation with Vya. I'd always envied Frost's ability to split their attention like that.

'We did,' I said. 'Honestly, I'd been thinking of getting a sibling upgrade, because you three—'

Storm threw a cushion at me, which bounced off my right horn. I laughed and helped Journey take off her coat.

Nova came in and froze. I glanced at her; her feathers were puffed up and her ears were flat back. She looked...upset? Why?

'Oh, Journey!' She rushed forward and enveloped her kit in her wings. 'You're soaking! Oh you poor darling!' She glared at me. 'You didn't make a rain ward over her?'

I stomped a hoof, letting out some nervous energy. I wasn't very good at rain wards, or any firecraft more complicated than moving things with my starfire. 'It's just some rain,' I said. 'She was wearing her coat and we came right back.'

She snorted and swept Journey away. I stared after them, wire tangling inside my chest. I stomped again and went to sit down at the low table with Frost and Vya. Vya gave me an uncertain look. Frost didn't look at me at all.

Vya leaned forward, long ears perking. 'Are you—?'

'So I still don't know how we'll find room for a companion animal,' Frost said quickly. 'I'm just not sure our spare room is large enough to meet their needs—'

Vya's gaze returned to his mate and they started arguing the merits of their home for a companion animal. I wasn't sure whether to be annoyed or relieved. After a while, feeling thoroughly an outsider, I made my way into my bedroom and collapsed on my pile of cushions. I sighed loudly and shoved my head under one.

'You too, huh?'

I poked my head out from under the cushion. Jenna was in the other nest—I hadn't noticed her under her blanket. She had a data crystal orbiting her cosmorb, her button board in her lap. She looked...tired.

As if she could read the question in my face, she said, 'I just needed a break. Everything's so unfamiliar here—again—and I guess I need time to process. And people keep wanting to go for walks...it's taking a lot of me.'

'What're you reading?'

'Hmm? Oh, Keera sent me some human novels. This one is what we call science fiction. It's an imagined picture of what the future will look like, with a story over the top of it.'

'We have science fiction,' I said. 'What's it about?'

'Well...this one is quite old, so actually, it's pretty inaccurate to what things actually look like. But it's about an android that breaks its programming and just wants to watch cheesy videos.' She paused. 'Do you want me to read it to you? I'm not very far in.'

It was such an odd suggestion. 'Yeah,' I said, surprising myself. 'I would really like that.'

I shifted so that my head rested on a pillow rather than under it. I closed my eyes and listened to the story, which was funny and heartfelt and oddly relatable, in spite of the extreme distance between what the fictional world looked like and what mine did. It was also interesting that, although Jenna said it wasn't accurate to human society, I could see so much of human culture and technology in it and the world it envisioned.

I got lost in the story and, for a while, the hurt and anxiety spiking in my chest and belly dulled.

THE OLD GOAT AND THE ALIEN

The next few days passed relatively uneventfully in a confusing mixture of tension and comfort. Lur and I took Journey to a copse of trees so she could watch us climb and we could show her the different leaves. Jenna and Vya uncovered some long-disused board games and set up a Leap Stones tournament, which I did terribly at because I always forgot about the portal tiles, and Frost won—well, Illusion won, in spite of the rest of Frost, anyway.

Nova told me how good it was to see me, and showed me her recent art—etched on thin glass and designed to be hung and catch the light, each shard an image of someone in our family. Teera asked me to help her cook and even let me make the dinner a little spicy. She showed me some tricks for cooking mushroom bread, which I'd never managed to raise myself. She told me she loved me, and when she pressed her cheek to mine, for once I didn't feel crowded.

Bloom and Night got into an argument, as if we were children, and rather than resolving it, spent the next few days pulling each other's tails and generally being nuisances. I fretted about it at first, but as time went on, it clearly became a game between them, the original quarrel long forgotten.

Jenna continued to read her book to me and when Bloom found out about it, she begged to be included. By the end of the week, Jenna was reading to the whole family in the sitting room, while Frost knitted, Bloom and Lur played cards, and Journey curled up at one of our sides, too young to stay awake, too new to understand the words.

The next week was a little more fraught. Teera was in a bad mood and continually sniped at me. Frost always seemed to excuse themselves from the room when that happened. I took out my stress by aggressively cleaning the kitchen, leaving the whole thing gleaming. Telling myself that she'd regret her terrible mood when she saw the nice thing I'd done for her, but such a moment never materialised.

Jenna witnessed one of the moments where Teera snapped at me for something small and followed me to the room. 'You okay?' she asked me. 'Sorry—I mean, I know you're not okay. Anyone can see you're not okay. But do you want to talk about it?'

'No.' I noted the anger in my voice. 'Yes. I'm sorry.'

Jenna gave me a fleeting smile. 'No need to apologise. Go ahead.'

I tried to sort through my feelings, through hundreds of little complaints and frustrations. Through the feeling of being slowly killed by papercuts. 'I don't...understand,' I said. 'I don't know what they want from me, except to be different than I am. No matter how many times I've asked them. I don't know why it still hurts so much. I'm not a kit anymore. I haven't been a kit in a hundred years. I thought I would outgrow this. I thought they would treat me differently. But every time I see them, it's the same.'

'You feel...powerless? Stagnant?'

I shook my head. 'I feel...like we should all be past this. Like they're children who can't help but whine and be petty, but they're meant to be the adults, you know? They're my parents! And then my siblings...I know Frost sees it. But they act like they don't. Or like it's *my* fault.'

'It's not your fault,' said Jenna.

Tears welled in my eyes. I stomped a hoof.

'May I touch you?'

I nodded and Jenna laid a hand on my neck, digging her fingers into the mane. It was a surprisingly welcome touch. The pressure grounded me, somehow.

'They aren't bad people,' I said, when I had enough control of my voice to speak without warbling. 'They aren't even bad parents, really. Just bad for *me.*'

'They don't have to be bad people to hurt you,' said Jenna. 'I'm sorry.'

I sniffed. 'Yeah. I know it's not, like...terrible. My parents love me and are often really wonderful. But it still hurts.'

'Yeah.'

'I just wish...anyone had ever acknowledged it, even once. That they aren't fair to me.'

'I see it,' said Jenna. 'They aren't fair to you.'

Her words were warming and bitter to me at the same time, a wash of recognition and safety that was unfamiliar to me, and bitter in its unfamiliarity.

'Jenna? You...don't have a good relationship with your parents, either.'

Jenna sighed. 'No, I don't.'

'Are they...good people who hurt you?' I hesitated. 'I'm sorry, I don't mean to push. We don't need to talk about it.'

She stared at the wall for a long moment, her lips pressed into a tight line, her arms folded across her stomach. 'No,' she said at length. 'I don't think they're good. They never...they never threw me out, or anything. They never cut ties. But they hurt me. Sometimes by accident, because they didn't understand my illness and didn't really try. Sometimes knowingly, because they didn't really accept who I am. I don't think they were capable of loving me as I am. They only loved who they wished I had been. And my brother...I saw him maybe once every five years, and he was happy with that.' She shook her head, and there were tears in her eyes. I couldn't tell whether she was crying from sadness or pent-up anger. 'I think good people would have at least pretended their love was unconditional. They couldn't even manage that.'

My core wrenched. 'Jenna...'

She looked at me. '*You* have been more family to me than I had on Earth. Our friends...they're more family to me. And maybe it's hard, living somewhere so different. Being so different. And yeah, Geminus' support for human travellers is practically non-existent. But I'm so, so glad I get to be here. And that I get to be here with you right now, hiding from your mothers with you.'

I didn't know what to do with the enormity of her emotions, or the painful sympathy and anger her words stirred in me.

I leaned forward. 'Could I hug you, please?' I asked, a little thickly.

Jenna wrapped her arms around my neck to hug me, as Bloom might. I rested my chin over her shoulder, my nose against her hair. I didn't know what to do with the rush of emotion inside me, or the sense that this was *right,* as right as hugging Journey or Frost, as right as family when it was good. She even smelled like family, somehow. I wondered how that had happened in just a handful of months.

It wasn't long before I pulled away, because that much closeness was overwhelming to me. But I gave her a shaky smile. 'Thank you,' I told her.

'Thank you,' she said, and smiled back.

Chapter Sixteen

I coped a little better the next week. I played with Journey and talked to my siblings and tried to savour the good moments with my mothers and let the bad slide off me like water off an oiled cloak. It didn't always work, but the edge of my frustration was gone now. I knew, I *knew* I wasn't imagining it. Jenna had given me that.

Our last night in Athelean, we all went out to a large hill just outside town. Lots of our neighbours were already there, either mixing or off to the side. Food and drink were swapped and shared and lots of hearty greetings went all around. The sky was awash with stars, a sparkling sea above our heads. We laid out several blankets for our family, and while the others went and greeted our neighbours, I settled down on a blanket woven into a bright pattern of blue and turquoise and watched Journey bounce and frolic and roll around to stare up at the stars.

Frost settled beside me. While Storm and Illusion watched Journey, Night said, 'Hey.'

'Hey.'

I looked at him. A sleek, tired black serpent. Of all of Frost, he and I had always related to each other the most. We were the 'grumpy ones', the ones who never said the right thing. When we were very young, before Frost had really grasped their nature as a system and their alters had taken over each head, Night had been the reason Frost and I bonded so quickly, I think.

'I don't really see what the big fuss is about meteor showers,' said Night. 'I know they look nice during Rainbows but it's not like we haven't seen it before, or like we couldn't do it from home. And we have a whole season for them, for stars' sake.'

I shrugged. 'I like having an excuse to be out at night. I could do without the rest of the village being here, though.'

Night and I met each others' eyes and chortled, as we had since we were children every time we had a griping session.

'It's been nice to spend more time with you,' he said quietly. 'We've really missed you. Being home all together, it feels kind of like old times.'

I nodded and looked away, a lump forming in my throat. 'Yeah,' I said, and left it at that.

He changed the subject. We talked for a while about the book Jenna was reading us, with its strange human ideas and high drama. 'Vya thinks the android is going to try to become human,' he said. 'That the reason it loves human media so much is that it craves human experiences.'

I snorted. 'The android is pretty clear that it wants to be an android,' I said. 'I think it loves human media because it enjoys feeling an emotional connection without actually having to socialise.'

'Sure you aren't projecting?'

I headbutted Frost's shoulder, causing Night to chortle.

Illusion suddenly lifted her head and cawed in alarm. 'Journey? Journey, darling, that's too far. Journey!'

'See you in a bit,' said Night as Frost got up to chase after our youngest sibling.

I nodded and looked up at the sky. I couldn't see any streaks of light among that glittering darkness, but it wouldn't be long. A cold breeze ruffled my cloak and chilled my ears. I snuggled down further, tucking my cloak around me better and pulling the hood over my head—it was Ever's work, so of course it sat very nicely just behind the base of my horns.

Members of the family came and went. We ate and talked and sat in a circle. I took my turn following Journey around the hilltop, and couldn't completely avoid exchanging awkward sniffs and hellos with my former neighbours. Then, as the meteors started in earnest, we all huddled together as a family under blankets and cloaks, our breath making clouds in the air. Journey sat with me for some of it, and I pointed up at the sky with my muzzle. 'Look at this, Journey,' I said, my eyes full of darting lights. 'Those are meteors. Hunks of space rock, burning up in our atmosphere.' Each of them streaks of vari-coloured light, the atmospheric spores of the season filtering the sky.

When I looked down at Journey, her eyes were full of stars and light as well, her tiny flame bright with interest.

Later, when she was tucked warmly between Nova's wings and on the way home with everyone else, I still stayed up and watched the meteors.

'Looks like it's just the three of us,' said Frost, coming to sit beside me.

'Aren't you three yourself?' asked Jenna.

Storm laughed. 'You know, how we count ourselves sort of depends on the day.'

We were silent a while. The chill of the night was piercing the blankets and I could feel it setting into my bones, but I didn't want to go home yet. With the hillside mostly abandoned, it was a beautiful kind of quiet now. And I couldn't quite bring myself to stop searching the sky for rainbow streaks.

'You know,' said Jenna. 'On Earth, we call meteors "falling stars".'

'They aren't stars,' I said.

'I know. But they sort of look like it, don't they?'

'They do,' said Illusion.

'They do,' I agreed.

When it got so late that Jenna started to doze, I asked Frost if we could head back to the house.

'Yeah. Yeah,' said Storm. They paused, then Night said, 'They're not so bad actually. Meteor showers.'

'Falling stars,' I said, liking the shape of the words in my mouth. It felt like poetry, somehow. Like human poetry, maybe.

Frost helped me drape a sleeping Jenna across my back and we headed home beneath a shower of falling stars.

The next morning, we packed our things. Neither Jenna nor I had brought much, though Jenna seemed to have accumulated all sorts of bags of food and jars of preserves from an overbearing Teera. We disassembled our nests and stacked the cushions in the corner. Jenna got a broom and swept up all the fur we'd left—mostly mine—though she struggled a bit since most human brooms have handles but ours do not.

We made our goodbyes on the doorstep. Journey very gently touched her nose to mine, so I pressed my cheek to hers. I felt tears sting my eyes; she had grown so much in just a few short months. She would be a new person the next time I saw her, and the next after that.

Nova reached up to touch my cheek with her paw, careful of her talons. 'Don't be a stranger,' she said. 'We'd love to hear what you're up to, out there in the city.'

I nodded. 'I'll try,' I said.

Her eyes softened, and she moved on.

Teera hugged me roughly, her arm around my neck, then said firmly to Frost, 'Look after your sibling!'

'I will,' said Frost. 'We always look out for each other.'

A lump formed in my throat, grateful for the distinction, surprised that Frost knew to make it.

'It's been lovely to meet you, Vya,' said Nova. Teera echoed it, sounding not quite convincing to my ears, but then I was a suspicious sort of person.

Vya smiled and nodded eagerly. 'It was lovely to meet you as well. Please feel free to visit us! We may even have a companion animal by then.'

'We *might,*' Frost said, throwing him three sternly amused looks.

Later, as the canopy-glider rode smoothly through the sky and all the fields in all their beauty rushed past, Jenna came to stand beside me.

I glanced at her. She seemed subdued, somehow. 'How'd you find it? Athelean, I mean.'

'Oh, it was lovely. It was actually amazing to see somewhere on Geminus so different to Lost Circle. Your sister Bloom took me on several tours. I feel like I got to see it all.' But though her words were cheerful, there was something dull about her tone, and her arms were crossed with shoulders high, something she had explained to me meant tension in a human.

I wasn't sure what to make of that. If she wanted to talk about something that was bothering her, wouldn't she just do that? But Jenna was my friend; there would be no harm in asking. 'Are you all right?'

She gave me a quick smile that looked halfway to a grimace. 'I'm fine. Just have a lot on my mind.' Then, oddly, she got out her cosmorb and looked at it a moment, then put it away, still completely inert.

I tried to parse this. 'Do you want to talk about it?'

146

THE OLD GOAT AND THE ALIEN

She shook her head, her shoulders rising even higher, so I left it at that.

Chapter Seventeen

It was good to be home. It took me about a week to get over the visit to Athelean. I moped around the house and read data crystals and ate only food I got from local cooks rather than cooking it myself, which seemed completely beyond me. I even got a messenger to deliver a few meals to me while on their route. I was lucky that Lost Circle had a large enough Messengers' Union that it wasn't considered rude to ask for things like that. The messenger even left me a note wishing me a tasty meal. I made a mental note to drop off something nice for them at the Messengers' Union when I was feeling better again.

Jenna worried about my malaise to begin with, but I assured her this was my normal reaction to long stays away from home. By the end of the week, I got back into something resembling routine. I brushed my fur and cleaned the house and started to think about picking up CU contracts again.

Jenna, though, kept mostly to her room and had little to say. Now that I was done wallowing in the misery of change, I was clear-headed enough to notice, and it worried me. She washed little and ate little and I rarely saw her. When I did, she seemed...forlorn, maybe. And certainly tired, in spite of doing very little. I got the sense there was more going on than the pernicious Pem, but she still refused to talk about it and I didn't want to press her.

So, two weeks after our return from Athelean, I found myself walking into the Internet Café. It was surprisingly quiet—I couldn't see any of our usual crowd around. I went up to the counter, where one of the other cooks, a silver-and-blue badger-shape named Pell, was busily refilling jars of spices. 'Oh hello,' he said as I walked up. 'Avari, isn't it?'

I nodded and shuffled my hooves a little. I always found interactions with someone who knew who I was but didn't *know* me particularly awkward. I was never sure what level of familiarity to expect, or express. 'Is Cloud in?' I asked.

'Oh no, she's taken the day off today. We had a big event a few days ago that she handled mostly on her own, so we all agreed it was best she take some time off. Can I get you anything?'

'Oh. Uh.' I supposed it would be nice to have something. 'You're a juice specialist, right? I'd love some juice.' Pell grinned, baring sharp teeth. 'I'd love to make something up. Take a seat and I'll bring something over soon.'

I nodded and did as he asked, wondering what to do. If I was honest, I'd come here almost automatically because I was thinking about Jenna. But now that I was here, I realised how much I wanted Cloud's opinion. Cloud was loud and silly, but she knew Jenna nearly as well as I did, and she understood humans far better.

After I finished Pell's juice, which was a delicious fruit blend touched by a nutty spice, I picked up my cosmorb and contemplated what I wanted to say. I formed a message to Cloud several times, unable to keep my emotions calm and cool as I hoped, uncertain whether I really had any right to send it. After all, she was having time off. She probably didn't want to hear from one of her customers at a time like this.

But then Jenna had said we were friends. And it did *seem* like we were friends; we played games and went for walks. She even messaged me sometimes. I just...had never initiated any of those interactions myself, and at this point, it felt like it was somehow taboo.

Finally, I sent it. Anxious energy and all. I wouldn't know if I didn't ask, and Jenna was counting on me.

Jenna is unhappy and she won't tell me why. Are you free to talk? I would like to do something nice for her to cheer her up.

As I put my cosmorb away, it warmed as I received a message. It was Cloud. She'd replied so quickly it seemed impossible that she'd already received and read my message.

Come to mine. I live in the middle home on Pyretree, not far from the café. Always happy to help a friend.

I stared at the message a moment, trying to parse the rush of warm feeling she'd sent with it. Was Jenna the friend, or me? My flame pinked a little at the thought. Ridiculous.

I shook out my mane, feeling like I was flicking off rainwater, and told her I was on my way.

Pyretree didn't take long to find. I had a fairly good map of the city on my cosmorb and I'd passed it many times on my walks without really paying attention to it. It was a squat tree with very dark bark and leaves that shifted from green to yellow to orange at the top, giving it the impression that it was licked with flame.

I was just trying to work out which of the five doors was the 'middle' home when one carved with clouds and stars burst open and Cloud skidded out of it. 'Avari!' she yelled. She bounded down the tree and took a flying leap to land right in front of me, sending up a cloud of dirt and leaf-mulch.

I didn't flinch but I did put my ears right back. Cloud was unconcerned. She wore a knitted jumper studded with beads painted with stars. She didn't sniff a greeting, only grabbed my hoof with her paw and gave it a firm shake. 'Lovely to see you,' she said. 'Come on up!' And then she turned tail, and I sneezed a little as one of her fluffy tails whapped my nose, and then she was bounding back up the tree.

Cloud's home, as it turned out, was a little smaller than mine, with only two rooms. It was probably the most cluttered home I'd ever seen. The floors and surfaces were clean, just...busy. There was a basket overflowing with data crystals in the corner, and the walls were absolutely covered in shelves of strange objects and portraits of humans and 'humansonas'. I looked at the figurines on the shelves. Most of them were of humans, or softer impressions of them. Carved wood, clay, and quite a lot of smooth synthetic material I assumed was 'plastic'. It smelled awful, and I wrinkled my nose after sniffing it.

Thankfully, the rest of her house smelled quite pleasant. Among the clutter were various potted plants and flowers, giving the whole home an incredibly fresh smell. I had rarely seen potted plants. It was a human habit, which I assume Jenna had taught her.

Cloud didn't have a low table and instead had some kind of human-style table with large stools. She sat down on one. I awkwardly climbed onto another, feeling horribly precarious. The stools were clearly made for cosmoran proportions but it still seemed very alien.

'So,' said Cloud, rubbing a paw across her whiskers briefly. 'Jenna needs cheering up?'

No small talk, no awkward greetings. Just straight to the point. In spite of the nerves of being a guest in an unknown and strange home, I relaxed a little. At some point, I had learned that Cloud was verian, too. As different as we were, it made talking to her a lot less fraught. 'Cheering up, distracting...something like that.'

'Did you have anything in particular in mind?'

'Well...I don't know. She enjoys the game nights you put on...maybe something like that?'

Cloud nodded. 'We could do one again. I was waiting until you both came home to run the next one anyway.'

'Yeah,' I said. 'I suppose a human board game night wouldn't be as good without your resident human.'

Cloud's ears twitched. 'And it wouldn't be as fun without you.'

I looked up in surprise, meeting her large, mismatched lilac-and-blue eyes. I couldn't read anything in her face; her flame flickered once, so faintly I wondered if I imagined it. I looked away, my body flushing. I tried to keep my flame from pinking.

I cleared my throat. 'So, uh. A game night. What would we play?'

'Hmm.' I glanced up at her; her whiskers twitched from side to side as she considered it. 'Well, I know she wants to learn more cosmoran-style games...what if we did a cosmoran game night instead? I'm not sure what would be best—I haven't played a cosmoran game in ages.' She glanced thoughtfully around her home. 'Actually, I'm not sure if I have any.'

'Oh. Well, I have plenty,' I said.

Her mouth quirked, revealing a single sharp tooth. 'Any suggestions?'

'Uh.' My mind drew a blank. I tore my eyes away from Cloud's toothy grin and fumbled my cosmorb out of my satchel. I pulled up the right list and passed it to Cloud.

Cloud surprised me by sitting back on her haunches and holding it with her paws rather than her starfire. 'What's this?' she asked.

'That's a list of all my board games,' I said.

Cloud's eyes widened. Her grin revealed another tooth. 'It's labelled "inventory". You keep an inventory of your board games?'

My ears flicked back. I shuffled my hooves. 'I have a lot of board games.'

Cloud's whiskers twitched. 'Adorable,' she murmured, and I was glad she wasn't looking at me because my starfire had flushed all kinds of pink. 'Hmm...I think something like Shines Hop might work best. It's very different mechanically and in theme from any of the human games I've played, but the rules are simple enough that she should be able to pick them up quickly.'

'Oh. Yeah, that's great.' I put my ears forward and tried to look politely interested and not like I was about to bolt out the door.

'I think I can put together a board game group for tomorrow evening. We can have it at the café again!' She grinned. 'What are Jenna's favourite snacks? I know she likes meatgourd paté...'

We talked things through for a few minutes, but it didn't take long to get everything in order.

'Good,' said Cloud. 'I'll see you tomorrow evening after closing, then!'

'Yeah.' I nodded once, then, and I really don't know why, I nodded again. 'I guess I'll be going then.' I turned for the door.

'You don't have to,' said Cloud. 'It's really nice to see you. I can't believe you actually messaged me, honestly.' She laughed. 'You're very reclusive.'

I hesitated a moment, not wanting to let that stand. I *was* reclusive, but...'I just don't like to impose,' I said, and that was the truth. Because I liked seeing Cloud.

'It's not an imposition. Assume I want to see you! If I'm busy or would rather not on a particular day, I'll just say so.'

Assume I want to see you. My chest felt tight and my face felt very warm.

'Uh,' I said, my mind completely blank.

Cloud stood up and stretched. 'I was thinking about taking a walk today,' she said. 'Maybe catching a tram to the Purple Garden. Would you like to come with me?'

Cloud and me, among the flowers, the sky grey as her fur, the breeze chill and ruffling her fur...

I took a quick step back. 'Nope! I, uh, I have some errands to run.' I backed out of the door. 'Thanks for your help today.'

'Oh,' said Cloud. She looked a little crestfallen but then brightened into a smile. 'Yeah! See you tomorrow!'

I hurried down Pyretree and back onto the nearest path, not sure why my heart was beating like I was being chased.

When I got home, I tentatively gave Jenna the news. She frowned at me from her nest. She was surrounded by data crystals and dirty dishes, her hair a tangled mess, her eyes shadowed. 'A board game night?' she said uncertainly. 'That sounds...nice.'

She wasn't as enthusiastic as I'd hoped. I nodded. 'Cloud's cooking special snacks for it again. We're playing a cosmoran game this time—do you know anything about Shines Hop?'

'No.' Then, a spark of interest. 'What is it?'

'It's a game about the season of Shines, when the spores from extra-planetary pollinators on Viridus are travelling to Profundus and the stars seem to change colour. You play as sky deities that are controlling the weather and migration paths of the spores and trying to pollinate the most plants on Profundus.'

'Oooh.' She sat up a little in bed. 'So cosmorans have sky deities?'

'Not really,' I said. 'It's more of a fantastical imagining.'

'What about the Starfire Ancient?'

I paused, considering. The question had rather stumped me. 'The...Starfire Ancient is the Starfire Ancient. It just...is.'

Jenna nodded and made a face. 'I really want to go. But I don't know whether I'll be up to it.'

'That's fine!' I said quickly. 'You can decide on the day. I'm sure it won't be an imposition.' I didn't tell her that the entire game night was to cheer her up. That would only put pressure on her to say yes when she might not want to. I wanted to help Jenna, but I didn't want to force my idea of 'help' on her. I'd been on the receiving end of that far too many times myself.

The next day didn't seem any different than those preceding it. I didn't see much of Jenna and assumed she wouldn't be up for the board game night. I was just trying to decide what to message Cloud about it when Jenna emerged from the washroom, hair washed and plaited, wearing fresh clothes.

'I'm ready to go!' she said. 'We're not late, are we?'

I blinked. 'Uh, no! No. I was about to ask whether you wanted to come, actually.'

She gestured to herself, as if that was answer enough and headed for the door. I followed her out, studying her slyly as we walked. There was still that tiredness to her eyes, but she held her back straight and walked with a determination. She wanted to do this.

Before we went inside, I said, 'We can leave at any time. If you want, I'll make up an excuse for us to leave. Just let me know.' Frost had done the same for me many times. It felt right to offer Jenna the same.

Jenna gave me an amused look but nodded. 'Thanks.'

We entered to a chorus of greetings from our friends. It wasn't as big an event as it had been previously. I saw Frost hadn't made it, nor had a handful of our internet café friends, but Cloud, Mers and Nila were settled around a table, each with a bowl loaded with snacks. I supposed it had been quite short notice.

'Come in, come in,' said Cloud. 'You're the last we're expecting. We can get playing! Did you bring the game?'

I pulled it from my pack and placed it on the table.

Cloud bounced excitedly. 'Yes! Okay, let's set up.'

As it happened, nearly everyone needed a refresher on the rules but me. I suppose everyone here was more used to human games than cosmoran ones. I felt anxious, standing up and explaining the rules to everyone like I thought I was in-charge or something, but everyone listened intently and asked questions and made jokes, and I quickly relaxed into it.

As we played, I really enjoyed watching everyone's reactions to the game—like Mers groaning when Nila seized the wind cards and diverted the spores toward their part of Profundus, or when Jenna got her first story encounter and spent a long time deciding whether to spend her precious divine fire on helping the inter-planetary travellers reach their destination safely.

Best of all was Cloud's mock-aggressive defending of her territory, threatening curses and divine retribution on anyone who took her winds. The sudden shift between her snarl and her laugh was a stunning transformation.

When the game was over, Nila was the first to leave, citing exhaustion. He had a condition similar to Jenna's that made him more tired than most. Mers left soon after. Then it was just me, Jenna, and Cloud. I mopped up the left-over snacks a little more freely now that the others had left. Jenna nursed one of Cloud's smoothies.

Cloud rested her paws on the table and her chin on her paws. She looked tired but happy. 'How did you find it?' she asked Jenna.

Jenna poked her straw around in the cup a moment. 'It was fun! I really liked the concept, and it was interesting how even though it was competitive, it was still satisfying to lose. The storytelling elements especially softened the blow.'

Cloud's tail flicked once. 'That's common in cosmoran games. Or the ones I know, anyway.' She sniffed. 'There's an elegance to the brutality of a long and painful loss, though.'

'Still pining after Monopoly?' I asked her, taking the seat beside her.

She sniffed. 'I was thinking of another human game, actually.'

'I'm sure you'll make us all play it one day.'

She looked at me sidelong. 'Oh, I will.' She grinned, baring her teeth.

Her grin made me feel warm and...embarrassed, somehow. I snorted and looked away.

Silence fell over us. Jenna stared at the table, picking at the base of her nails.

Gently, Cloud said, 'Stay as long as you like. I've still got quite a bit of cleaning up to do.'

'I'll help,' I said quickly. I stood up so fast that my forgetech leg pinched uncomfortably and I winced. It had been on for so long today that it was already becoming quite sore. I glanced at Cloud, uncertain how she would take it if I were to remove it. People were rarely unkind about my leg, but sometimes people were visibly uncomfortable to be reminded of it.

Cloud caught my glance and raised her eyebrows. 'Something the matter?'

'Oh. No. My leg is just pinching a bit.'

Her expression softened. 'Oh. Well, I hope you know you can do whatever feels comfortable to you here.' She turned away and started picking up dishes from the snacks table disappearing out through the kitchen.

I stared after her. I wondered how she'd known to say exactly what I needed to hear, and then left so that removing it wouldn't be a spectacle. I disengaged my forgetech leg with a burst of blue energy and leaned it against my seat. The muscles in my shoulder shivered, and for a moment, I felt both relieved and bereft. Always an adjustment.

I went to the snack table and picked up what Cloud had left behind and followed her into the kitchen. She thanked me brightly and started washing up, humming to herself, her tails twitching in time.

When I returned to the main café, Jenna actually stood up and helped me return the tables and seats to their usual formation, which was a surprise. There seemed to be a change in her, though I wasn't sure what had done it.

When Cloud returned, I thought it was just about time to say our farewells.

'I heard back from my family,' Jenna said abruptly. She kept her eyes low, but they sparkled with moisture. 'I've, uh, been processing it. Maybe not very well. But this evening was really lovely.'

Though we'd been halfway to the door, Cloud gestured to a nearby table and we all sat down.

Jenna scrubbed at her face like it was dirty, then said, 'I didn't have a great relationship with my family, back home. Or many friends, if I'm honest. I had online friends, but sometimes they seemed so very far away, you know? I wanted everyone to know why I'd disappeared, and that I was safe. My friends were really encouraging. It'll be hard that we won't be able to call and chat to each other now. That it takes so long for the messages to travel. But we'll manage. But my parents and my brother...' she trailed off, her mouth pressing into a thin line.

'Family can be difficult,' said Cloud.

Jenna nodded. 'Yeah. You know, I never really felt like they liked me. And when I transitioned, that feeling only increased. They were never really *open* about it, but...it was little things. Little barbs. Well. And big ones. I don't know. I'm an adult. I shouldn't have to care what they think. But I do, somehow.' She shook her head. 'I always do.'

Cloud made a sort of sympathetic chirping sound and boffed her head against Jenna's shoulder. Jenna leaned against her, tears running down her cheeks. 'They said...pretty terrible things. About me coming here. And the worst part is...it's kind of true? I *did* want to get away from them. From everything. Even though part of me thinks that even if everything had been perfect at home, I would have moved here.'

'It feels like you belong here,' I said quietly. 'I can't imagine life without you now.'

'Me either,' said Cloud. 'You're going to have to fight me if you want to go back.'

Jenna gave a sort of choked laugh. 'I reckon I could take you.'

'Don't be so sure. I'm very wily.'

We said our goodbyes not long after that. On the walk home, Jenna asked me, 'Did you transition?'

I thought about it. We didn't have the concept in quite the same way as humans. 'I did. I don't know what it's like for humans, but I had some treatments. Not everyone does. Socially, it was easy. Thankfully, people could see in my starfire the moment I knew. We don't have to guess at gender the way humans do.'

'Were your parents weird about it?'

I blew air a moment and looked up at the sky. At the stars sparkling through breaks in the canopy. At the strings of lanterns trailing from tree to tree. 'They were, a bit. Our history tells us we were once shapeshifters, you know,' I told her. 'Changing ourselves is our birthright. So it's common and accepted. You can see it in starfire, sometimes, if people want to share it. Cloud transitioned. Nila, too. But...' I trailed off, chewing on the thought. 'In practice, with family, it can still be complicated. Parents sometimes...I don't know. Put expectations on their kits. And while it didn't really matter, I could still sense they were sad to "lose" those expectations. That incorrect picture of who I was. They were never bad about it. But weird...maybe, yeah. A bit weird.'

Thinking about it brought up those confusing emotions, now long laid to rest. The sense that—for a while, at least—they had constantly been comparing me to who they'd thought I would be in their minds. It had been a long time since I'd really felt that way. I wasn't mad at them about it—not that, anyway. I'm not sure it was something they'd been able to help. But I had wished it didn't have to be that way.

'Shapeshifters,' Jenna murmured. Her eyes looked very bright. 'Really?'

I shrugged. 'We think so. I said "history" but it's...somewhere between that and myth, if that makes sense. I think there are even some actual shapeshifters out there, in the Firecrafters' Union. Illusion talks about it, sometimes.'

'I suppose you are still shapeshifters,' she said. 'Since the stars decide what shape you'll be. I don't know of any other creatures like that.'

'I like that,' I said.

'I wish...' she trailed off, staring at the ground.

'You wish?'

'Nothing,' she said. 'It doesn't matter.'

I let it lie. We talked a little more when we got home, and I went to bed knowing that Jenna had had a good evening, at least.

Chapter Eighteen

I sat wedged between Nila and Jenna while the canopy-glider took off. Keera was the first to take off her safety harness, hopping out onto the middle of the floor and immediately setting up an elaborate cosmorb relay. Shade and Mers joined her, murmuring questions as they set up their own displays.

We were on our way to the Cleaners' Union Conference in Moons Cliff, a mountain city only a few hours away by glider. I watched Cloud bounce over to the window and coo excitedly at the view. Jenna soon joined her.

'This is weird,' I muttered under my breath for the tenth time that day.

Beside me, Storm laughed and knocked their horn against mine in a playful sort of way. 'Is it weird when I come along to support you?'

I didn't reply. It wasn't weird when Frost came along to support me because Frost was my sibling and only friend. Except, I supposed, that wasn't true anymore. Jenna and Cloud had both wormed their way into my life. Even Shade, Nila, Mers, and Keera seemed to consider me worth travelling across Viridus for. If I thought about it, I felt the same about all of them. They were kind, fun, interesting people. I was lucky they wanted to spend time with me.

As if they could hear my thoughts, Storm chuckled and relaxed back in their seat.

It didn't feel like long before I heard Jenna gasp.

'That's it!' Cloud bounced up and braced her paws against the window. 'That's Moons Cliff!'

She sounded so delighted that I found myself joining them at the window. Below, the thick forests of Lost Circle and beyond had given way to the rocky brush of the mountains. Brightly-furred creatures skittered up the rocks as ably as a goat-shape. A four-winged serpent kept pace with the glider, watching us with beady-eyed curiosity before spiralling up and out of sight.

Among the rocks, I began to make out cavehomes, notable only by their carved doors and the hard stone paths cut into the cliff-face. And those were only the peripheral cavehomes. As we glided into the city proper, we began to see the enormous rocky structures of the ancient city, the vast rune-carved over-lapping stone rings that floated over it as much of a historical marvel as the floating islands at the heart of Lost Circle.

The glider gently landed in the shadow of those rings, on a small plateau with room for the spread wings to gently cease their flapping and then fold inwards.

We exited in a bit of a rabble, with lots of jostling and laughing and general buzzing excitement. It was a bit annoying but it also had something of the feel of family.

Nila trotted over to walk alongside me. 'So where's this convention?' He gazed up and around at the city. I wonder if, like me, he felt overwhelmed by its openness and shrunk by its vast rings.

'It's in the Heartcave, down there,' I said. I trotted to the edge of the plateau and pointed down at a distant door embedded in a large rock. It seemed a little grander than many of the others around—or larger, at least, as it was difficult to make out details from here. 'But I don't need to be there until noon.'

'So we have the whole morning free?' Mers laughed with one head and whooped with another. 'Let's explore! We've never been to Moons Cliff.'

'I know my way around,' said Keera. Her long ears twitched thoughtfully. 'My aunt lives here.'

'You have an aunt?'

'Why is that a surprise?'

'I dunno,' said Nila. 'You just don't reveal that much personal information.'

Keera shrugged. 'It's not usually relevant.'

Jenna came up alongside me. She looked a little nervous of the large drop, so I offered that she could rest her hand on my shoulder, which she gratefully did, tangling her fingers in my mane. 'It sort of reminds me of Athelean,' she said. 'Only...higher.'

'A lot higher.'

'Yeah.' She laughed nervously. 'Are all cosmoran cities formed out of the landscape like this? Athelean is built into hills, Lost Circle is grown from trees...'

'Pretty much,' I said. 'We do our best not to disturb our environments.'

Keera made a suggestion I missed and the group started a slow descent down a switchback path. It seemed plenty wide but I remembered Jenna's slip on the climb up the Flowering Ancient, so I made sure I was behind her and Frost was in-front. We brought up the rear so that we didn't slow down the others.

As Jenna carefully paced forward, both hands touching the rockface as she went, she muttered, 'Haven't cosmorans ever heard of railings?'

I snorted. 'We have railings.'

She glanced back at me, her expression wry. 'Have you considered using them?'

The next few hours were a bit surreal to me, but also pleasant enough. We walked around the city and let Jenna take in the sights. We visited a small cavecafé lit by natural crystals in the walls, with seating and tables carved of the same. It felt like we were eating inside a cosmorb. They brought us drinks and a local dish (mushroom sausages filled with a sweet paste) which we shared alongside the picnic supplies we'd brought with us. The server seemed quite startled by Jenna but was quickly put at ease by her friendly manner and how easy the rest of us were in her company.

Then we walked around a bit more, finding some small gardens growing among the rocks, or the occasional tenacious flower bursting out of the rocky surface. All the while, my nerves grew. I checked the supplies in my pack constantly. I had the Lost Circle CU's blessing to present my new cleaning solution at the conference and while I was confident in the solution's quality, I was less sure of my ability to pitch it.

As the heartstar drew near to its zenith, I nervously let the group know that I was going to head to the CU to prep for my presentation. This caused much excited chatter and actual bouncing from Cloud. 'Do you want company while you set up?' she asked. 'Ooh, do you need help? I could be your fabulous assistant. I'm really good at holding things and looking pretty.'

She sat back on her hind paws and mimed displaying an object around, batting her eyelashes and swishing her tails.

Everyone else laughed but I felt my flame pinking. 'Oh,' I said, trying to force my flame back to its resting magenta. 'I think it's better that I do it on my own. Not that you're not! Good at it. You are. Uh.' I coughed and turned a pleading gaze to Frost.

Night stuck his tongue out at me and Illusion's eyes danced with amusement.

'Anyway,' I said. 'I've gotta go now. My presentation is in the Foxfire chamber, if anyone wants to watch.'

'We'll be there!' said Cloud, dropping back to all fours. The others chorused their agreement and I fled toward the Heartcave. As it turned out, the Heartcave was the largest cavehome of Moons Cliff and had several entrances. I found the nearest one and followed a long tunnel down to the Heart Chamber, where there was a circular desk with several people manning the reception. I was marked in and given a pin and a sash with my name on it by a plump, cheerful pig-shape and pointed in the direction of the Foxfire chamber—one of many tunnels coming off the Heart Chamber like the rays of a star.

The Foxfire chamber was a large room of carved stone with enough cushions on the floor to seat perhaps fifty people. Fire-coloured crystals hung from the ceiling on threads, the reflections of the forgetech glowlights causing them to appear to dance with flame-like light. It made me quite nervous—in the past, I'd never presented to a larger gathering than twelve. The Lost Circle CU must have a lot of faith in my new solution. I only hoped I would do it justice.

Though I'd arrived perhaps a half hour early, there were already some people seated and talking quietly in the audience, and a mouse-shape forger came up and fitted me with an amplifier gem for my sash, testing that it was resonating well with the forge-drums at the back that would broadcast my voice around the room.

I went up to the desk where I'd be presenting and unpacked everything I needed for my demonstration—a jar of dirt, a jar of water, the current standard cleaning solution, and my cleaning solution in a spray bottle. I'd have to do a bit of a trick with my starfire to get this to work properly, but I'd practised enough in my workroom the last few weeks that I was confident I could do it.

Gradually, audience members trickled in, some I recognised from past conventions or the Lost Circle CU, but most entirely unfamiliar. The room had nearly filled by the time my friends arrived, squeezing onto the back row together. Jenna smiled; Cloud waved; Frost winked and stuck out one of their tongues.

I took a deep breath, activated my amp-gem with a touch of starfire, and started my presentation. 'Our traditional cleaning solutions have had a big problem with chemical run-off,' I said. 'There are, of course, more environmentally gentle solutions, but these tend to leave a tacky residue that makes them impractical for most uses. Building on the work done by Astera of the Everlight Cleaners' Union, I have created what I believe to be a practical *and* environmentally friendly cleaning solution.'

A bunch of starfires flashed, signalling a desire to ask questions. I started to sweat. 'Questions after the demonstration. Let me show you how it works.'

First, I covered the table in a scattering of dirt and water, smearing it around and then baking it with a blast of heated starfire. There were a few 'oohs' from the crowd—it was mostly cleaners in the audience, and like me, they'd likely had little practice with even simple firecraft. I warmed with both pride and embarrassment. I showed them Astera's cleaning solution and how it cleaned the mud off reasonably effectively, but left lots of residue. A few audience members came up to check my work.

Then I did the same trick again, but used *my* cleaning solution. Not only did the mud lift up quickly, but the residue evaporated into the air. A few other audience members came up to inspect it themselves. One sniffed the table closely, while another ran their paw across the surface. 'Completely clear!' they declared it, and drummed their paws on the ground in applause, which the rest of the audience quickly joined in with.

After that, I gave out the recipe and everyone broke into groups to discuss the applications and whether it could be improved. This was always a very nerve-wracking part of the presentation for me, as I hated to think I had missed something obvious after so much work. But while there was some discussion about lowering the amount of viricar sap, on the whole it was accepted as a fine recipe they'd take back to use in their own unions.

The audience gradually dispersed, still talking, and my friends came up to the presentation table while I packed away my things. 'That was amazing!' said Jenna. 'I didn't know you could make actual fire with starfire!'

'Oh it's not so hard,' said Cloud. 'Cooks like me use that trick all the time. I didn't know you could do it, though!'

'I learned it specially,' I said, my flame pinking.

Nila grinned. 'That's dedication!'

'Ah. Thanks.' I shuffled my hooves.

'So what do you get, for doing that?' Jenna said.

I blinked, one ear going forward and one back 'Get?'

'You know. A prize, or...something?'

'Oh. It wasn't a competition. No prize. But I really think people might use my solution. Maybe it'll even become the new standard for a little while.' My core warmed at the thought.

Jenna looked thoughtful, no doubt comparing this to whatever strange habits humans had for union conventions. I couldn't have been happier with the result. All anyone could hope to do was contribute something that helped others. Maybe even make a lasting difference. When I took on cleaner work, I did the first. When I presented the new cleaning solution, I had possibly achieved the second.

We spent the rest of the day in small groups that split and rejoined and split again. I went to some exciting CU presentations, which Frost dutifully attended with me—Night and Storm were both pretty bored by them, but Illusion could find something to love in the most irrelevant of lectures. The others went to explore Moons Cliff and I joined them in-between lectures.

In the evening, a few hours before our glider ride back to Lost Circle, we ate at a beautiful outdoor cliff-side restaurant that overlooked the mountainside below. Jenna fed strips of squash to a winged serpent that begged at her feet like a hatchling. Frost and Mers were deep in conversation about the challenges of dating as plural chimaera. Keera and Nila were explaining the role of cleaners in human society—it was fascinating, in a horrifying sort of way—when Cloud suddenly stood up.

'I know there's not much time left before the glider home,' she said. 'But there's one last thing I'd like to do.'

And so, in the last hour before we needed to return to our canopy-glider, we found a small flitter to carry us up to the Moons Cliff rings. I don't know how she had managed to scare up a pilot at such short notice, but the flitter was just about big enough for us all to fit in; about the same size as a canopy-tram and a similar open-topped design with railings, but with no rail to follow and with large solar wings that vibrated like an insect. The flitter swooped and glided around and through the rings, sometimes so close that it felt like I could stretch out my nose and brush it against the rock if I wanted to. Jenna even briefly reached out with a hand, only to pull back self-consciously.

The flitter really gave us a sense of their scale, of their incredible size and how small we were in comparison, a little firefly to its coiled dragons. I realised they were gently moving, spinning in place so subtly that it was startling to notice.

I glanced at Cloud, staring at these vast, ancient structures with her flame and eyes both sparkling, her tails twitching contentedly behind her. 'Thank you,' I said. 'This was a wonderful suggestion.'

She grinned at me with one sharp tooth bared. 'I just wanted to share something beautiful with you. And—and the others.' Her ears twitched and she looked away, her flame pinking. In silence, we watched the rings together as the flitter glided back down to land.

I carried that feeling—the elation of watching the rings slowly rise above us as we landed, the electric warmth of doing so side-by-side with Cloud, the familiar, comfortable murmur of my friends nearby—with me on the glider home.

It had been a perfect day. As we got off the glider, Jenna had us all wait—she'd received an important message on her cosmorb. She set up the keyboard and anxiously checked it. I hovered beside her. The last important message she'd received had thrown her into weeks of depression from which I didn't think she'd fully recovered yet. She read with her brow furrowed, her teeth pulling at her lip.

Then suddenly she smiled and looked up at all of us. 'It's happening!' she said. 'It's a message from Elm—the gardener's have finally finished growing my treelding. I have my own house!'

As everyone pressed in around her to offer her hugs and cheers and congratulations, I felt that beautiful, happy feeling inside me shatter like glass into sand.

Chapter Nineteen

When I was barely more than a kit, I moved to Lost Circle. I knew that I couldn't stay at home any longer, couldn't face my mothers' constant disappointment. But I hadn't counted on how hard it was to be separated from my siblings by such a great distance; to hear from Lur and Bloom only through messages, rather than watching them race around causing chaos at home. What it was like to have lost Frost, who had been the only company I ever wanted for my whole life.

It was good to be alone, but it was terrible to be lonely.

Then Frost had come to stay, and while I grumbled about them every day, I was utterly, embarrassingly relieved to have their company. We shared meals and went for walks, and it seemed they had no real plans of returning home. I let it become my new normal.

And then they'd let me know that a treelding had become available that fit their specifications. And they'd moved out.

Now, I watched Jenna plan her new home, practically buzzing with excitement. When she had energy, she went to the market and got some more baskets to aid in moving, and she got permission for a flitter to carry her things across the city. Sometimes her human friend, Elm, stopped by to help and the two discussed what furniture she needed and how she might lay out her new home. Sometimes, she asked me as well. I smiled and said things. I don't know what, but they seemed to meet with her approval. I could feel myself fading into her past with each passing day. By the end of the week, she'd be gone and our time as housemates would be history.

When moving day arrived, I dutifully helped carry her baskets to the flitter. I was a little surprised by how much stuff she had accumulated in the handful of months she'd spent on Viridus. I hadn't really noticed the way her stuff had crept out of her room and into the rest of the house until it was all packed away. Now, somehow, my house looked empty and almost sterile without it. Without her cushions and blankets. Without the beads she'd been stringing into bracelets, or the data crystals she'd left around the house, or the strange human nick-nacks our friends had bestowed on her.

I rode with her in the flitter, the driver a chatty pigeon-shape who ahhed and cooed with Jenna in excitement for her big day. I didn't like her and instead kept to the back of the flitter under the pretence of keeping all the baskets securely strapped down. The flitter swooped through the trees with nimble speed, the wind ruffling my fur and dragging at my flame.

'Here. This is it!' Jenna bounced in her seat and pointed.

The flitter set down outside a ground-level treelding, made up of several trees planted as the walls and grown together at the top to create a roof. Though fairly recently gardened, it already had a beautiful spray of foliage above the roof, and the tree walls had already fused. A broad plot of freshly turned earth stretched out beside it.

Jenna got out and ran to the door, running her fingers across her name written out in simple runes. My flame juddered and it suddenly felt hard to swallow. There was something intensely emotional about the way she touched her name, about this sudden quiet moment between her and her new home. After a moment, I cleared my throat and came to join her. 'It's a good door, solid,' I said, knocking it lightly with my hoof. 'If you want it carved, there are some really talented folk at the Woodcarvers' Union.'

Her fingers hovered there a moment and then she drew back. 'That would be really nice, actually,' she said. 'I suppose I'll have to think of what design I'd like.' She tried the door—it had a handle, like the one for Bloom's room, designed for someone with hands rather than a bolt that gave way to pressure. It opened easily at her touch, and I followed her inside.

It felt like the inside of an instrument—a heartbite or hollowmuse, one of the ones with a resonating body. The gardeners had done a wonderful job of smoothing the interior walls—they were still curved—as the trunks curved as a whole, but there was no way to differentiate each trunk individually.

There were, as far as I could tell, a few rooms: the kitchen, the sitting room, a human-adapted privvy and washroom, and two empty rooms, presumably for nestrooms. It wasn't that much different in layout from my house, actually. The nestrooms were a little larger, and the small kitchen was enclosed rather than open, but otherwise it felt quite familiar.

It was the floor I found the strangest; I was used to the warm hollow sound of hooves on wood, but here the floor appeared to be made of stone slabs and each hoofstep seemed to be swallowed up by it.

Jenna asked, 'Help me bring all the baskets inside?'

I nodded and went out to pick up what I could, balancing baskets on my back with starfire. At Jenna's direction, I put various baskets in particular rooms and it wasn't long before we'd fully unloaded.

'Do you want help unpacking?' I asked her, but she shook her head. She opened one basket and took out a bunch of cushions, throwing them down on the sitting room floor and then sinking onto one pile. After a moment, I settled on the pile beside her, carefully tucking my legs under me. My ears kept twitching back and forth; I tried to still them. I didn't want to project anxiety at her, no matter how uncertain I was.

She had her head in her hands. Her hair had come partially loose from its plait during the flight and hung around her face.

I touched my nose to her shoulder. 'Jenna?'

She lifted her head; her face was splotchy-red and wet with tears.

Panic bubbled inside me. What had gone wrong? Was it Pem again? Had I said something careless? I didn't want her to move, true, but I didn't want her to feel unhappy about it! Before I could formulate an apology, Jenna said in a cracked voice, 'I can't believe I have a house.' She pressed her hands flat to the floor, as if sharing her energy with them. She shook her head. 'On Earth it's...it's difficult. To get a home. There are so many of us and even though there are lots of houses to go around, somehow most of us don't get one to ourselves. I've lived a lot of places I wish I hadn't, with people I'd like to forget. Not—not *terrible* places. Just...lonely. Lonely and crowded at the same time.'

I didn't like to think of her like that. In some glass-and-concrete house with no cushions and strangers penning her in. Worse, there were surely other Jennas out there. Kind, fun people lost in the sea of other humans, weighed down by their horrible culture of money. Was it just what happened when there were so many people living on one planet? How had it come to be like that, when Jenna said the poor far out-numbered the wealthy?

'Well, you don't have to live like that any more,' I said.

'I haven't for months,' she replied. Her smile was watery but warmed me all the same. 'It means so much to me that you took me in. You were never anything but kind.'

I sighed and released a miserable bleat, resting my chin on the cushions in front of me. 'That's all you,' I said. 'I can't take credit. I didn't want you to live with me.' I'd thought it would be better—easier—if she'd been put in the CU's temporary accommodation, and Frost had pretty much forced me to take her. The thought of that now—of Jenna in some small room in the CU with no friend or guide to show her around, was repugnant to me.

'But you took me in anyway,' she said.

'I did. I'd do it again in the space of a breath,' I said.

'Why are cosmorans so kind?' she said, flopping back on the cushions.

I considered what to say. That we weren't that kind. That we had a violent and terrifying past that we hardly remembered, darker than the humans' own. That we hurt each other all the time, and with our long lifespans, it could be hard to forgive. But what I said was, 'Maybe you bring out the best in us.'

'I'm really glad we're friends,' said Jenna. Her voice was thick. And when I looked at her, tears streamed down her cheeks and her nose was very red.

I scooted closer to her, so that my flank rested against hers. 'I'm glad we're friends too,' I said. 'I don't know what I'm going to do without you.'

She gave a watery laugh. 'You're not getting rid of me that easily,' she said. 'I'll still drag you out on adventures with me all the time. I'll make you cook dinner with me and listen to me read my human books.'

I sighed. 'You promise?'

'I promise.'

We stayed there a long time. Then Jenna sat up and wiped the tears from her face. 'Okay.' She took a shuddering breath. 'I need to unpack now but I hurt too much.'

I stood up, my forgetech leg needing a little shake to unlock, and shook out my mane as I stretched. 'Just tell me what goes where,' I said.

By the end of the day, we had nearly everything put away and it looked less like an empty shell and more like a home. Dishes were stacked in the kitchen. Cushions were heaped in the sitting room. We'd even managed to put up shelves in the nestroom so she could store her baskets and data crystals more easily. Throughout the day, other friends dropped by to help. Nila put up shelves. Elm brought a box of kitchen utensils and cooking ingredients for storage. Cloud came by with enough savoury pastries, preserves, and smoothies to feed twice as many people, which we all gratefully devoured.

Now Elm and Cloud joined us on the floor, finishing up our pastries and talking animatedly about Jenna's new home and house-moving in general.

'You know, it was nearly a year before I got planning permission for my home,' Elm said. They sat poker-straight even while the rest of us sprawled on our cushions, holding their pastry carefully. They took a long time to eat. They seemed to nibble at it slowly over time.

'A year?' Cloud lapped at her smoothie, then shook her head. 'That doesn't seem right. It would be a big imposition on your host.'

'Elm didn't have a host,' said Jenna.

Elm nodded. 'It's true. The TU took me in on temporary accommodation. I was one of the first humans in the city, you know, and nobody quite knew what to do with me.'

'When did you come to Lost Circle?' asked Cloud.

'Oh, about ten years ago. Eleven years, now I think about it.'

'Did you get a traditional treehome like Jenna?'

Elm shook their head. 'I waited for a treehome in one of the treeldings to open up. I live in Mudwallow Tree.'

I flicked my ears forward. 'Over by the little lake? It's nice over there.'

Elm smiled. 'I quite agree.'

'It doesn't seem right,' said Cloud. 'When I applied to move from Villeas, they had a treehome available for me within a few months.'

I glanced at Cloud in surprise. It was hard to look at her for too long. She'd flipped onto her back with her paws curled, baring her round belly. I was not made of stern enough stuff to weather that level of cute. 'You're from Villeas?' It was a forest town a few days away by canopy-glider. I'd just always assumed Cloud was a Lost Circle native; she seemed to know so much about it, and be so settled. Even after several decades here, I still sometimes felt like a newcomer.

Cloud stretched, her paws kneading the air. 'Yep. Moved here maybe forty years ago? I love living in a forest but Villeas was a bit sleepy for me. I'd never have been able to make a go of the Internet Café there.'

'Ever the business-person,' Jenna teased, and Cloud air-swatted a paw at her.

'Do you plan to join any of the unions?' asked Elm. 'You don't need to work, of course, I'm just curious.'

Jenna sat up and rubbed her hands along her legs in an almost nervous motion. 'Well...actually, that's what the dirt plot outside is about. I'd like to take up gardening again.'

Everyone took a moment to take this in. I wondered what to say.

Gardeners used starfire to shape the growth of plants. They were absolutely integral to cosmoran society.

And I had no idea how Jenna could be one of them.

'Not...not gardening like it's practised here,' she said. 'Though I'd definitely be interested in learning that. Gardening like it is back home. Growing plants and flowers with my own hands. Keeping them healthy and flourishing.'

'But...don't flowers grow themselves?' asked Cloud.

'They do, but some flowers need more help to grow, or grow in certain ways. And gardening is also an art; about creating something beautiful using growing plants. It also means people can grow certain plants in safety, ready to be sent to new homes. We call those plant nurseries, on Earth.'

'Plant nursery.' I tried out the words. They felt strange in my mouth, the word 'nursery' having connotations I couldn't completely grasp.

Cloud suddenly rolled over, her eyes wide and shining. 'Jenna, I would *love* to see a human garden! Do you want help?'

Jenna laughed at Cloud's sudden intensity. 'I'll definitely need help getting set up. I used to teach gardening at home; I could teach you as well.'

'Wow, yes!'

The conversation carried on from there. The day wore into evening and gradually everyone said their goodbyes, until it was just me and Jenna left.

'Thanks for your help today,' Jenna said. 'It meant a lot to me.'

'Oh. Sure.' I stood up and stretched. 'I'll head home now, I guess.' The words felt strange to say to Jenna. 'Home' no longer meant the same thing to us.

I headed for the door, but Jenna moved to intercept me. 'Wait. I...' she hesitated. 'I don't know how to say this. But...you know about me and my family. And I did have friends on Earth but somehow never very close. And then being aromantic and asexual as well, I didn't have much hope of finding my own family. But you've...you've really been that for me. And I know it's a big deal, me moving out and all. But I hope we can be like you and Frost, you know? Still family.'

Tears stung my eyes and I nodded. 'Can I hug you?' I asked her.

Her eyes widened and she nodded. I put my chin on her shoulder and she wrapped her arms around my neck, tangling her hands in my mane. 'We will always be family,' I promised, then pulled away.

She wiped a tear from her eye and nodded, giving me a watery smile. And then I headed out into the cool evening air toward home.

Chapter Twenty

I sat on the lake shore, watching Journey paddle toward Bloom, lit by Bloom's starfire as she kept her sister buoyant. 'You're doing great!' said Bloom. 'Longer strokes! Splashier! SPLASHIER!'

'Funny, I don't remember splashiness being an important component of swimming lessons,' I said to Lur. My brother lounged beside me, rolled onto his back with his legs out at all angles. I'd always envied his ability to look comfortable. Sometimes, I wondered if I was fully capable of relaxing. There was always some tension in me, I guess.

'According to Bloom, splashing is the entire *point* of swimming,' said Lur.

'I'm surprised to see you both here,' I said. 'I thought you'd probably visit separately, since Bloom moved away.'

Lur sighed. 'Yeah. Well, I've been seeing a lot of her. I'm not sure it's working out as well as she planned.'

'What's wrong?'

Lur shrugged. 'Not my place to say. You'll have to ask her.'

I nodded; that seemed fair. 'What about you?'

Lur quirked his head at me. 'What about me?'

'How've you been?'

Lur shrugged, which he turned into a stretch, paws kneading the air. 'It was a bit lonely at first, when Bloom left. But I think both of us have been looking forward to a bit of space.'

I frowned, my ears going back. That definitely hadn't been Lur's stance before. Bloom and Lur were twins; closer even than me and Frost.

He must've changed his mind.

Lur snorted. 'Not surprised you can't imagine it. Didn't you have a breakdown when Frost moved out?'

'I did *not* have a breakdown,' I said, which was sort of true because 'breakdown' barely covered how poorly I'd taken it.

'Sure, sure.' Lur grinned at me, baring pointed teeth. 'Honestly, I think we both want to work out who we are when we're apart, you know? Bloom wants to start a family, like Frost. I want to start a career, like you. We still love each other and we'll always be best friends. We just want to be other things as well.'

'That's...a very mature approach,' I said. I shouldn't have been surprised. Lur had always been shockingly wise for someone so much younger than me.

'Yeah well...it's not without its challenges.' He shifted so he could watch Bloom as she picked up our little sister, who bleated her laughter.

'What's this about challenges?' Frost settled beside us.

'Frost!' Lur flipped over and gave them a tongue-lolling grin.

'Sorry we're late,' said Vya. A winged serpent curled around his neck like a scarf, tucked under his sun-hat. It lifted one of its feathery wings from its face and blinked at us lazily in what I thought might be a greeting. 'Is Jenna coming?'

'I think she got held up at the Gardeners' Union,' I said. 'Her initiation has been...complicated. And long. Apparently, she's the first human ever to join.'

'Oh. Should we be worried?'

I shook my head. 'She can handle it. She's been handling it. And Elm is there today for emotional support.'

Beside me, Storm snorted. 'Jenna *and* Elm are dealing with it? In that case, if anything we should be worried about the GU.'

'Exactly.'

'Who's Elm?' asked Lur.

'A frighteningly competent human traveller,' said Vya. 'Their sunderthrice companion is one of my clients and sometimes, I think they only come in for access to my supplies. No expertise required.'

I baaed appreciatively. Sunderthrices were six-legged creatures whose fur formed hardened scales and had claws nearly as long as Vya's. They were about the size of Journey and had ten times the energy and one tenth the understanding. I didn't know anyone else brave enough to keep one as a companion animal.

There was a shriek from the water as Journey tried to climb atop Bloom. 'Well, that's our cue,' said Frost. 'Anyone else jumping in?'

'I'm good here,' I said, and Lur and Vya agreed. Frost stood up, tossed their hats to the ground, and sprang into the lake, creating a massive splash and pulse of water from the sheer bulk of water they displaced.

I snorted as stray droplets hit my face. Vya's winged serpent shrilled in displeasure. Vya cooed to it and stroked it gently along its feathered body. I watched as Frost resurfaced, lifting a shrieking Bloom and Journey on their back.

'Sometimes I think how weird it is, how much things have changed,' said Lur. He watched our siblings splash and play with a thoughtful expression.

'I thought you wanted things to change,' I said. 'Time to start your career, etc.'

'I do, I do. It's just also strange, you know? I remember when it was just the six of us, and Bloom and I were the babies of the family. Now we're responsible elder siblings, and Frost has a mate, and I hear you have friends...' He shook his head, his ears flapping.

'I hope they haven't changed in a bad way?' Vya asked with a nervous laugh.

'No, no! It's all good. It's just, when we're all together like this...it's, I don't know. A bit surreal, sometimes.'

I nodded. 'It's like that, with Jenna having moved out. I think...I think it's a positive thing. She's so happy to have her own home, and it's nice to have my own house back. But it also doesn't feel quite right yet. Like sometimes, after we've spent the day together, it feels weird that we aren't both going back to Antlervine Tree. And sometimes the house feels quiet, even though she never made much noise.'

'No breakdowns?' Lur asked.

'No breakdowns,' I replied firmly. Though sometimes I wondered if I might have, if not for how happy Jenna was to have her own home at last. Easier to feel happy for her knowing she was achieving a long-held dream.

Vya shifted where he sat, so that his large, furry feet faced the lake. He moved the winged serpent to his arms, cradling and stroking it. 'For me, change has only been good. Sometimes, I wonder how I lived without Frost. Even this little girl has become impossible to imagine life without.'

Impossible to imagine life without. As much as I'd hated first Frost and then Jenna moving out, I didn't think I'd ever felt that way. Our relationships had changed, and that was hard for me, but I did still love my solitude. I wondered if there would ever be someone who made me feel that way. The thought was frightening, and yet I found myself longing for it at the same time.

The afternoon wore on. I wondered occasionally where Jenna was, a needle of anxiety pricking my core, but I reminded myself that she could handle it. That she was far more capable than I was. The others left the lake and we headed to the Purple Garden for the market and to grab something to eat.

The market wasn't unusually busy, but I noticed Journey's ears go back and her head lower as we approached. She seemed reluctant to go in, her eyes very wide, her nostrils flaring. 'Hey,' I said, coming to stand beside her. 'It's okay. I don't like crowds either, but there's nothing to fear here.'

I'd been overwhelmed my first time visiting a city, too. Sometimes I still felt overwhelmed, though thankfully it was becoming less common. In Athelean, I could list everyone who lived in the village if I needed to. In Lost Circle, that was impossible. There were thousands of us. I let Journey hide under me and walk between my legs. She was still so small, she didn't even need to lower her head, though her ears did tickle my ribs.

'See?' I said. 'We can get used to this.'

I got her a sweet seedpop to eat. To my delight, she picked it up with starfire—a little wobbly and I wasn't entirely convinced she wouldn't drop it, but that was still huge. That seemed to cheer her up quite a bit, and when the sugar hit, she even ventured out from my legs occasionally.

Lur walked beside me and kept making faces at her beneath me. Bloom and Frost kept finding things to get for her—hats, coats, leg warmers...the list went on. Their packs were bulging by the time we walked all the way through the market, and Journey had been cooed at by just about every vendor we passed. She was a particularly endearing kit—just a leggy little faun peering nervously out from under me, her tiny wings still fluffy and folded on her back.

'You're doing great,' I told her. When I'd been a kit, it had taken me years to risk venturing away from the protection of my mothers, but it seemed Journey had a more adventurous spirit. I hoped that meant my mothers would have more patience with her than they had with me, too.

We made it out into the Purple Garden and even found a low floating rock to have our lunch on—though it required a bit of a skip from a terrestrial rock to get to. These were dotted around the place; lost fragments, perhaps, of the islands floating far above us. After watching Bloom leap across the gap, Journey pawed at the ground and looked determined to do the same, but I picked her up and carried her across. 'It's good to try new things,' I said. 'But you're still just a kit.'

She squirmed in my starfire but forgot her frustration the moment I put her down. She followed Bloom around the little rock, investigating the edge of the rock together. Below, the tall flowers rustled in the breeze, petals and pollen puffs passing in a flurry.

I stared off toward the market, where many starfires still moved and twinkled, and glanced at my cosmorb, still inert.

Vya came and settled beside me. 'Lakeweed wrap?' he asked, offering me a little food parcel of spices and paste wrapped in crispy dark leaves. I had my cosmorb orbit me and accepted the wrap. On a tentative nibble, it was absolutely delicious, with an unexpected bite of spice. 'Bloom is going to hate this,' I said.

'Already thought of that,' said Vya. 'There's some porridge and fruit I think she might enjoy. The wraps are from Flicker's stall, by the way. Ey really has a gift for flavour.'

I hadn't tried anything from eir stall in a while, but I remembered the little pony-shape and eir colourful aprons. I'd have to stop by and thank em next time I went to the market.

My cosmorb drifted past my eyes, no warmth or glimmer of a message. My eyes tracked it anyway, my ears flicking back.

'Not heard from Jenna yet?' Vya asked.

'No.' I took another bite of the lakeweed wrap, which had just the right mix of crunch and squish.

'She knows we're here?'

I nodded. I'd sent her an update each time we moved on but I still hadn't heard from her.

She was with Elm. She was fine.

Right?

We carried on with our trip. I tried not to worry. I knew Jenna's health was still up and down, and that it was not always easy for her to respond to messages. Perhaps she'd had another message from her human family and was processing that. Perhaps her session at the Gardeners' Union had run particularly long, or triggered the awful Pem again.

I knew it had already been complicated. All sorts of new equipment and assessment criteria had been created to cope with the fact that Jenna had no starfire and gardening as it was practised on Geminus used starfire to manipulate the growth of plants. And then of course they'd also needed to create all new plans for her as a *teacher* because she had plenty to teach them as well.

We finished our picnic and took Journey to frolic around the fields. I showed her how to jump from stone to stone—very low, shallow, terrestrial stones. She was surprisingly agile for so small a thing. I'd thought that might be the case, as a fellow hoofed cosmoran. It turned out she didn't have the same kind of innate grip as me, though, so I had to catch her a few times when she slipped. I noticed she instinctively flapped her wings when she jumped or fell—perhaps she would actually be able to fly when she was older, the only one of our siblings with the ability. Thankfully Nova would be able to show her how to deal with all of that.

As the sun set, Bloom picked up an increasingly sleepy Journey and we said our farewells. Lur promised they would all visit again soon. However soon they might be thinking, I hoped it would be even sooner.

As we watched their canopy-glider take-off, I checked my cosmorb again, just in case I hadn't noticed the message come in. Still nothing. I put it in my pack and tried to clamp down on my increasing worry.

As I walked through the door at home, I felt a flash of heat through the fabric of my pack. I fumbled it out, tossing the pack on the floor.

I activated it and a message flared up on the screen. *This is Elm. Jenna has had bad news. I'm staying with her overnight. Meet us here in the morning.* And then another flash of heat and the message was appended: *She says she's sorry she didn't make it to your family visit.*

I stared at the cosmorb. Elm and I hadn't harmonised our cosmorbs—there was no way for them to have messaged me but through Jenna's cosmorb.

I waited for a follow-up, for some clarifying details, anything. But no other messages were forth-coming. Stars! I couldn't cope with this. Though I sometimes turned down the emotional settings on my messages, I found myself bitterly wishing humans could send emotions with their messages.

Bad news. Jenna had received bad news. About what? Had the GU rejected her? I knew she'd been terribly worried about that as the initiation process dragged on and on. The work she'd already done with them had delighted and challenged her by turn. Her greenhouse designs were going to be built soon. She'd be devastated if anything threatened that.

Unless it wasn't related to the GU. Unless, perhaps, she'd received another message from Earth.

Stars, I wanted to message back demanding to know more. I couldn't cope with knowing so little. But it sounded like Jenna needed to rest. If she'd decided it could wait until morning, then I needed to respect that.

So I restrained myself. I went to my nest and curled up with my cosmorb against my chest. I couldn't keep my eyes closed and spent most of the night staring out the window into the moonslit forest.

I must have eventually fallen asleep because I startled awake at the feeling of sunlight on my face. I got up. My body felt heavy with exhaustion, but I wasn't going to let that stop me. It was only a little past dawn and Jenna was normally an early riser. I threw a pack together and hurried out, catching a canopy-tram even though Jenna's treehome wasn't a long walk. The tram stopped only a few minutes away so I hurried out onto the forest floor and over to Jenna's.

Her treehome was looking even more homely now. I could see her garden plot had been furrowed and seeded in a human manner of neat rows. A basket of wildflowers hung beside her door, overflowing with creepers and joyous petals.

Jenna answered my knock. Her hair, normally so neat, was a tangled mess. Her eyes had dark smudges beneath them, which I knew was a sign she hadn't slept. But when she saw me, her entire body sagged in relief and her eyes glimmered. 'Avari...' I could see her hands open and close with the desire to hug me. I leaned in and pressed my chin to the back of her shoulder, letting her throw her arms around my neck. I could tell she needed it.

After a moment, I pulled away and she ushered me inside.

'Elm?' I asked.

'Asleep.' Jenna sat down at her oddly raised table, and I sat across from her. I was glad she'd sized her seats for cosmorans, as there was a lot less flexibility on seats like this than there was on a good pile of cushions. 'They spent all night cleaning the house. I don't think they knew what else to do.'

That didn't sound good. 'Do you want to talk about what's happened?'

Jenna rested her elbow on the table and pressed her hand against her forehead. 'No. But I need to anyway.' She stared at the table a moment, her lip pressed into a thin line, her eyes still gleaming with unshed tears.

She got out her cosmorb and sent it drifting over to me. A small data crystal orbited it. I connected to it and found the message still glowing on the screen.

Jenna Hughes has been found to have unlawfully travelled to Geminus. Her presence is required at the Geminus Galactic Council on or before Mirrorsday 14 The Lovers for a moot. Failure to attend will lead to instant return to Earth.

My fur stood on end. I repressed a shiver. 'That's in two weeks,' I said. The words sounded hollow even though there was a maelstrom inside me.

Return to Earth.

Could they do that?

'Elm says there's been a mistake. That the entire visa program has been a shitshow and they're trying to shift the blame for their mistakes onto me.' The odd human phrase barely fizzled in my starfire, the meaning clear enough.

'Will the Travellers' Union back you? And the Gardeners'?' I asked. 'You're a member.' And the right to travel was a sacred right of all cosmorans.

Jenna wasn't a cosmoran.

But Jenna was *family*.

'Elm says if the TU doesn't back me, it'll create a whole bunch of problems for them.' Jenna gave me a mirthless smile. 'In fact, they said they'll make sure of it. I asked if I need a lawyer, but they said there aren't lawyers here, there are guardians.'

Guardians. Guardians! I stood up. 'No, that's right. Frost is a guardian. So is Nila.'

Jenna nodded. 'You contact Frost,' she said. 'I'll message Nila.'

I sent the messages quickly, letting my panic and urgency bleed into the signal.

'Do you have a plan?' I asked Jenna.

Jenna released a long, ragged breath. 'I...do. I'm—I'm a human gardener. I have zero experience with cosmoran bureaucracy. But shit like this...ugh.' She rubbed her face. 'Shit like this happened to me all the time on Earth. I'll talk to a guardian first, and then I'll see about the rest. I'm not just going to let this happen. I don't want to go back. I can't—I can't go back, Avari—' She started to cry.

I hesitated, then got up to settle beside her, so she could lean against my flank. I knew physical comfort was important to her but it also felt so terribly inadequate in the face of everything.

'You're not going back,' I said. 'You're settled. You're a member of a union—maybe two, if the Gardeners' Union will vouch for you as well.'

'I completed my initiation yesterday,' Jenna said quietly.

'You—you did? Jenna, that's great! Congratulations!'

She rubbed her eyes and gave me a watery smile. 'We were going to start building the greenhouse tomorrow. I suppose that won't happen now.'

'It might,' I said. 'Don't go cancelling everything just yet.'

She was quiet for a long moment. The weight, heat, and pressure of her body against mine was mildly upsetting but I tried to keep that in. It was easier because she was a friend; a friend was worth sacrificing for.

'Where is the Geminus Galactic Council?' she asked. 'I haven't looked it up yet.'

Ah. I braced myself, because I knew she wasn't going to like this. 'It's on Profundus,' I said.

'Profundus? Like the *planet?*'

'It's not as far away as you think,' I said. 'It's our twin planet. I know you've seen the star system maps. Travel between Viridus and Profundus has been as casual as travelling anywhere on the same planet for centuries.'

'You've...you've had space travel for centuries?'

'We've had portal travel for centuries,' I said. 'Space travel is a bit more recent.' Which was probably a big part of why the Otherworldly Travel Commission had decided to use portal technology to handle human travellers. Unfortunately, they'd made a mess of it. Perhaps portalling across galaxies wasn't as straightforward as portalling between binary planets.

A groan drew my attention to the doorway to Jenna's spare room. Elm shuffled in. All my fur stood on end and I couldn't help but snort in surprise. Their hair was rumpled, their beard tangled. They wore loose trousers and a poorly-fitted stained top.

'G'morning,' mumbled Elm. They shuffled into the kitchen, swayed a moment, and then laid their head on the counter.

Jenna got up. 'Elm's not a morning person,' she confided. 'Elm! Let me make you some coffee.'

Coffee? The word was fuzzy. I couldn't latch onto the meaning.

Elm mumbled something unintelligible while Jenna poured some powder into a mug and boiled some water. It smelled horribly bitter and earthy. I wrinkled my nose. 'What is that?'

'Humans drink a stimulant called coffee,' she said. 'It's meant to be tasty and many humans require large amounts of it to function, so early travellers to Viridus prioritised finding a substitute.' She shook a jar of the strange black powder and set it down. 'On Earth, it's made of ground up beans. Here, it's the roots of three different flowers. One for the stimulant aspect, and two for the flavour.'

I watched her make it with interest. It seemed to involve straining the water through a cloth full of the powder, creating a stinky, muddy drink. She made two mugs, one for herself and one for Elm.

'Would you...?' she hesitated, reaching for a third mug.

'No! No thanks.' I tried to moderate my tone but couldn't stop my nose from wrinkling again. Watching her take a sip of it made me feel weirdly unwell, so I left them in peace to drink it and tried to occupy myself by poking at my cosmorb.

When they finished, the shadows under Jenna's eyes were a little less pronounced and Elm managed to smooth their hair and beard into some kind of order. I briefly felt hopeful before I noticed Jenna's lip quivering. No amount of stimulant was going to make this okay.

But Jenna squared her shoulders. 'I was looking up legal proceedings this morning,' she said. 'And it relies a lot on character references, right?'

I blinked, trying to make sense of this. My mind still felt sluggish, still processing this unthinkable news. 'Uh,' I said.

'It does,' said Elm. 'I've had to provide them before for members of the Lost Circle TU. Avari, as the cosmoran host and first cosmoran to interact with Jenna, your testimony will carry a lot of weight with the Galactic Council. So preparing a statement to speak on Jenna's behalf is essential.'

My ears perked forward. 'I can do that,' I said.

Jenna tapped her lips. 'Are you willing to help me collect references? You'll need to record people, I think.'

'I...yeah!' I had never been more determined to interact with people. 'Of course.'

'And Elm, you could collect references from the TU members?'

'Certainly.'

Jenna took a long, shuddering breath. 'Okay,' she said. 'Okay, that's a start. But I need representation. Avari, Frost and Nila are both guardians.'

Elm straightened, suddenly looking several times more awake. 'And they'd be willing to defend you?'

'I'm certain of it,' I said. 'Do you want me to see them about it, or...?'

Jenna was quiet for a moment. 'I...want to see them myself as soon as possible,' she said. 'But...just this news is exhausting me, and I already overdid it yesterday. I need to divide up the work. If you can speak to them initially and ask them to visit me if they can help, please do that. Then with references...we'll divide and conquer.'

I found the phrase a little odd, but Elm nodded.

Jenna touched Elm's elbow. I was surprised at the casual intimacy of it, but Elm only looked around with soft eyes. Perhaps Elm had a more compatible tolerance for physical contact than I did.

A little more discussion about plans went on, Jenna dictating lists to Elm of what each of us needed to do. At times, she almost seemed to break again into tears, but I watched her blink them back and push on each time. In those moments, fleeting though they were, she looked terrifyingly bleak.

My last look at the room was of Elm plaiting their beard while calling someone and listening intently, and of Jenna giving me a tight smile.

I smiled back, trying to warm my starfire to an encouraging colour, trying to force my ears forward. Then the door closed and I slumped. I stood there for a long time, completely still, the breeze a chill ripple through my fur, mist stirring about my legs. I waited for the tight squeeze in my chest to pass. Then, when it didn't, I forced myself to walk away.

Chapter Twenty-One

'No. No, this won't do at all.' Frost paced the room, their tail lashing behind them. I sat on a large cushion with Glimmer, their winged serpent, happily twining herself around my horns. Every now and then, one of her four wings would flop into my eyes, but I didn't mind. Somehow, physical contact with animals had never over-stimulated me the way it did with other cosmorans and humans. If anything, it was soothing.

'Jenna is working on it,' I said. 'She and Elm think they can get Jenna support from both the Travellers and the Gardeners. They've asked me to collect statements on Jenna's character as well, but they thought it would be best if Jenna was defended by a guardian.'

Storm said, 'She shouldn't be on trial at all! She's a protected traveller, a citizen of the world.'

Illusion fluffed up her feathers indignantly. 'However she got here, exile is only for criminals. We don't send people away for making mistakes, only for committing harm. The fact that this is going to the Geminus Galactic Council...'

Frost continued to pace, Illusion and Storm muttering to each other.

Night looked at me. 'Without a guardian, she has no chance at all,' he said bleakly. 'They aren't being fair. I don't know why. We're defending someone else in an on-going battle right now and we can't abandon them, but Jenna's issue is definitely pressing.'

Anxiety pinched. 'So you can't defend her?'

'We can, but our attention will be divided. You think Nila will help?'

I thought of Nila, the laughing hyena who, like so many people we met, was completely charmed by Jenna—and not just because she was a human. 'I think he will, yeah.'

Storm breathed out heavily through their nose, and Illusion looked distant, no doubt working out exactly how much time they had. Night said,

'Nila's help will make all the difference. I expect he's busy too, but together we have a chance. You contact Nila and collect the statements, as Elm suggested. We'll visit Jenna now and get started as her guardian.'

They gestured with a claw toward the door, but I couldn't bring myself to move. Frost couldn't devote their whole time to Jenna's defence. They'd said things like 'we have a chance' and 'our attention will be divided' and 'Jenna's issue is pressing'. As calmly as they'd said it, that was terrifying.

Illusion's feathers raised as she looked at me. 'Avari? Hey. Hey.' Frost walked over and Illusion put her face in front of mine, so that I had nowhere to look but into her eyes. 'We've got this. Jenna's not going anywhere.'

I knew she was just trying to calm me down, but it still helped to hear it said aloud.

'Can you repeat that for me?' she asked.

'Jenna's not going anywhere,' I said, and it felt good to say it. I turned for the door.

'You can stay a bit, if you need to,' said Storm.

'No, no I'm all right. I'm going to go find Nila.'

The moment I stepped outside, I messaged Jenna. *Frost is going to help. They'll visit you soon to get started. I'm going to try to find Nila as well.*

It was an agonising few minutes before Jenna replied, *That's good news. Things are always easier if there's someone knowledgeable backing you. Can I call you?*

I hated voice calls, but this was important. *Go ahead.*

My cosmorb pulsed with heat and I accepted Jenna's call, setting my cosmorb to hover in front of me. There was no-one around, but I still felt sort of exposed.

'Hi,' said Jenna. Her voice was a bit distorted but still reassuringly familiar. 'I just wanted to say thank you, properly. I...was really worried there wouldn't be a guardian I trust available.'

That was news to me. 'You seemed so in-control before,' I said, though as I said it I thought of those bleak moments she quickly pushed through.

'There's nothing to do but keep moving,' Jenna said firmly. 'That doesn't make it easy. I think...I think maybe I'd be tempted to just cry and shake for a few days, honestly. This...this has been such a shock. But after all the shit with my immigration and now this...I think Elm is right. I think they're trying to shift the blame for the faulty immigration system onto humans.'

Everything she had been through on her way here was unfair. The portal she'd applied for had appeared far earlier than expected and without notice and she'd had no option but to rush through. She'd ended up far from help and forced to rely on me, instead of someone qualified, and frankly I hadn't made it easy for her. She'd had to find all her own supplies, had to struggle with the Gardeners' Union just to be initiated, and all that while also battling her own illness.

'I can't believe after everything that's happened, they're trying to pin this on you,' I said.

'Weirdly, I can,' Jenna said grimly. 'I don't like it but...it's not the first time.'

That shocked me, and I didn't know what to say.

'I don't think this is just about me,' said Jenna. 'I think this is about humans. There are so few of us here, and everything we do is the "first" for so many cosmorans. Very little is in-place to support us. If we start getting accused of crimes for things we didn't do...' she trailed off. 'It's not just about me. So I'm doing my best to hold it together.'

'If you need a break–'

'You know I'll take one,' said Jenna. 'I don't have a choice. But I have to do as much as I can. Can you add Keera and Mers to your list?' she added. 'I'll talk with Frost about it but...I think it might help to have some human statements about their experiences travelling here, too.'

'I can do that.'

'Thanks.'

About an hour later, I found myself in the Internet Café. Nila wasn't there;. none of our usual crowd seemed to be in, but Cloud caught my eye from the kitchen and came bounding out to see me, leaping the counter like she was skipping a puddle.

'Avari!' She bounced over, flame bright with excitement. 'Can I get you anything?' She frowned. 'Wait...are you okay?'

I considered lying but it made me wrinkle my muzzle. 'Not really,' I said.

Her tails lashed the air behind her, her concern plain. 'Do you want to talk about it?'

Did I? Could I? For a brief moment, I felt panic spike at the thought of revealing something so personal about Jenna. Then I realised that I was supposed to collect character statements on her behalf anyway, so surely I would be expected to explain the situation. 'It's Jenna,' I said. 'The Geminus Galactic Council thinks she came here illegally. They want to send her back to Earth.'

Cloud's ears went back. 'What? How would that even be possible? She came via portal! And why would that mean she'd have to go back to Earth?'

I shrugged and stomped a hoof to let out some of the restless energy that had been building up inside of me. 'Frost has agreed to be her guardian. I'm meeting Nila to ask for him to do the same. And I'm supposed to collect character statements from people who know her.'

Cloud's eyes stared past me a moment, her expression uncharacteristically solemn. 'Character statements. Okay, I can help with that.' She whirled and started for the kitchen, calling over her shoulder, 'I'm getting you cake!'

The cake was decorated with sprigs of sweetflower and minty blue leaves. The whole thing was creamy and wonderful, and I got a spark of energy from consuming just a few bites. Which probably meant it was dreadfully unhealthy, but sometimes that was called for.

Before long, Cloud emerged from the kitchen and came to join me at the table, resting her chin on her paws. 'Okay. I've spoken to all the staff here and they're all writing up statements for Jenna now, and we can record them after. Honestly, it sounds like Pell is going to write a novella's worth of reasons why Jenna is wonderful. I can help contact our friends and all staff are encouraged to ask any regulars for a reference on Jenna. Who else are you planning to ask?'

'Oh. Uh...Ever, some of my neighbours at Antlervine Tree, and I was going to go around the market as I know Jenna's friendly with a lot of the folk there.'

Cloud nodded. 'Sounds like a plan. Who would you prefer to take? I'm taking the day off to help.'

I blinked. 'You are?'

'Of course. Jenna's my friend. We can't expect her to face this alone.'

I stared at her a moment. For someone so round and fluffy, she remained one of the toughest, most practical people I had ever known. I wanted to say, 'Thank you'. I wanted to say, 'This is so helpful.' What I said was, 'You're amazing,' in a tone so warm I wondered that it had come from me.

Cloud's ears twitched. Her flame pinked slightly. 'Well. Obviously,' she said, but she seemed more flustered than blustery.

My flame pinked as well and I looked away. We divided up the work. Cloud would handle the market and Ever, and I would seek out Nila and the rest of our friends. It was a relief to have her help. While I knew none of our friends would hesitate to stand up for Jenna, I worried that I would struggle to convince her acquaintances. I doubted Cloud would face that problem; she was charming and an absolute whirlwind besides. She could sweep anyone up with her.

My task was easier than I'd worried. Over the next few days, I met up with friends and acquaintances and got their agreement to write statements in support of Jenna. Mers even planned to get some of the kits they cared for to write something—apparently, Jenna had been an educational guest to teach the kits about humans.

Nila was harder to get hold of, but we arranged to meet up in the Internet Café. I walked in to find Nila already sitting at a table and sipping from a smoothie with one of Cloud's strange wooden stirrers inside it. He stood up as I approached, his expression worried. 'Is everything okay?' he asked. 'You said it was urgent. I'm sorry I couldn't see you sooner—I was in the midst of a guardianship issue that got messy.' His ears hovered half-back, his flame flickering nervously.

'I'm fine,' I said. 'It's about Jenna.' As I'd gotten a lot of practice since I'd received the news myself, it didn't take long to spill the whole story. Nila asked me more questions than anyone else had—particularly around the circumstances of Jenna's arrival.

'This whole thing stinks of someone trying to cover up for their mistakes,' Nila said. 'Especially considering a portal issue affected Elm as well, however long ago. Jenna cannot be held responsible for something out of her control. Nor can she rightfully be uprooted from her life, no matter the circumstances that brought her to it.'

'So you think she has a chance?'

Nila considered a moment, his flame dimming thoughtfully, then nodded. 'More than a case. Guardianship is about justice. I don't think anyone could say that forcing Jenna back to Earth is just. There's no difference between cosmorans and humans under Geminus law. She has just as much right to be here as we do, even if she had come here illegally. The difficulty will be in convincing the moot of that. Make sure you send any character statements to me and Frost, and we'll see what we can do.'

'I can do that. What else should I do?' I shuffled my hooves, anxious to get started on the next phase of Jenna's defence.

'Be a good friend to Jenna,' Nila said. 'Frost and I will be doing a lot of that as well, as her guardians, but the more support the better.'

I hesitated. 'Is there nothing else?' I wanted to run around the city collecting statements, or petitioning the unions, or contacting people on Earth—anything. Something practical. Something tangible.

'That's the most important thing,' said Nila. His flame turned a worried dark blue and his ears drooped. 'We'll be on our way to Profundus soon enough.'

I made my way back to Jenna's. I noticed that the garden patch out front had now had little seedlings poking tentative tendrils out of the dirt. She must have been out to garden, in spite of everything. The thought made my ears perk hopefully.

When I knocked, it was Elm who answered the door. They looked tired, though I noticed they had gold and blue beads threaded into their goatee. Elm put a finger up to their lips, which I knew from Jenna was a human request for quiet. 'Jenna fell asleep maybe half an hour ago,' they murmured.

I nodded and walked in. I was not particularly built for quiet, and I cringed at the loud clomp of my hooves against the floor. I flopped onto the nearest cushion just to stop my hoofsteps. Elm sat beside me, perched straight-backed as ever, and picked up a cup of coffee that still steamed.

'How is she?' I asked. 'She did some gardening?'

Elm nodded. 'She directed me. No energy to move after all the calls and visits she's made. I think she's coping well. We're focusing on distractions right now but her energy is really low—as you might expect from someone going through something this stressful, let alone someone with ME.'

I put one ear forward. 'You two seem...close.' I really wasn't sure how to ask this in a way that wasn't awkward. Maybe there wasn't a way. But before I could even form the question, Elm smiled tiredly at me.

'I thank fate every day that Jenna was brought into my life. I don't want you to get the wrong idea—it's not a romantic thing. Neither of us are wired that way. Aromantic, both of us. But just as important.' Their expression grew distant, their mouth pressing into a hard line, and they added quietly, 'I would tear the world apart for her.'

It was a feeling I shared, but something about Elm's intensity rang of a different note in their relationship than mine and Jenna's. We lapsed into silence for a while, my tail tapping a quiet rhythm against the cushions. Then I asked, 'What will you do? If they send her back to Earth?'

Elm's expression hardened. 'That's not going to happen.' They drained their cup and set it aside with a quiet clink.

'But if it did?' I asked.

'If it did,' Elm said. 'I'd go with her, if she let me.'

We studied each other across the table.

Elm raised their eyebrows. 'So, do I pass?'

I quirked my ears. 'Pass what?'

'Jenna says you're her protective older sibling. Do I have your approval to be Jenna's platonic partner?'

The thought of Jenna describing me that way warmed my chest. 'Jenna doesn't need my approval for anything,' I said.

'She doesn't,' Elm agreed. 'But I'd like it, anyway.'

I snorted. 'She chose you. You pass. But yeah, I like you. You get things done and you have a cool beard.'

Elm actually laughed in surprise, before catching themself and glancing nervously at Jenna's nestroom. They stroked their goatee thoughtfully. 'You like the beads?'

'And the plaits,' I said. 'I never got the hang of plaiting.'

Elm considered. 'Hmm. Might be harder to do with starfire. I could plait yours, if you like?'

For a moment temptation and repulsion warred within me. A beautiful beard versus the horror of being touched. Eventually, I said, 'Maybe another time.'

Elm nodded. 'I'd like that.'

I got out my cosmorb and we did our own things. I tried to read one of my adventure data crystals but my focus kept slipping. I realised I'd been reading without taking anything in and had to backtrack. Eventually, I picked up a data crystal from Jenna's basket that she'd read to me before. Re-reading was easier because it was okay to miss things. Plus, reading it reminded me of Jenna's gentle voice shaping the words and soon I was completely absorbed. I was vaguely aware of Elm cleaning things around me, and occasionally stepping out to take calls but the details passed me by.

'Avari?'

I surfaced from the data crystal to see Jenna standing in the doorway of her nestroom. Her hair was dishevelled and the room was cast in sunset pinks and yellows. She clutched a small cushion with a seedling embroidered on it to her chest.

'Hey.' I stood up hastily. 'I didn't want to disturb you.'

'You didn't. Elm?'

I glanced around, ears swivelling, and picked up their voice outside. 'They're taking a call.'

Jenna nodded, the tension in her jaw loosening somewhat to hear that they were nearby.

'They're a good friend,' I offered.

Jenna smiled shakily. 'The best.'

I stomped a hoof and put my ears back in mock offence. 'And what does that make me?'

'The world's grumpiest big sibling,' she said. 'My favourite old goat.'

I scowled even as my core warmed. 'It's gonna be okay, you know?'

Jenna nodded and took a shuddering breath. 'Yeah. Yeah. It's gonna be okay.'

Elm made us dinner—a creamy sauce over mushroom pasta—and I stayed up late with Jenna. When she finally fell asleep, I left her in Elm's hands, trusting they would look after her.

THE OLD GOAT AND THE ALIEN

Chapter Twenty-Two

G uardianship is going well. Nila and Frost take it in shifts. They've been drumming up support for Jenna on the backs of the character statements you collected. They agreed with Jenna that it affects humans more widely and have been hugely helpful getting in contact with other humans across Geminus. Their guardianship has made the whole case official enough that the unions are confident backing Jenna. But more than that, they're supporting her. Talking her through her trauma around it, going with her on outings, helping her get all the travel in order. They've even arranged for meals to be delivered and for the CU to send a cleaner around each day.

It looks like we'll be travelling to Profundus at the end of the week, on Aurorasday, for the hearing on Ancientsday.

Elm's message faded from the screen as I looked away. Once again, I found myself wishing that humans could include emotions with their messages. As overwhelming as I often found it, I couldn't help but want some emotional context to Elm's words. Did they feel confident? Or was this more of a tentative positive?

I prepared for the journey. We'd be staying at least a few days, so I packed things to do. Clothes, I left alone. Profundus was almost entirely aquatic and I didn't have anything that would suit the environment. I collected some things from the market at Jenna's request. I didn't get to see her much—she was too busy with her guardians preparing for the hearing.

Before the sun rose on Aurorasday, we gathered at the canopy station for the canopy-glider that would take us to the Geminus Portal. Rain fell in thick sheets, roaring through the trees and drumming against the glider before us. I wore a wide-brimmed hat and waterproof cloak which slicked off the rain. Elm wore a long coat patterned in flowers and a hat as well, and Jenna wore a bright green poncho with a brimmed hood. Nila and Frost huddled below a shroud of firecrafted rain ward, which Illusion kept up while Nila, Night, and Storm spoke quietly. The rain sizzled against the shield and turned to mist.

'Why can't you do that?' Jenna asked me.

I tilted my head at her, causing a thick stream of water to slide off my hat. 'Why would I bother? A hat does just as well and doesn't require years of mind-numbing study.'

'It's cool, though,' Jenna said.

I snorted and stomped a hoof, though privately I also thought it was cool. Just not cool enough to take time away from my work for the CU.

Before long, the glider opened and a few hours later, it set us down in the Shadow Glade, a broad open space in the midst of a thick forest with dark trees. In that space, there seemed to be shadows hovering and darting through the air, intangible to touch.

The Geminus Portal dominated the empty space. Two enormous trees had curved and twisted together to form the frame of it, anchoring the energy in the earth. The land around it was strange. Coral and seaweed grew there as comfortably as it would in the ocean. Eerie in its displacement and vibrant growth, a testament to the power of the Starfire Ancient, who had itself planted the seeds of the portal trees. Cosmorans had studied it for centuries to learn how to recreate it. Of the portal itself, it was like a doorway edged in golden light, and through it were murky waters lit by faint splinters of distant sunlight.

I hadn't been here since I was a kit; I remembered my fear and reluctance to enter this strange place, shadow-speckled and gazing straight into the depths of an otherworldly ocean. As we disembarked from the canopy-glider, I breathed in air that had a salty sea tang despite being days away from the nearest Viridian ocean. The rain cast the entire scene in a haze. I had packed away my hat and cloak and my fur was already heavy with water.

I looked to Jenna, looking small and wet between Frost and Nila. She had changed into a waterskin made of tightly woven flexible fibres. It was blue flecked with orange and designed for the water, but she still looked small and wet and frightened between her guardians.

Frost and Nila both looked imposing and distinguished beside her in spite of the rain, each wearing the glinting golden amulets that marked them as guardians on active duty. I had never really thought of either Frost or Nila as huge before, but of course they were both larger than I was. Something about how they held themselves made them seem larger still in this moment.

Elm stood behind them, in a grey-green waterskin, their arms crossed and shoulders hunched. Without their usual style, they looked oddly vulnerable. I let Jenna and the guardians pass and fell into step beside them.

'Ever been to Profundus?' I asked them.

'Just the one time.' There was something more abrupt than usual about how they said it. I remembered that they'd been dropped on Profundus when they first arrived. My ears lowered in sympathy.

I decided not to press them but I kept pace with them. 'Well, when we go through the portal, we'll be in the ocean. But you'll be able to breathe as long as you have your forgetech bubble. Do you have it?'

Elm lifted up the sleeve on their skin, revealing a chunky bracelet lit with forgetech runes. I got mine out of my pack and strapped it around my ankle as well. 'Exactly. That will make the water around you breathable—and a little easier to swim in, or so I've heard. So hopefully you won't get tired as quickly as you might normally.'

Elm nodded once, sharply. 'And if it comes off?'

I perked my ears, getting a better grasp on Elm's nerves. 'It won't come off. They're designed to stay on and they aren't fragile so they shouldn't break.'

'But if it did?'

'But if it did,' I said, as patiently as I could, 'then Illusion would cast it on you until we found you a new one.'

'She can do that?' Elm said.

I nodded. 'She's particularly interested in firecraft. I think she would have joined the Firecrafters' Union, if the rest of Frost had had any interest. She probably will, one day.'

'Okay.' Elm visibly took a deep breath. Water ran in streams down their waterskin. 'Okay. I'm ready.'

I hesitated a moment. Jenna was receiving a similar pep talk from her guardians. I saw her glance over her shoulder at us, concern in her eyes—not for herself, it seemed, but for Elm and for me.

For me?

I wished I could offer Elm any stronger reassurance—offer for them to hold onto me, like Frost had for Jenna climbing the Flowering Ancient. But the truth was that just the thought of hands in my fur and weight dragging me down made my chest tighten and my core pulse far too fast. I'd do my best to look after Elm but looking after myself was going to be more than enough trouble.

As we approached the portal, a group came through from the other side, swimming up surrounded by pale blue fire undampened by the water. They emerged through the portal one by one, the fire snuffing out as they stumbled onto land. There was quite a mixed group—an elephant-shape, a rat-shape, a phoenix—and two were actually aquatic-shapes. A seal-shape swam through with no fire on the Profundus side but then it flared to life on the Viridus side, allowing them to swim through the air as if it was water. A golden catfish-shape followed them, the last of the group, swimming swiftly toward the waiting canopy-glider.

'I didn't realise there were bubbles for Viridus as well,' said Jenna.

'You haven't met any aquatic cosmorans?' asked Frost.

Jenna shook her head.

'Deep breath,' said Nila. 'It can be disorientating. You can hang onto me if you need to.'

Jenna nodded and the three of them walked through the Geminus portal. There was a strange moment where it seemed almost like they had entered zero gravity, their bodies weightless, their fur lifting and swaying. Then the fire bubbles bloomed around them, swirling and amorphous, and they swam a little ways away to make us room. Jenna stared around with wide eyes, then looked back at us and smiled, gesturing.

I looked to Elm, thinking I would reassure them, but they had their eyes fixed on Jenna. Their chest raised as they took a deep breath, and then they stepped through the portal and were consumed by that same amorphous bubble of starfire.

I looked down at my forgetech leg. I'd been going back and forth over whether to wear it for the whole journey. It would give me more traction in the water when it worked well, but it still needed tuning and if it seized up, it would be a hindrance. I made the decision, unclasped it from my leg, wincing as I did so, and used starfire to store it safely in my pack.

Ahead, the portal still stood, watery and golden-edged. My friends tread water on the other side, waiting for me. I took a step forward, limping without my forgetech leg. I flexed my short leg, which ended just below the shoulder, trying to take some comfort in the lack of pinching and pressure on it now.

As I stepped through, it was a shockingly familiar sensation; like plunging into a lake, but slowly. The icy chill against my muzzle, sinking into my fur. The sudden awkward weightlessness. I tread water, wheeling my legs. When would the bubble kick in? Surely this had been too long? Already it felt like my lungs were burning for lack of breath.

Everybody talked about how panic attacks felt like drowning but nobody talked about how drowning felt like a panic attack. My adrenaline spiked at the familiar sensations, made realer and more terrifying than ever as I gazed about this terrifyingly empty space.

Then warmth bloomed around me as the bubble flared into life, amorphous blue starfire surrounding me. My movements became less strained, the water more gentle. I gasped in fire that tasted like cool air. My body warmed as the water became tepid instead of icy. I breathed in and cool air flooded my lungs, fresh and welcome.

But I still tread water awkwardly. Still felt like at any moment, I might be dragged deeper. And this place *was* deep. Hazy blue and green in all directions, vision fading at the vastness of the distance.

'Avari?' Jenna swam toward me, slipping through the water like she was born to it with the aid of her forgetech bubble. She stopped in front of me, the tail of her hair drifting up behind her. She tried to find my eyes; I struggled to meet them.

She needed me. I needed to focus. But my eyes drifted down to the darkness below, to the ocean depths that seemed infinite in their distance.

'Avari. We want you to breathe with us,' said Frost at my ear. 'Can you breathe with us?'

I tried to nod but my head just sort of jerked.

'In...out,' said Frost. 'In...out.'

In. Out. My breath caught each time. I breathed too fast. Couldn't seem to get hold of it. Even with the forgetech bubble, the ocean seemed to press in on me, too vast for my tiny body to withstand.

'In...out,' said Frost. I watched their chest rise and fall. Took comfort in Illusion and Storm watching me in concern while Night kept an eye on Jenna. We were here for Jenna.

Gradually, my breathing became more smooth. I kept at it for a long time. Around me, my friends waited. Nila and Elm spoke quietly, the words eluding me. Frost and Jenna breathed with me.

Energy still fizzed inside me but I wasn't sure what else to do. It wouldn't get better than this until I was back on Viridus. Back with my hooves planted firmly on the ground. My eyes sought Jenna's.

'Okay?' she asked quietly.

I nodded, because this would have to be okay enough.

Nila and Frost led us out into the oceans of Profundus. I quickly realised we were not in as much of a void as it had first seemed. Large rocks teeming with seaweed and other long-tendrilled aquatic plants jutted up on both sides, providing us with a sort of tunnel to follow. At the other end, at all levels and heights, cosmorans swam, each one a tiny lantern of starfire.

Hardly anyone else we saw used forgetech bubbles. Here, most cosmorans were naturally aquatic. Manatee-shapes with golden speckles, sea dragons with long snaky bodies and rows of spade-like flippers, swordfish-shapes and shark-shapes with gleaming scales that reflected the light of their starfire.

There were buildings here too, I realised, watching people come in and out of them. Some were naturally formed into rocks or even the walls of the vast crevasse below us, cavehomes like the aquatic versions of the buildings we saw in Moons Cliff. But others were...bubbles. Mostly opaque, floating untethered in the ocean and yet unmoving in the currents. They floated at all heights and distances and it was hard for me to imagine what they might be like inside. What did home look like to an aquatic-shape? What did it look like when it was fully flooded with water? My brief childhood visit centuries ago gave me nothing to go on.

Nila swam with lazy, dog-like strokes. Frost was able to use their long thick tail to propel them like a crocodile. Jenna swam with confidence, some of the tension leaving her as she paused frequently to take in the crushing void of Profundus with avid wonder. I hoped the bubble was making this easier on her.

Only I swam awkwardly, lop-sidedly. I knew others with only three legs managed fine but I had never had the practice, never trusted myself enough to try. The bubble did help, though, the flames making the water lighter, easier to move through. I shuddered at the thought of trying to swim with the full weight of the water dragging me down.

It wasn't long before Nila signalled for us to follow them. Maybe half an hour's swim from the Geminus Portal was a large transparent bubble much like those we'd seen floating around. Inside it was a suspended island of rock around which floated several vessels that resembled canopy-gliders. Instead of wings, they had flippers, and they weren't enclosed.

I followed the others in. The bubble didn't contain air, as I'd expected, but instead was a sort of viscous membrane with more water on the other side. We swam to the island—which I supposed was the Profundus version of a canopy station. Nila searched the waiting vessels until he found the right one and called us over.

'This will take us to Ocean Throne,' said Nila. 'That's where your trial with the Galactic Council will take place, and I've booked lodgings for us all together there. Do you know how to ride a tide-cutter?'

'No,' said Jenna, but her eyes were bright. 'Tide-cutter?' She studied the vessel before us.

'It's a little more involved and restricted than gliders and flitters,' said Frost. 'Those prongs out at each side are handles for hanging on.'

'But we have a long journey and activating the safety gems is expected,' said Nila. 'They work the same as in the canopy-glider. You just can't get up and wander around.'

While Jenna asked more questions, my gaze ran over the tide-cutter. The idea that there was no surface to stand on was disturbing, but then I supposed that was how everything worked down here. As far as I knew, aquatic-shapes didn't even sleep in nests. The water was their nest as well as their air, I supposed.

Out of the corner of my eye, I saw Elm frowning at the tide-cutter as well, but before I could ask them anything, they started talking to Jenna.

We made our way to the tide-cutter. Its body was rough like coral and in just as many colours. Its flippers were lit with forgetech just like the wings of a glider, long and spade-like. The pilot waved us over; a fish-shape with rainbow scales and a bright smile. He sniffed toward us politely.

'Welcome, welcome! First time on Profundus? I don't like to assume, but you're looking at the tide-cutter like you've never seen one before.' He had a pleasant manner and addressed this last comment to Jenna, who smiled nervously.

'I haven't seen one before,' she said. 'How does it work?'

'Oh, the usual. Forgetech engine which powers these flippers here and that little spiral tail back there that propels it. I interface with the controls via this.' He gestured with a fin toward a crystal orb embedded in the pilot's slot. 'And from there it's fairly simple. Only a little more complicated than swimming your own self, and a lot faster. I'm Flare, by the way.'

'Jenna,' said Jenna.

The rest of us introduced ourselves in turn. Flare nodded amiably. 'And you're all on your way to Ocean Throne?'

'Yes,' said Jenna, a little nervously. I wondered if she thought Flare might judge her for that, but Flare did a little wiggle of excitement.

'Excellent! Oh you'll love it there. Ocean Throne is just a gorgeous city. The seat of the Starfire Ancient itself, of course, but architecture like you've never seen. I always prefer to be on the Ocean Throne route, but you know, sometimes the Transport Union requires me elsewhere. Well, okay! We're setting off in about 10 minutes. Get yourselves settled in each of these seats and make sure you activate your safety gem—it's a long journey and we don't want anyone getting tired...'

I swam awkwardly into the 'seat' behind Frost—essentially a space between two prongs with a gem embedded in the side of the cutter. It was a little awkward to get myself situated. Even with my forgetech bubble, I wasn't a strong swimmer and navigating swimming a little up or down in order to get into place certainly didn't come naturally to me. But once I thought I was in vaguely the right place, I activated the safety gem. A harness of shimmering fire wrapped around me, holding me in place. It felt secure rather than restrictive. It was nice to think that I'd be carried rather than having to swim. That I'd be tethered to *something* in the absence of normal gravity.

Jenna was in the seat across from me. She caught my eye and smiled.

'You look almost excited,' I said. I didn't bother to keep the grumpiness from my voice, knowing she wouldn't mind.

She laughed. 'I sort of am? All that time I was waiting to move to Geminus, I never imagined anything like this. Of course I knew Profundus existed, I just...didn't know it was possible for me to really experience it. This is *magical*, Avari.'

I tried to smile and warm my flame. It was hard to hold in the apology that this visit couldn't be under better circumstances. My mothers might think of me as a ruiner, but I wasn't going to ruin whatever joy Jenna managed to wring out of this horrible situation.

It wasn't long before the tide-cutter lurched into motion, the flippers beside us paddling in slow, smooth motions that sent us gliding through the ocean at increasing speeds. Flare piloted us through currents so thick they were tangible stripes of colour against the darker ocean. They curved us through wide open spaces that glittered with animals: diving birds with their wings pinned to their sides, huge schools of fish that stroked the water with their many fins, vast crystal jellyfish that sent out waves of crystalline calls that rocked the tide-cutter with their force.

The water rushed past, cool but not cold, streaming through my fur and washing harmlessly across my face even at the incredible speed of the tide-cutter. The tide-cutters movement was almost rocking, the flippers taking up a natural rhythm of pushing and gliding. With my chest still tight with anxiety and the vast emptiness still open beneath my hooves, I welcomed it when it lulled me to sleep.

My eyelids fluttered as I rocked and swayed in weightless water, my semi-conscious thoughts fluid and changing like the world around me. When my eyes opened and I surfaced from the disturbed pool of my dreams, I found the tide-cutter slowing to 'dock' inside another bubble much like the one we'd started at. The waters here were colder, the floor of the ocean taller like walls around us. An aquatic mountain range, it seemed, covered in plants with long swaying stalks, bright flowers, and glowing pods.

Shaking a little, I deactivated my safety gem and drifted free of the tide-cutter.

'Thanks!' Nila said to Flare, who flipped their tail in a friendly farewell.

Elm swam over to me, long arms cutting easily through the water, hands acting like fins. 'Where's the Council building?'

I looked around. There were fewer bubbles floating out here around the craggy, plant-covered mountains. Nothing stood out to me as particularly large or grand. 'Perhaps it's in the mountain?' I swam closer to Elm. 'How's Jenna? I fell asleep on the way over.'

Elm cast a glance at Jenna, who was treading water with Nila and Frost, clearly in conversation. She was nodding and frowning. 'Quiet,' Elm said. 'As much as she's loving seeing a new planet, she has a lot to think about.'

I wanted to talk to her. Give her a chance to express her feelings, and try to reassure her. But then she had two guardians right now and that was their explicit job. They were professional supporters. She didn't need my help. I wondered if Elm felt as useless as I did.

'Where's the throne?' I said. 'Given this is Ocean Throne and all the talking up the pilot did, I thought there would be more to see.'

'Perhaps it's just the mountain,' said Elm. 'More a poetic throne than a literal one.'

'Mm.' I was non-committal. Perhaps humans named their cities more poetically, but that didn't sound very cosmoran to me.

Frost waved us over with one heavily-clawed paw and we swam over. I couldn't tell whether Elm was just as slow a swimmer as I was or whether they were choosing to keep pace with me, but I was glad not to be left lagging behind regardless. 'The Throne part of Ocean Throne is down there,' said Frost, gesturing.

'You've been here before?' I asked, surprised.

Frost nodded. 'A few times. Most guardianships don't require interplanetary judgement, but it does happen from time to time.' They led us down the mountain, toward what I had thought was just one of many shallow caves but as we drew nearer was clearly a shaped archway of rock and coral in twisting lines. Frost went in first and then the rest of us followed.

Swimming out in the open had been terrifying, but as we descended into the cave, lit only by lines of glowing aquatic lichen striping the walls with blue, I found that swimming subterraneously was just as disconcerting, if in a completely different way. The tunnel led us down. It made me feel trapped in a way I couldn't place. This wasn't what I expected from the Geminus

Galactic Council. I suppose, in my head, I'd imagined we'd be somewhere with air and...gravity. A ridiculous bias considering it was on an ocean planet.

The tunnel eventually opened out into a vast chamber, the walls no longer craggy lichen-lit rock but now smooth slate with orb-like wispy lanterns floating around the space. People spoke in pairs or small groups—fish-shapes and dolphins and other aquatics. One particularly large figure appeared to be a hippo-shape such as you might see around Viridus. They had a forgetech bubble strapped to their leg but it didn't generate a swimming field for them—presumably, it was just helping them breathe.

There was a central figure waiting in the middle wearing a sash. A seahorse-shape who seemed very absorbed with their cosmorb. Rather than letting it float free, they held it curled in their long tail, and as we approached they looked up in excitement. 'Oh! Hello!' Their dark eyes found Elm and Jenna. 'You must be the Jenna Hughes group. The hearing isn't until tomorrow but I'd be happy to show you to your rooms. While it's perfectly safe to sleep with forgetech bubbles, we thought you might find a more familiar environment more restful so we've put you in a terrestrial suite. I hope that's okay?'

Nila looked to Jenna. 'If it's okay with you?'

'Uhh...yeah. Yeah. That would be nice,' she said. I struggled to read her tone—was she frustrated? Disappointed? Mostly she just sounded sad.

The seahorse led us down a series of long tunnels, first down, very deep down, and then up again. Surprisingly, at the top the water stopped and we were able to climb out into a spacious and comfortable cave with three chambers branching off from it. The seahorse-shape didn't emerge, but called from the water, 'If you need anything, you can contact me via your cosmorb and I'll see what I can do.' With that, they descended again, disappearing back down the tunnel with surprising speed.

Nila investigated first. 'Nestrooms, it looks like.'

Frost sniffed the cushions around the low table in the main cave. 'And just a nice room to relax in, I guess,' said Storm.

Illusion sneezed. 'Bit dusty though.'

'Well, I d-don't expect these rooms get a lot of use,' said Elm. 'It's n-nice to be somewhere a bit more familiar, though.'

I dipped my head in assent. I had not been relishing the thought of trying to sleep inside my forgetech bubble.

'It's comfortable and we're all together,' said Jenna. 'Since we have to b-be here, I'm glad of it.' As much joy as she'd taken from the journey, I could hear the resentment in her voice.

Now that we were on land, I was really starting to feel wet. I hadn't swum in a long time, and my fur poured water onto the floor. 'Are there any towels?' I asked. I'd normally shake myself first but I didn't want to drench the furnishings.

Frost investigated the baskets and tossed me a large towel, which I started to scrub against my fur. The others started to do the same. I noticed Elm and Jenna were shivering.

'Are you cold?'

'A b-bit,' Jenna stuttered, teeth chattering.

'Could b-be w-worse,' Elm said, then made a face.

While the rest of Frost dried themselves, Illusion watched the humans excitedly. I noticed her tail was twitching. 'Could I try a trick on you?' she asked them. 'I can dry you right up!'

My stomach shifted in misgiving. Firecraft could be spectacular, whether successful or in failure. 'Is that...safe?' I asked.

Storm looked around at me. 'We're experienced. Illusion's as good as any firecrafter.'

'It's not even proper firecraft,' said Illusion. 'Just a trick. A humble trick.'

I laid my ears back. I didn't like it when Illusion started calling things 'humble'. Humble was not her way.

'Y-yes please,' said Jenna at the same time Elm said, 'What exactly—?'

Frost's starfire flashed white-hot at the same time Illusion's eyes glowed the same. White fire washed over the human pair.

'Frost!' I snapped at my siblings. I rushed forward to Jenna.

The fire faded, leaving Jenna's hair and clothes gently steaming. 'I'm fine, Avari, really.'

I didn't put my ears forward and sniffed her carefully. She patted my nose and gently shoved me away. Though she didn't have the strength to move me, I went. She *looked* okay.

'What happens now?' Jenna asked.

Nila and Frost exchanged looks. 'Everything is as ready as it can be,' said Nila. 'Frost will double-check—'

'Quadruple check,' said Night.

'—but it's really your call what happens now.'

Jenna nodded seriously, wringing her hands. 'Well, we have all the statements recorded and ready. And I know mine by heart.'

Nila nodded. 'We've got a recorded back-up, too.'

Jenna smiled tightly. 'I want to do it in-person. But I do know it. I think...' She tucked stray hair behind her ears. 'I want to go out.'

I shifted my hooves, one ear forward and one back. We'd had a huge day following two weeks of big days. With all the travel we'd done already, Jenna would likely be suffering horribly already on the day of her trial—though I supposed she might have gotten quite a lot of rest on the ride over.

Her eyes found mine, as if reading my thoughts. 'I'm on a new planet,' she said. 'And if things go wrong, then maybe I'll be back on Earth soon. I want to enjoy it.' She grimaced, and added, 'I want the distraction.'

'Your case is solid,' Nila said gently.

Jenna nodded. 'I know. But if any of this was fair, I wouldn't have been summoned here in the first place. I want to enjoy today.'

'I think that's a great idea,' said Storm, while Night nodded his agreement.

'Well,' said Nila. 'Are you three happy to stay here and check everything over, and the rest of us will go out with Jenna?'

Frost nodded while my core seized.

Me, go out? Again?

Jenna had asked for it and she *would* probably love it. We were on an entirely new part of Geminus. Knowing Jenna, she'd have a great time going around and seeing everything and making a hundred new friends.

I whuffed as I considered it. I couldn't think of anything worse, personally, but...

Well. It wasn't about me.

'How are your energy levels?' I asked her. I knew the journey down had been hard on her. Too much physical activity on top of a heavy emotional weight. But only she could know what was too much.

211

'I'm tired,' she said. 'And...a little sore.' I knew her well enough now to know what she wasn't saying; that it would only get worse, even if she rested now.

Nila's ears perked. His tail gave a single, worried swish. 'You could ride on me, if that would help? You'd still have to hang on, though. It's not as easy to ride underwater, I guess.'

'In some ways...' Jenna said slowly. 'Yeah. I'd like to take you up on that. What is there to do in Ocean Throne, anyway?'

I picked up my bag. 'Let's find out.'

THE OLD GOAT AND THE ALIEN

Chapter Twenty-Three

I didn't want to swim again, but Jenna's eagerness in spite of her worries and her tiredness was motivation enough. I wouldn't let her down. Elm, I noticed, similarly chose to venture out again with us. I was glad Jenna had a friend like them.

When we emerged from the council building out into Ocean Throne, I was again struck by the vastness of it all. The steep lichen-covered walls rising up all around us. The chasm below, so deep that my vision faded into mist and shadow before I could perceive the bottom. Infinitely deep, perhaps. I tread water and starfire, feeling the uneven pace without my forgetech leg.

I glanced at Jenna. She had her arms around Nila's neck, her grip gentle as she floated just above him. She looked around with a bright excitement that didn't entirely hide the tension in her body. I wondered how much of that was nerves and how much pain after a day of heavy exertion. On her other side, Elm watched her with a worry that mirrored mine, but when she looked around, they smiled encouragingly. 'Where to first?' they asked.

'I can look up things to do,' I said. 'Most settlements have event calendars.'

Jenna waved me down. 'No, no. Let's ask someone!'

Hard to think of something I would like to do less, but Nila fixated on a starfire glow in the distance and paddled toward it, towing Jenna. I knew I should follow, but I hesitated. My swimming gait still felt uneven. And the starfire glow was almost consumed by the murky distance.

I didn't like this place, so far from the sky, so devoid of gravity and direction and clarity. I didn't like being forced to come here to defend a friend who had done nothing wrong.

As I trod water, Nila and Jenna grew more distant with Elm trailing behind. The void around me yawned. The depths below seemed both dark and hungry.

I didn't want to be here, but Jenna needed me. I didn't know how to cope with the scale of Jenna's need. I didn't know where to put all the fear building up inside me, making my body tight and tense, like I was on the verge of explosion.

If Jenna was forced to leave, it would be awful for her. And the thought of her hurting hurt me, too.

But more than that, it would be awful for me.

Some time in the last year, she had become indispensable to me. My best friend, as close or closer than Frost. And when I thought of them sending her back to Earth, I wanted to shake and scream and hide and cry and break things and...

I wasn't like Elm.

I couldn't go to Earth. Not only was travel there extremely restricted, I didn't think I could cope with being so far from the home I loved. So far from the family I loved.

But I loved Jenna too, and if the Geminus Galactic Council exiled her there, I would be forever broken.

I had only just begun to learn what it was to be whole.

The emptiness around me yawned wider. The others were a distant speck of starfire and shadow. My strokes faltered. My chest hurt and my breaths came too quick and too thin. Jenna was leaving and I was alone in this terrifying place and I couldn't swim right and at any moment something might emerge from the darkness below and eat me. The darkness itself might encroach and swallow me whole. I could feel its malevolence, its intent. To take everything from me. To leave me trapped and failing.

The pressure in my chest increased. My strokes grew more sluggish as I focused on my breathing. I tried to slow it down but I wasn't getting enough air. Could feel myself growing light-headed. The darkness closed in around me, suffocating.

Voices in the dark. A touch like fire at my shoulder. I startled and stared into the eyes of Jenna. She said something, but her words were muffled and distant. I tried to tell her not to worry about me but the words wouldn't come. My lips wouldn't part. Sealed shut.

'Should we go back?' she asked and her voice was very small.

I tried to hold onto that. I searched for the part of me that could pretend I was okay, at a cost. Scrambled for it. I needed to act okay for Jenna.

I tried to say something. Tried again. Time stretched. 'Nnno,' I managed finally. 'I'm...fine. Really.'

Jenna watched me with worried eyes. I put my ears forward and tried to look alert and ready. It didn't come easily to me. I hated lying about my mood—lying about anything, really—but Jenna needed me.

I tried my best for the next hour. I trailed the others while Jenna spoke with a family of fish-shapes and was led to a coral garden by a crab-shape. Profundus was every bit as beautiful as Viridus, full of light among shadow and shapes emerging from mist. The wildlife here was stunning: many-finned eels, creatures with fluffy rodent-like torsos and fish-like tails, crustaceans almost as large as cosmorans with long, grasping legs and four claws. Vast shoals of sea creatures swept past us. Fish that glittered like gems, jellyfish with cat-like heads, and small blue six-legged turtles among them. It was beautiful; it was also overwhelming. There was too much to see, too much to fear, and far too much swimming, which only grew more exhausting over time.

Jenna looked tired too, and sort of brittle in a way that worried me. But she was also full of smiles and squeals of delight as we explored this new world. This was good for her.

I needed to be there for her tomorrow, and I wasn't sure I'd be able to do that if I stayed with her today.

I sent a message to Frost. *Would I get in your way if I came back?* I let my anxiety seep into the message—just a little of it. Just enough that Frost would get the idea.

Immediately, I got a message back. *You wouldn't get in the way. We can't talk much but would enjoy the company.*

I got the sense the message had mostly been from Storm, but there were other notes of emotion in there from the rest of Frost and I knew they all meant it, even Night.

I couldn't quite face heading back alone, swimming out into the vast emptiness, but I found someone with a small tide-cutter—a paddler, they called it—and begged them for a lift back to the Throne. Since most vehicle owners were in the Transport Union or at least understood the responsibility, I was reasonably confident they'd take me, and so they did.

I asked the seahorse-shape on reception for directions back to the Hughes suite and emerged soaking onto the floor, the forgetech bubble fading. I collapsed, shivering, and rested my chin on my knee.

Frost emerged from their room. All of them looked worried. 'Can I dry you?' Illusion asked.

I flicked my tail once, not having the energy to nod. White fire washed over me and the water steamed away into the air. It was a little uncomfortably warm but I was so glad to be dry, I found I didn't mind.

I knew I should probably haul myself to my nest but I was so tired and the effort of the day pressed on me like a physical weight. Frost bustled around for a few minutes then brought their work over and sat beside me. Most of them were busy with their cosmorb and various data crystals, but Night laid his head beside mine, not quite close enough to touch. A rare and welcome affection from the least affectionate part of Frost. It was blessedly quiet, too; Frost didn't need to speak aloud when they were just speaking to themselves. There was little but the clink of crystal on crystal, the occasional crackle of starfire, and the sound of claws scraping on stone when Frost shifted.

For a long while, I didn't say anything. At some point, Frost brought me some cushions, which I gratefully sank into, my body sore from so long lying still on hard stone. I wondered what Jenna was doing now. I wondered if she was tired or ill. If Nila and Elm would think to keep offering to return home, since Jenna would never bring it up on her own. Nila was a trained guardian and Elm spent more time with Jenna than I did, yet I couldn't let go of the thought.

At length, I asked into the silence, 'What will happen if Jenna gets sent back to Earth?'

'She won't,' Night replied irritably. 'Exile is for villains, not travellers.'

'But if she did?'

Night sighed and lifted his head. He considered me, tongue flickering, lidless eyes unblinking. 'If she did...'

'If she did, we would work out how to get her back,' said Storm. They were still focused on the cosmorb, but one ear pointed toward me. 'She had already applied to move here. I've seen her application. There's no reason it would have been rejected. And I know you hate travelling but we could visit her together until she came home.'

'But it won't come to that,' said Night. 'So don't worry about it.'

I wished it was that easy.

When Jenna arrived, Nila was carrying her. She looked wan with dark circles under her eyes, almost as ill as the day I'd had to rush her to Vya. Nila stopped by my side so that Jenna could give me a pained smile and touch the side of my face. Then tapped Nila who whisked her off to her nest.

Elm stopped beside me. They didn't look great themself, but they were entirely focused on where Jenna had disappeared.

'How is she?'

'Good and bad,' said Elm. 'It's always a trade-off, with things like this. As long as she thinks it was worth it, then it was.'

I dipped my head. 'And what about you?'

Elm raised their eyebrows at me. 'It doesn't matter how I am, as long as Jenna is okay.'

'It does,' I said. 'She's going to need you.'

Elm shrugged and looked away.

I considered my own energy levels. I still felt exhausted in both body and mind. But at least I'd been able to spend the last several hours resting at home. Elm had been out there, even though they seemed to hate the ocean as much as I did.

'Sit down,' I told them gruffly.

'Sorry?'

'Sit. I'll make you something.'

I went through our bags and found the brown sludge drink Elm and Jenna were so fond of. There was a small kitchen so I heated up the sludge drink and served it in a steaming mug for Elm, then when Frost and Nila joined, I served them some freshflower tea. When Nila joined, I learned that though Nila had eaten while out with Jenna, Elm and Frost had both failed to eat, so I rummaged in our bags again and found some sourspice soup to heat up and serve with some seasoned flatbread.

Elm and I ate in silence, but Nila and Frost talked quietly about what Nila had seen and how Jenna had enjoyed the outing. It sounded like they'd explored some ancient caves for a good bit of the day, and that Jenna had spent a few hours among longsharks, petting them and feeding them strips of food at the local herder.

Would those be her last experiences on Geminus, and I had missed them? How long did it take for the GGC to exile someone to another planet?

I kept these thoughts to myself. Elm was exhausted, and Nila and Frost needed all their energy to support Jenna. I finished my tea, mopped up the last bit of my small serving of soup, and made my way to the unfamiliar nest the council had provided. The walls glowed faintly with pink lichen casting a strange hue around the room. I burrowed into the cushions and waited for morning. Sleep visited me in fleeting, stressful dreams.

Chapter Twenty-Four

We floated outside the entrance to the Geminus Galactic Council, a vast archway of crystal and coral that light flickered through like electricity. Beyond, I could already see that there was a cavernous chamber lit by the hazy glow of floating werelights.

'You're sure you're okay to give your statement in-person?' Frost asked me.

I nodded, though I felt like my insides were tied in knots. My fur all stood on end, no matter how hard I willed it to lay flat. I felt like a vast invisible predator was closing on us...or not on us, but on Jenna, floating between her guardians, looking so incredibly small. She was only forty years old. I understood that she was well into maturity for a human, but now all I could think was that Journey would be forty in the blink of an eye. That Jenna was barely more than a child, faced with being ejected from her home and separated from her friends.

Despair threatened to suck me in like a whirlpool, but I resisted it with all my might. It wasn't time to despair yet. Jenna needed me.

She hugged Elm tightly. She murmured something to them, too quietly for me to hear. Then she turned to me.

I put my ears forward and calmed my flame, doing my best to project peace for her even though I felt like I was coming apart at the seams.

'Nila and Frost think this will be easily solved,' she said, and in the shake of her voice I could hear, 'but I'm not so sure.'

'It will,' I said, even though expressing certainty about the future had always been hard for me. 'You're not going anywhere, Jenna.'

She stared at me, her human face no longer startlingly expressive to me, only the face of my friend as her eyes welled up and her mouth trembled. 'Can I hug you?' Her voice was thick.

I leaned forward, putting my chin over her shoulder and pulling her close. She wrapped her arms around my neck and buried her face in my mane. I knew she was hiding her tears in it; I didn't care.

'I never knew what my life was missing until I met you,' I whispered. Tears burned in my eyes, too, and my flame juddered and sparked. 'You must belong here, because you've made everything so much better.'

She hugged me tighter.

Nila approached, an apologetic look in his eyes. I flicked an ear in acknowledgement and pulled back from Jenna. Her eyes were reddened and her face was splotchy and some of my fur was stuck to it, quickly washed away by the ocean waters.

'Okay,' she said. 'Let's do this. I'm—I'm ready.'

She squared her shoulders a moment, then swam through the glowing archway, flanked by her guardians. There was nothing I could do for her but follow.

The council chamber yawned around us, a cave thick with coral, lichen, and aquatic plants. Seagrass danced around us as we passed and long fronds of brightly-coloured weeds threatened to tangle my legs if I swam too close. There were fish in here, too—all sorts of small aquatic creatures, glittering and fleet as they danced among the werelights. I wondered if they were fed here. I could think of no other reason they would choose to hang around. Glowing filaments hung from the ceiling, strung with shining pearls. I had no idea whether they were decorative or natural.

For all its wild beauty, I couldn't shake that this was a place of judgement. Of Jenna's judgement. And indeed, the council floated above. Five cosmorans: a stern gull-shape with a red-slashed beak and shining black-and-white feathers; a crocodile-shape with golden spines along her back and a void-dark gaze; a turtle-shape with translucent flippers and a shell engraved with a dizzying mandala; a wolf-shape with brilliant white fur and eyes that blazed as red as their flame; and an octopus-shape with arms that curled and uncurled curiously as it watched us, each arm either gold or blue, matching the shining blue rings that marked its golden flesh.

'Jenna Hughes,' said the octopus-shape. 'I am Glimmer of the Geminus Galactic Council. You are here to discuss your illegal immigration, is that correct?'

Jenna glanced at Nila. 'I am here to discuss my immigration,' she said, and Nila nodded encouragingly.

'I am Ven of the Geminus Galactic Council,' said the gull-shape. 'Does a guardian stand for you?'

'Frost of Lost Circle stands for Jenna Hughes,' said all of Frost in unison. Their voice echoed in spite of the water.

'Nila of Lost Circle stands for Jenna Hughes,' said Nila, and his voice was more sonorous than I had ever heard it, with a hint of hyena-growl.

And on went the council, introducing themselves and asking sharp questions which Jenna or her guardians would answer. The turtle-shape was Aurora and watched Jenna with hard eyes. The crocodile-shape was Marsh, and she punctuated her questions with a snap of her long toothy maw. The wolf-shape was Lorum and, after introducing themself, they fell completely silent, watching not just Jenna, but me and Elm as well.

I shifted uncomfortably under that gaze. I didn't want to be part of judging Jenna. She deserved better; that was why she had guardians, afterall. People who understood the law and were upstanding in their community. I was just an everyday cosmoran, and not a particularly well-liked one either.

I didn't like the tenor of their questions. Had she known the portal wasn't for her? Had she made any attempt to report her portal use to the GGC? Did she know the person the portal had been intended for? But Nila and Frost were both quick to quash unfair phrasing, and Jenna spoke haltingly, recalling the hours of preparation her guardians had done with her.

Then it was time for Jenna's statement. She took a long, steadying breath, stirring the water and flame surrounding her. She looked so small in this vast chamber, before the arrayed council, each of them twice or more her size. But she gazed at them unflinchingly. 'I applied for the immigration program and followed every step of the process,' she said. 'I had thought it would be a few years before I saw my portal, but no strict date was given. When the portal appeared to me, I was in my garden, alone. There was nobody else around it could have been for. And I panicked, as I knew the portals are only open for a short time, and entered; much less prepared than I would have been with warning.

'And then I was on another planet. Alone. In a forest full of plants and animals I had never seen before, with nothing and no way to contact anyone.

I was terrified. I had been led to believe that a portal would take me to the Otherworldly Travel Commission. This was not the case. If Avari and their family hadn't found me, I don't know what might have become of me, with no food, no knowledge, no transport, and no communication.' She let that hang in the air a moment, and I saw anger, bright as a flame, sparking in her eyes. 'I was brought to Lost Circle where the Travellers' Union thankfully took me under their wing, but there was still very little in place to help me as a *human* traveller. If Elm, a human official there, hadn't been there to help guide me, I might have really struggled.

'The only thing I have done is take a portal I believed was meant for me and then start a life here as best as I could. These were not the circumstances I would have chosen. To blame me for them, when so many other human travellers have similar stories, is deeply unjust. And my life is *here* now. My friends and family are here. My work is here, my home is here. I did not come here as a tourist and I did not live as one. You cannot send me to Earth without ripping me out of my life. That would not just be unjust. It would be cruel.' She clenched her hands at her sides.

There was a pause as the council took that in.

'Jenna's statement that other humans have similar stories is verifiable,' said Nila. 'We have collected references from hundreds of human travellers. We've prepared a selection. The rest is available for your perusal.'

Nila picked up his cosmorb and set it to hover and project. The data crystals around it spun faster and faster, and then a holovid lit the space before us: a sparkling, flickering image. 'My name is Zhang Li,' said the first figure. 'My portal arrived years later than I was told to expect. It left me in a cave, in complete darkness...'

The human told her story, and then another appeared, and then another. They spoke, in tones of fear, frustration, and sometimes wonder, of the unexpectedness of their portals and the danger of their arrivals. Some, like Jenna, quickly found help from nearby cosmorans. Others struggled alone for hours or even days. Some faced injury, illness, and starvation before help was found. It was deeply upsetting to hear and I couldn't help but look at Jenna through it all, watching with her jaw clenched and her eyes shining. Those awful things those people had gone through...it could have been her.

The council listened in grim silence. I had no idea what they made of it.

'Thank you,' said Marsh. 'We will review the rest of the statements separately.'

'Well,' said Glimmer. 'I think that's the formalities out of the way. Let's move on to the character references, shall we?' It swam down to a clump of rocks below and unhooked a bag of a strange material, then started to unpack all sorts of jars and wrapped parcels from it. It moved with hypnotising efficiency, using not just starfire but its eight arms. 'Is anyone interested in some refreshments? I've brought enough for everyone, I think.'

'I picked up a few meal sacks from the café on the way as well,' said Aurora. His starfire flared and the sacks materialised in front of him.

'Show off,' Marsh grumbled. She lashed her crocodilian tail and nudged Glimmer with her muzzle. 'Are those seaweed wraps?'

'Mm-hmm.'

'I'll have one, thanks.'

I stared, my ears slowly laying back. They were going to...have a picnic? In the midst of an important meeting to decide Jenna's fate? I looked to Frost for support, but Frost was already unpacking food from their own pack, Storm talking to Nila while Illusion offered things to Jenna and Night quietly focused on unpacking.

'Is this...normal? For cosmoran legal proceedings?' Elm asked. They looked as shocked and uncomfortable as I felt.

I snorted out a bubble of fire and water. 'I hope not. This is my first time before a council.'

'Mine, too. It...isn't like this on Earth.'

'Is it better?' I asked.

They shrugged and accepted a strange-looking pastry Night offered them. It was dark and oily-looking and not at all like anything I'd ever seen before. Profundus required food that could survive underwater, I supposed. 'It's different. More formal.'

Much as I'd disliked many things Jenna had told me about Earth, I would have vastly preferred something formal right now. The idea that they could threaten Jenna with exile, when both Nila and all of Frost thought there was no grounds for that even if she *had* come here illegally...and that then they would have a *picnic* while her fate was decided...

I wished I could stomp my hooves to let out some of my frustration and restless energy. I hated swimming.

Night offered me an oily-looking pastry as well but I shook my head vigorously. I had no desire to try frightening, unfamiliar food when Jenna's freedom hung in the balance.

I noticed that the wolf-shape, Lorum, also didn't eat. Their red eyes burned as they stared at me. I quickly looked away.

'Alright,' said Marsh. 'Let's hear the references.'

Nila picked up his cosmorb and put a data crystal to orbit it, spinning faster and faster. There was a flicker, then a flare, as a holovid glitched into the space between us. An image of cat-shape, pixelated and sparkling, appeared before the council, bars cycling down it as the projection refreshed. 'My name is Cloud of Lost Circle,' said the projection, and my chest tightened at the familiar, warm voice. I could just about make out some of the patterns of her fur now that I was looking, though the colour was all washed in blue and pink. 'Jenna Hughes is a dear friend and a fixture of my local community.' There was a blur behind her as her tails lashed. 'She is a regular at my café and helps host board game nights, as well as running a monthly drop-in session on human culture, which is always well-attended. She is also the reason I met a dear friend, Avari, who gave her room under traveller's hospitality. My life would be poorer if she wasn't here, and would be poorer still if she left. I'm sure everyone who knows her agrees, because she is generous with her time, her skills, and her energy.' There was a pause, then holo-Cloud bared her teeth and added, 'So don't do anything as ill-thought and irresponsible as sending her away, because—' The holovid cut out as Nila disconnected the crystal.

'Strong words,' Marsh remarked. She took another bite of the seaweed wrap Aurora had supplied.

'Maybe not the right tone,' Elm murmured under their breath, but I couldn't agree. This whole situation was so incredibly unjust. It felt good to hear Cloud call it out as it was.

The next holovid flickered into life, this time a millipede-shape clicking xir legs together anxiously. 'Uh...my name is Ever. Sorry, Ever of Lost Circle. I first met Jenna Hughes not long after she arrived on Geminus, where she politely requested clothes, as she had none of her possessions with her. I got the sense that, uh, that she was nervous of me to begin with, but she quickly overcame that and was effusively grateful for my help. She often visits even when she has no need of my services and has offered her help to me in my shop as well. She has a good heart and I consider her a friend.'

Next came a badger-shape I didn't recognise. 'My name is Wind of Lost Circle. Jenna Hughes has been my apprentice at the Gardeners' Union for about a month, though I feel I have learned just as much from her...'

Then a monkey-shape draped in beads. 'My name is Velo of Lost Circle. Every week at the Purple Garden market, Jenna Hughes brings me lunch and watches my stall so I can take a break...'

'My name is Keera of Lost Circle. Jenna Hughes is my friend. I'm verian and she helps me make sense of other people in social situations...'

'My name is Vya of Lost Circle. I am a healer of cosmorans, humans, and animals, and I first met Jenna when she was very ill and came to me for treatment. Since then, she has brought me two wounded animals and notified the Animal Healers' Union of three more she was unable to catch...'

'My name is Mers of Lost Circle—'

'My name is Shade of Lost Circle—'

'My name is Nova of Athelean,' said my mother. 'I met Jenna Hughes on the way to my youngest kit's hatching day, when she first arrived in Geminus. She seemed then to be a sweet and friendly young human, and has since become part of the family due to her friendship with my eldest kit, Avari.'

'Jenna Hughes is good. Helpful,' said my other mother, Teera. 'Looks after my eldest kit, Avari, who needs extra help sometimes—'

My siblings and even former neighbours had nice things to say about Jenna, as well. And the list from Lost Circle went on and on. Cloud had tracked down far more people than I imagined. Names and faces I had never heard of before, mentioning small ways Jenna had improved their lives or was part of their communities. Representatives from the TU and GU spoke, as well. Not just members, but officials who offered Jenna their protection—and consequences, should she be removed from their care.

As the last holovid faded, the white wolf-shape, Lorum, spoke for the first time since their introduction. 'We've heard much from people absent. What of those present?' Their red eyes bored into me.

I couldn't do this.

227

Much practised words now lodged in my throat, unable to gain the lift required from my thin and struggling lungs. My tongue felt thick and sluggish. All my fur stood on end, my mane flaring out even as I ducked my head.

Jenna needed me but I couldn't do this. What if I misspoke and cost her the trial?

Lorum stared at me, fire in their eyes.

Frost left Jenna's side to come stand beside me. Illusion smiled encouragingly; Night gave me a serious nod. Frost was not my guardian, but they had always been there to support me, nonetheless.

Jenna turned toward me, her expression so full of trust in spite of the intensity of her situation.

I could do this.

I *needed* to do this.

I could no longer pull the script from the static of my brain, but I would find words.

'My name is Avari...of Lost Circle. I was...the first person on Geminus to meet Jenna Hughes,' I said haltingly. I kept my eyes on Jenna. 'I was travelling with my family to my sibling's hatching day ceremony. I left the path to be alone but found Jenna instead. She was confused and a little frightened, but she was kind. I...was stressed and didn't know what to do with her. My family reminded me that, under traveller's hospitality, it was my responsibility to help and house her. I...resented that responsibility. Resented Jenna. I'm not...I don't get along. With people. Or I didn't, then. But living with Jenna changed everything for me. She became my first real friend. She helped me make other friends. My life now...it...my life is unrecognisable. I was so unhappy. And so lonely, though I didn't realise it.'

I took a deep breath. 'Jenna is family. The idea of her being sent away...it terrifies me. And it doesn't make any sense. She belongs here.'

Jenna's eyes were red from crying, though the tears were lost in the ocean waters. I was glad that mine were, too.

The trial moved on. Elm told their story of Jenna, both from the perspective as a Travellers' Union official, and as Jenna's life partner. I picked up bits and pieces of it; showing Jenna around Lost Circle, going on trips

228

together, Jenna's work for the TU. But most of it seemed muffled and distant as my thoughts turned inward, to the crushing fear that all would go wrong.

Nila and Frost both made their legal case for her, as well. That all travellers have the right of welcome. That all people have the right to travel. That there was no difference between humans and cosmorans under Geminus law, and that no cosmoran had ever been exiled from Geminus. That Jenna had never knowingly broken any rules, and that her application would likely have been accepted in time regardless. That even if she had, it would be cruel to unsettle her now.

Even in my state of body-freezing panic, I could tell that the council had long been convinced. Ven the seagull-shape was openly nodding; Glimmer the octopus-shape had ceased handing out refreshments and listened with calm empathy. Even though Lorum still had me fixed in their red-eyed stare, I began to relax.

'We need to retire a moment to discuss what you have presented,' said Aurora. He gestured with a scaly flipper to the door. 'Feel free to go about your business, but do not go far. We reconvene in an hour.'

And with that, they exited the council chamber via a sea-grass shrouded tunnel at the back. Following Nila's lead, we left through the coral archway we'd first entered through and out into a garden of rainbow seaweed. I was glad to have ground so near to me, rather than swimming back out into the ocean void beyond the council building.

Jenna floated close to Elm. They held hands, which must be inconvenient in the water but which seemed to calm her. 'That went well, right?' she asked to the group. Her plaited hair drifted behind her, swaying in the faint current like an anxious tail.

'It went perfectly,' said Storm. Their ears flicked forward. 'You are very loved.'

'It was an easy case,' Nila agreed.

Jenna looked back toward the coral arch, and I knew she must be thinking about the council deliberating her case beyond it. Wondering why an easy case required an hour for the council to come to a conclusion. Perhaps wondering why an easy case required a trial at all. 'It wasn't how I expected it to go,' said Jenna. 'Where I come from, legal cases are more...formal. And it doesn't matter how other people feel about you.'

'What, really?' Illusion looked to Elm for confirmation.

Elm nodded, tightening their grip on Jenna's hand. 'It comes up a bit, but it wouldn't be the key to the success like it is here. And certainly, nobody would be sharing a picnic during legal proceedings.'

'Weird,' said Nila.

It did sound strange. If you were going to exile someone, why wouldn't it matter that they would be missed? That they were a key part of their communities?

But then again...what if Jenna had been more like me? If she'd just stayed home and made no friends but me...would she have been exiled back to Earth? That didn't seem right. Or what if her disability had prevented her from leaving her nest, as she'd told me it did for many people with ME, and might well for her one day?

There were people like Needle who were too unwell to get out and make friends. That didn't mean they didn't deserve to live freely in their communities.

I hoped Earth's legal process was fairer, in that sense. Lighter on punishments, more understanding of people's unique situations. But I understood very little of how it worked here, and nothing at all of how it worked on Earth.

'How're you holding up?'

My head jerked up in surprise. Jenna smiled tiredly at me, her head resting on Elm's shoulder. 'Doesn't matter how I am,' I said. 'As long as you're okay.'

'It matters to me,' she said. 'Elm, could Avari come here for a bit?'

'Of course.'

I translated that as meaning that Jenna was too tired to swim unnecessarily, so I drifted over to her. 'You did great,' I told her. I pressed my forehead to hers.

She stroked the side of my face, just once. 'You did, too. I know all of this is really hard for you.'

I sighed in agreement. 'If you get to stay, it'll all be worth it.'

'Yeah,' she said, and she sounded subdued. 'Yeah, it will.'

Lorum swam out into the garden with long, confident strokes despite their terrestrial shape. They fixed their red wolf eyes on Jenna. 'The council is ready to deliver its verdict. Come with me.'

Jenna nodded, eyes wide. Her fingers curled into my mane, only to pull away as Nila and Frost nudged me aside and took up their positions on either side of her.

Chapter Twenty-Five

Among the glittering shoals and dancing grasses of the council chamber, we awaited the verdict. I couldn't read anything from the council members; I struggled to read people at the best of times, and their starfires were oddly neutral. Glimmer was no longer snacking or handing out food. Aurora watched Jenna with what I hoped was kindness. Lorum's red eyes moved from person to person with a focused intensity I still found unsettling.

'I have been nominated to speak for all the council,' said Ven, the gull-shape. 'We have contemplated your situation and the evidence submitted. We find you innocent of all crimes. We find you a positive influence in your community. But you were still never supposed to be here.' Ven's eyes, dark voids that sparkled with stars, fixed on Jenna as he stared down his long, red-slashed beak.

Jenna seemed to shrink where she floated between her guardians, her arms coming to cross her belly in an incredibly vulnerable motion. 'Among the millions of intergalactic immigration applications the Otherworldly Travellers' Commission received from humans, we cannot say that yours would certainly have been approved, though we saw no reason to have denied it. There was nothing exceptional about it.'

The words cracked like a whip. I looked from face to face, snorting out a cloud of bubbles and fire, but I still could make nothing out from the stoic array of councillors.

Nothing exceptional. What a disgusting phrase. What a reprehensible way to reduce a person. And what an absolute *lie*.

I surged forward in the water, a retort hot on my tongue, but Frost bumped into me. Illusion shook her head and Night made sure to hold my eyes. Storm remained fixated on the council.

'However, we find you are now too embedded in your community to fairly remove you without causing harm to you and those who rely on you,' Ven continued. 'Jenna Hughes, formerly of Earth, the Geminus Galactic Council confirms your protected status as a traveller, and furthermore grants you citizenship.'

For a moment, there was silence broken only by the sound of Jenna choking. Then, 'Oh my god, *thank you!*' She surged upward in the water, kicking with delight. Elm swam over and hugged her, then Frost and Nila did the same, a big spinning mass of excitement.

My chest swelled and my starfire flared warmly. The verdict was still echoing around in my mind like the bright chiming of bells. Jenna was going to stay. *She was going to stay!*

'Congratulations,' said Ven, echoed heartily by the other councillors. Jenna thanked them and emerged from the huddle of friends, opening her arms toward me. I swam forward and rested my chin on her shoulder. Her arms curled my neck, her fingers curling into my mane.

'We did it,' she whispered.

'*You* did it,' I said. 'You're so ridiculous that you've befriended every cosmoran in Lost Circle and none of us can bear to part with you.'

She grinned at me. 'So it's a good job I'm not going anywhere, then.'

I snorted and pulled away, and she only smiled wider.

The council swam forward to chat with Jenna and her guardians, so I drew back and watched, enjoying the warm glow that still suffused me, knowing I had only a limited time before relief caused me to collapse as the stress of the last few weeks came flooding in. I watched as Jenna introduced Glimmer to the human greeting of shaking hands, and the octopus-shape's delight at the action, insisting on shaking with each of its eight arms. That was Jenna; already making friends with the people whose judgement she'd feared only moments before. Even Lorum, the red-eyed wolf, watched with a softness I hadn't perceived before. Personally, I didn't think any of them deserved her friendship, or her forgiveness. But as angry as Jenna had been...she probably knew that.

In spite of being deep beneath the ocean on an unfamiliar planet, in spite of the glittering fish and long coral-spined eels that darted past me or bumped curiously against me, I found myself smiling.

We all left the council chamber and made our way back to our suite. We laughed and congratulated Jenna, but also we all sank onto our various cushions in exhaustion. And as people gradually dozed off, all of us together, my thoughts turned back to the trial.

I couldn't shake the thought that it should never have happened. It looked like most of Frost was resting, but Night's eyes were still open. 'Night?'

'Mm?'

I rested my chin on a cushion. 'If there is no difference between cosmorans and humans in Geminus law...why did this trial happen?'

There was a long pause where Night said nothing, his dark eyes glittering thoughtfully. 'We've been going back and forth on that for days, with ourselves and with Nila,' he said. 'But I think it must be that there is pressure from some group to have humans treated differently.'

'But why?' The idea was startling. People were people! Cosmorans didn't believe in borders; we never had.

'Well...Illusion will disagree with me—I can feel her disagreeing with me even while she's mostly asleep. But, Avari...there's more anti-human sentiment out there than you think. Maybe this was a practice-run for how people would take that.' Night paused. 'It didn't work.'

I looked at Jenna where she dozed, curled up on a large cushion. I was glad she had won her trial. I hated to think that there were unknown forces out there trying to force her or any other humans out.

A few days later, once Jenna had recovered a little, we made our way back to the council gardens. Jenna wanted to properly take them in, now that the anxiety of the trial had been lifted.

While we chatted and looked around, two cosmorans swam up to us, a rainbow-hued manta-shape and a silver dolphin-shape. The dolphin-shape wore trailing white robes, while the manta-shape wore wreaths of white water lilies. Both were painted in whorls of white and gold, the mark of the Starfire Servants. Both had a pearly sheen to their eyes that I had never seen before.

Frost and Nila hurried to bow, which was awkward in the water. I slowly followed suit. Jenna and Elm watched curiously.

'There is a human woman here,' said the manta-shape Servant.

'Uh...I guess that must be me,' said Jenna. There was something hesitant about her. I wondered if she recognised their similarity to the Servants of the Flowering Ancient, or whether that was too long ago and too far away for her to make the connection.

The manta-shape swam closer to Jenna, who sniffed politely toward xir. Xe studied Jenna closely, xir pearly eyes strange and focused. 'This is her,' xe said.

The dolphin-shape nodded and flipped her tail. 'Come with us,' she said.

Nobody moved. Frost and Nila glanced at each other in alarm.

I swam forward, drawing their attention back to me. 'What is this about? Jenna has just been through a really harrowing trial.'

The dolphin-shape said, 'The Starfire Ancient has invited this human to an audience.'

My ears went back. I didn't know whether to run or prostrate myself.

Jenna squeaked, 'Me?'

Chapter Twenty-Six

The journey to the Burning Reef was not much like the Elder Grove, and yet the same strange weight of peace settled on me, a reverence that came as much from outside as within as I swam the dark waters, following the flames and trailing white wreaths of the Servants of the Starfire Ancient.

Jenna's arms encircled my neck. She was lightly tied into place, the exhaustion of the last few days overwhelming her too much for her to swim under her own power. She hadn't ridden on my back like this since the terrifying day she'd fallen ill, but the water made light of her. We'd left the others behind. When she'd asked if anyone could come with her, the Servants had told her only one was permitted. And to my surprise, she'd chosen me.

Gradually, the darkness gave way to a distant aura of shifting colours, then to pricks of light in the distance burning in the black deep like stars in the night sky. Swells of shining dust drifted past us. It made the darkness less hollow.

I felt Jenna shift on my back, leaning forward. 'What are those lights?' she whispered.

'I think that's the Burning Reef,' I said, with less certainty than I felt. I had never been here before, but I *knew* that was the Burning Reef. Could feel a familiarity with those flames in spite of their total novelty. Those flames called to mine.

As we drew nearer, those flames grew into coral, each a different shape, some branching, some with long feelers, some flat brackets clinging to rock. Each alight with a starfire like flame, the only fire that can burn even in the ocean. I could not help but feel reverence tinged with wonder: this coral was not cosmoran. It was not crystal at its core, and yet I knew it for kin. Much like the golden trees of the Elder Grove.

And much like the Elder Grove, I had a sense that it was...aware. That it felt my passage through its chill waters and took note.

Initially, the reef reminded me of a vast, rocky garden, but as we journeyed deeper, I realised there was structure to it. Archways and pathways, a labyrinth of stone and starfire. Even now, as we swam above, I saw Servants and pilgrims alike swimming the pathways below, their pace contemplative, their energy reverent rather than lost. And at the centre of it all, a latticed-dome temple of flaming coral, at once natural and otherworldly. Fish and sea creatures of all kinds swam in and out, brushing against the coral or the starfireless anemones that swayed and grasped at the current with their long feelers.

'I thought this would be a...a church, or something,' Jenna whispered as we approached the vast structure of the Heart of the Reef.

The word fizzled in my starfire for a moment before I got the meaning of it. 'Is it not?' I asked.

'Churches usually have...I don't know. Roofs. Walls.'

'We're underwater,' I pointed out.

'I...yeah.' She seemed to process this as we followed the Servants through a lattice of coral-clad stone, the flames gently tickling my fur. 'I like this better,' she said.

Curious fish with six fins and silver scales flitted up to me and bumped curiously against my side before darting away. I heard Jenna giggle as she got the same treatment. We swam through more layers of latticed coral, and as we did, a sort of...thrum...went through me. Like I was resting in a healing chamber with the resonance turned on, but instead of the bright, high singing I was used to, instead it was a core-deep pulse, something primal that caused the fire within me to roar. I wondered if Jenna could feel it. Was she quiet because she was exhausted, or was she quiet because something about the fire here called to the dust in her?

At last, we came to the centre of the dome. A roiling ovoid floated at an angle, oily black and yet also aflame with the reflection of the fire all around it. The ovoid itself was larger than the whole of Antlervine Tree, than even a canopy-station. The pulse of it was stronger than ever now; I could feel my fur prickling, my core shaking.

The Servants stopped before it, turning tail to stare at me and Jenna. 'Go,' said the dolphin-shape. 'The Ancient is waiting.'

'Is this a portal?' Jenna asked. Her voice shook and her hands tightened in my mane. Was she afraid?

'No,' said the manta-shape. Then, almost as if the idea had never occurred to xir until now, xe added, 'No harm will come to you.'

'Avari?' she whispered in my ear. 'I'm...none of the portals looked like this.'

The pulse continued to thrum through me. Almost a heartbeat, something I had only experienced second-hand when Jenna's body touched mine.

'It's okay,' I said, filled with the truth of it. My fire harmonising with the fire around me, my core thrumming in a beautiful beat. If a small part of me was afraid, I knew it to be irrational.

I belonged here.

And, when Jenna murmured her assent and pressed her face into my mane, I swam between the Servants and stretched out my neck until my nose touched the oily membrane of the ovoid. It felt oddly slick and pliant, and then with a great sucking tide, we were pulled in and everything was fire and shadow.

VEO CORVA

Chapter Twenty-Seven

We floated in a void of distant stars. No water, no earth, no membranous ovoid in a coral temple. All of it meaningless in the face of the Ancient.

It towered over us even in this vast space. Larger than a treelding, as large as the Flowering Ancient whose canopy brushed the atmosphere. Dozens of wings, some trembling, some curling across its body, some incredibly still. Bands of eyes surrounded it, each made of vari-coloured flame, each blinking and looking around independently, as if there was much more to see than just the tiny cosmoran and human supplicants before it. And in the centre of those wings and eyes, the shadowy shape of an enormous snake, that flickered and reformed into a cat, that flickered and reformed into a spider, that flickered and reformed into a fish. On and on it changed, wings furling and unfurling around it.

My entire body quivered, full of energy and awe. This was the original cosmoran. The other half of the tree from which all cosmorans hatched. This was the Starfire Ancient.

It pulsed, energy rippling through me. Every part of me felt that pulse. It resonated deep within my core. But now something else came along with it. A whisper of thousands of voices, speaking a language I couldn't parse. My reverence became tinged with confusion. I was cosmoran; I understood all language.

Jenna sat up on my back. 'I don't know,' she said. I turned my head, but she wasn't looking at me.

The shadow at the heart of the Starfire Ancient continued to change, shifting from a wolf to a butterfly to a phoenix to a scorpion.

Another pulse, full of incomprehensible whispers. I concentrated but there was neither the static of a word my starfire couldn't translate nor the clarity of understanding.

'Do I have to choose?' asked Jenna. Her voice shook and her fingers tightened in my mane. 'Can't I be more than one thing?'

The Starfire Ancient became a dragon, a giraffe, a ram. Some of its many flaming eyes shifted to me. Another pulse. Jenna spoke, but her voice fell away as the whispers all around me became one, coherent and piercing.

Fear not, grandchild. This is a moment of joy.

Then the whispers became disparate and alien once again, fading with the pulse of energy.

Jenna said, 'Something strong and soft and comfortable at rest. Something that when it bears its teeth, people take notice.'

More whispers, as strange and distant as stars.

Jenna said, 'I am.'

The Ancient ram inclined a head with horns incredibly similar to mine. Jenna rose from my back, the ropes falling away. I stretched out my neck, reaching for her, but she was already too far.

Was this safe? She was in the domain of the Starfire Ancient. I knew to my core that the Starfire Ancient would never hurt a cosmoran. But Jenna was human, and fragile in so many unexpected ways so far from the world that birthed her. She was so tiny in the vastness of space. Before the vastness of the living deity that had created my kind.

My fur stood on end. The Ancient had every reason to hate humans. I thought of the First Heartbreak. Of all the cosmorans that had looked on Jenna with fear or hate because of the cruelty of others of her kind. Would the Ancient understand that not all humans were like that? I tried to open my mouth to plead with it, to tell it that Jenna was one of us, that humans could be as good or bad as any cosmoran, but there was a pressure building that crushed the air from me and robbed me of my voice.

Jenna drifted out up and ahead, rising before the Starfire Ancient. I tried to swim toward her but my movements were meaningless in this place. There was nothing to gain purchase against.

But Jenna...she looked relaxed, except for a strange clenching and unclenching of her hands.

The rings of flaming eyes surrounding the Ancient broke and snaked toward Jenna like ribbons of vari-coloured fire. They circled her, wrapping ever tighter. Enclosing her legs, her arms, her torso, her head, even the tail of her plait. She became a woman not of flesh but of starfire eyes, burning star-bright and yet I couldn't look away. Her pose didn't shift.

Then the fire flared brighter and she became a ball of flame and she screamed *so loudly* and I was screaming too, my voice swallowed by the void, my desperate strides and strokes accomplishing nothing, getting me no nearer.

Please, I begged the Ancient with every part of my mind and soul. *Don't hurt her. Let her go. Let her go!*

The Starfire Ancient shifted again. No longer a ram, but a cat with oversized canines. The fiery sphere burst, the rings flying back to the ancient. But Jenna wasn't inside it anymore.

Instead, there was a cat. A burly smilodon, long-toothed and high-backed, with a tall brushy ruff that followed her spine and sandy fur that shone gold in the dancing light of the Ancient's fire. A cosmoran.

'Oh my god,' said the smilodon-shape, her voice a deep purr and yet utterly familiar. She lifted her paws and stared at them. Claws emerged as she flexed them. 'Oh my god!'

The Starfire Ancient shifted again, and again. Swan, vole, shark. It pulsed again, the whispers lost to me.

'I will, I promise I will!' said the smilodon-shape. She turned to look at me, her short tail wiggling in excitement. 'Avari!'

The terror of before had fast melted into confusion. I felt sluggish, overwhelmed. 'Jenna?'

And then we were shunted away from the Starfire Ancient, away from the wings and the eyes and the sparkling void, and I felt something membranous break at my back, and then the world shifted on its axis and we were ejected from the oily ovoid. My back gently bumped into a pillar of coral as I tried to get my bearings, righting myself in the water. The smilodon-shape spun out beside me, laughing and struggling to swim as might a fruit-fur kit in water for the first time. Indeed, her fur was as short and soft as the fruit-fur of any hatchling.

The Servants of the Ancient approached. 'Who is this?' asked the manta-shape. 'Where is Jenna Hughes?'

'It's me!' said the smilodon-shape. 'I'm Jenna! I'm...give me a moment, I think...' Her starfire flashed and in a burst of light her whole body changed. A human again, drifting in the water. I swam hurriedly over to her.

'Are you okay? What did it do to you?'

She looked like herself. Dark hair in a long plait. Smiling, flat human face. Her waterskin was unchanged.

'I'm fine,' she said. 'I'm better than ever. Avari...I'm cosmoran now.'

'You're...?' I trailed off, staring at her.

There were stars in her eyes.

Epilogue

Cloud and I arrived at the flitter spot at the same time. 'Hi!' she said, bounding up to me, her tails curled into question marks. 'It's been too long!' She sniffed me politely and I stuck out my hoof to shake, human style. She laughed and touched her paw to it.

I hadn't seen her since before Jenna's trial. She looked as bright and excited as ever, her blue-and-grey calico splotches making her look like a brewing rainstorm, her wide eyes bright and sparkling. She was wearing a red lace cloak with a hood that accommodated for her ears. Like me, she had baskets hanging across her back, though hers looked stuffed compared to mine, the lids barely hooked closed.

'You still smell sort of like ocean,' said Cloud, wrinkling her nose thoughtfully. She had a very pale pink nose. It looked like velvet.

I sighed, my ears going back.. 'Yeah. I keep washing but the salt smell is really soaked in. I think some of it must've got into my core.'

'I like it,' she said. My ears perked in surprise, but she only slitted her eyes and looked away in a mysterious cat-smile.

Above us, the flitter descended, wings whirring, from the floating islands above Lost Circle's Purple Gardens. They looked not so much like a collection of floating rocks as a small shattered island, each part with its own tiny ecosystem growing on it.

But we weren't heading to the satellite islands. We were heading to the enormous central island dominated by the large blossom tree growing from it. The Circle Tree. From here, we couldn't really make out much of the surface, but I knew preparations were likely already under way.

'So what's the big secret?' Cloud asked.

I shuffled my hooves and lowered my head to look at her. 'Uh. Secret?'

Cloud laughed, her whiskers dancing. 'I *know* you know what it is. Nila says Jenna has some big reveal for us, other than celebrating that she gets to stay on Geminus.'

I stared fixedly at the flitter as it carefully landed on the bare patch of short grass in front of us. Jenna hadn't told me she was planning to reveal the Starfire Ancient's gift to her today, but I knew she'd been planning to tell people soon. It was something I still struggled to get my head around myself. Jenna could transform between human and smilodon-shape almost at will, and her human form was no longer completely human below the surface. It was something Vya and Illusion were working together to investigate.

Jenna was cosmoran now. More than that, she could shapeshift. It wasn't *true* shapeshifting. We knew that cosmorans' past could take any shape granted by the stars, and were not limited to two as Jenna was. Nor had any cosmoran ever taken the shape of a human.

There were stories, of course, of cosmorans granted shapeshifting by the Starfire Ancient. And even talk of a few shapeshifters still alive, somewhere, working with the Firecrafters' Union to pass on the magic. But it was still incredible that Jenna had two shapes. It was also a little frightening to contemplate, but Jenna seemed delighted.

'Penny for your thoughts?'

The words felt oddly staticy. 'Sorry?'

Cloud rolled her eyes. 'It's a human saying, expressing a desire to pay someone to hear what they're thinking.'

'Oh.' I paused. 'Weird.'

Cloud grinned, revealing her pointed canines. 'I know, right? Come on!' She bounded up and into the flitter, and I could do nothing but helplessly follow, as always seemed to be the case.

The flitter driver shouted a warning and the flitter took off. Cloud and I watched the ground fall away, both of us resting our chins on the rail. Lost Circle was huge, one of the largest cosmoran settlements on Viridus, nestled in the largest forest on Geminus, and yet it quickly shrank below us, becoming a patchwork of toy trees and map-line paths. After a moment, Cloud leaned her head very gently against mine. I swallowed hard and my flame danced nervously, even as my core soared.

THE OLD GOAT AND THE ALIEN

When the flitter landed, my forgetech leg got locked and I stumbled off the flitter. Flame pinkening and skin burning with shame, I set about loosening it again so it would work properly. While I fixed it, Cloud just stood beside me and chatted as casually as ever about what she'd made for the picnic, what her human friends on Earth had messaged recently, what her plans were for the next board game night. She was so nonchalant that my embarrassment had entirely faded by the time I was ready to head off. It was nice to head to the picnic together, Cloud silently keeping pace with my heavy hoofsteps.

It was beautiful up here. I'd only been a few times before, when Frost had dragged me along to festivals held here. It wasn't normally permitted for people to visit, so we'd had to get special permission, which Elm had sorted out as efficiently as they did everything else. Distantly, I could see the Circle Tree, a lone and towering figure. The roots of the tree created a vast curving shelter, keeping off the worst of the wind, and the ground was largely clear of tall brush thanks to the tree's hunger.

At this distance, I could make out that there were a few people there but not much detail. I focused instead on the journey over, a trail that cut through brambles, bushes, and tall waving grasses studded with purple flowers. Cloud no longer chattered but the quiet was comfortable. When we caught each other's eyes, she would smile and look away, tails twitching lazily. When I looked back the way we'd come, I could see others arriving by flitter. We both flared our flames at them, a polite greeting at a distance, and Cloud got on her hind paws to wave.

When we arrived within the sheltered curl of the Circle Tree's roots, Jenna, Elm, and Frost were already there and setting up. Jenna was placing pots of various flowers around, attracting delighted songbees and flutterbugs that filled the area with music and light. Frost was laying out various quilts and woven blankets, Night and Illusion arguing with each other over the placement while Storm laughed with Elm, whose arms were laden with baskets.

We all greeted each other with warmth and friendly sniffs and muzzle-touches, and then Cloud started unpacking her baskets, which included a small fold-out table, and lectured Elm on the proper way to set up a buffet. I watched for a moment, my core warmed with some barbed but not unpleasant emotion I couldn't name, and went to join Jenna instead.

She smiled up from where she was settling a pot in the dirt, careful to keep it level. 'I'm hoping people will enjoy some flowers around us,' she said. 'I know cosmorans don't usually cart plants around with them but I wanted to brighten things up.'

'It looks good,' I assured her. There was something about the patches of colour and scent they brought that brightened up the area, and it seemed very Jenna. They all bloomed so beautifully, petals open to the sun. 'Did you garden these?' I asked.

Her smile turned lop-sided. 'Not the way you mean,' she said. 'Just the human way with hands and dirt. I do want to learn cosmoran gardening, but...it's not something I'm likely to pick up myself, and nobody at the union knows I'm part-cosmoran yet.'

'And how's your energy?' I asked her.

Her smile fully became a frown. 'Well...not great. I've overdone it with the planning, I think. I'll probably suffer tomorrow. But it'll be worth it.' She nodded determinedly.

A screech of laughter came from behind us; I turned to see Cloud rolling on her back in hysterics while Elm blushed but looked pleased.

'Are you really going to tell everyone today?' I flicked one ear back and stamped my hooves lightly to ground some restless energy. 'Cloud was asking me about a "big reveal".'

Jenna started to fuss with the plants, hiding her expression. 'That's the plan. I figure it'll be better to get it all over at once.'

I thought of her wrapped in the flaming eyes of god. Of the shock of our companions when we returned. Of the shock I still felt.

'Are you sure?'

Her shoulders tensed. She didn't look up.

I sighed. 'I'm sorry, Jenna, of course you're sure. It's just...it's a lot to take in.' And I wasn't sure everyone would take it well. Even if Jenna wasn't the first or only shapeshifter, even if she wasn't a true shapeshifter like our stories told us...she had still been given a gift from the Starfire Ancient. Maybe it was a gift people would resent. Or wouldn't understand, as strange as it was.

People were difficult, and not everyone was kind. Or realised they were being unkind.

Jenna brushed the dirt and leaf mulch from her gloved hands, peeled off her gloves, and faced me. 'You're excited for me, aren't you?' She gripped one arm with the other, gloves crumpled in her dangling hand. It was difficult to see sometimes, as small as she was, but even in this form, her dark eyes were filled with as many stars as any cosmoran.

I shifted my hooves and lowered my head to look at her eye to eye. 'I'm a grumpy old goat,' I told her. 'I hate change just because it's change. But—'

'But?'

I sighed. 'But of course I'm happy for you. I know you. And maybe I'll get to know you for a lot longer than I would have.' I had been trying so hard not to think about the fleeting nature of human lifespans. Now it felt like a muscle I hadn't known I was clenching had relaxed.

And my thoughts kept returning to the words of the Starfire Ancient, resonating in my core and fiame. *Fear not, grandchild. This is a moment of joy.*

Mostly, I kept thinking that joy and fear were not mutually exclusive. That Jenna was going to face things I had never and would never have to. That although she wanted to belong to both humans and cosmorans, there were going to be people who'd make her feel like she didn't belong to either.

Jenna couldn't hear my worried thoughts and she was still learning to read flames. She only smiled at my words. 'I hope so. Wouldn't that be wild?' she said. 'We can be friends...I don't know, for centuries? Does that happen often here?'

We lived for hundreds of years. Mates found each other, then separated and found new mates. Friends changed. The world changed.

But some things lasted. 'It happens when it matters,' I said. It would happen for us.

As more folk arrived, the picnic started to come together. Cloud oversaw the layout of all food and drink, pointing people to this table or that blanket with strict instructions. Ever brought a large patchwork canopy made of scrap cloth in all patterns and colours, which Frost and Vya helped set up, sheltering us from the heartstar's rays as well as the constant rain of blossoms. A group of musicians set up on one of the roots, perched all in a line. I didn't recognise them at first, but then I noticed the familiar jackalope-shape testing out the position of her drums.

'Hi Keera,' I said as I wandered over. She was setting up the drum set with the same precision and intensity she put toward setting up her human tech devices. 'I didn't know you were a musician.'

I sniffed politely toward her but she only flicked one long ear at me while she tested reaching the drums with her hind feet.

'I'm a member of the Musicians' Union,' she replied tersely. 'This is my job.'

I had thought forgetech was her job, but I didn't say as much. Maybe I had devoted myself wholly to cleaning, but that didn't mean other people couldn't have more than one passion.

Other folk from the Internet Café arrived and formed a cluster on a blanket embroidered with a large human hand. I went to greet them. Mers invited me to a lake trip later that week. Shade fluffed her feathers and continued to read her data crystal. Nila inclined his head to me, uncharacteristically quiet.

I gestured for him to step aside with me. 'You know about Jenna's plan?' I asked in a low voice.

He nodded his broad, spotted head. 'She has to do it sometime,' he said. 'It's not the kind of thing you could keep secret, even if you wanted to.' He studied me, ears perking thoughtfully. 'I'm not her guardian anymore,' he said. 'But if she needs me, I'll be there.'

I dipped a small bow in thanks.

Nila hesitated. 'Want to join us?' He nodded toward the café crowd.

I hesitated. 'Maybe later.'

It was so much busier than I'd thought it would be. There were people from the market, people from the Gardeners' Union, and a lot of people I didn't even recognise. There were other humans among the crowd, too. Just a few, but more than I had ever seen in one place. It struck me how different these humans looked from Jenna and Elm in shape, size, and dress. Perhaps humans were just as varied as cosmorans afterall.

'Avari!' A familiar cackle accompanied my name. I turned just in time for my silver-furred raccoon-shape sister to launch herself onto my back, throwing her arms around my neck.

'Personal space,' I grumbled. I gave a small buck, shaking her a bit, and she laughed and skittered off my back. 'How's Lightning Valley?'

She smiled and her flame flared a warm and cheerful orange. 'It's everything I wanted it to be,' she said. 'I have so much to do! I joined six unions.'

I snorted. 'Made any friends?'

'Obviously! I do miss Lur, though. Is he here yet?'

'Haven't seen him.'

She sniffed the air and then her ears perked and she spun around. 'They're here!' she bounced over to them, her long stripy tail flowing after her. And there they were, coming up the same path I had only a short while earlier. Nova waved one taloned bird-hand while my lizard-shape mother scolded our brother, whose fox face transformed from subdued to excited as he clocked Bloom.

I looked for Journey, but couldn't spot her among my clustered family. Perhaps she was riding on Nova's back again?

I started toward them, then felt a tickle at my flank. A little fawn had reared up onto her hind legs, tiny feather-wings flared and trembling as she sniffed at me.

'Journey!' I sniffed her back and she bumped her nose against mine. Warmth sparked in my core. Even as young as she was, she remembered me.

Journey play-bowed, tuft-tailed rump in the air, wings fluttering, and I found myself bowing back. She squeaked at me and started to gambol around, and though I was a bit large and heavy, I bobbed around as well. Delighted, she started to race in circles around me. I spun and plucked at her tail with starfire as she went, causing her to shriek and kick and run faster.

Finally, she stopped, panting and rubbed her face against my chest, her muzzle disappearing into my mane and beard. 'I missed you, too,' I said, and resolved that I would visit more. This was worth any vitriol my mothers spat my way.

'Who's this?' Cloud appeared from behind us, as silent as ever, and sniffed politely at Journey.

Journey circled under my legs and peeked uncertainly up at her, but I gave her a gentle nudge and she stepped forward to sniff back. 'Cloud, this is Journey. She hatched only a year ago.'

So incredibly young. She still had her fruit-fur, all short and soft, but she was already becoming so brave and clever.

Cloud smiled, baring sharp teeth and slitting her large eyes. 'I'm Cloud,' she said. 'Your sibling is a dear friend of mine. We play human board games together.'

Journey's ears perked at the word 'human'. Jenna had made quite the impression on her.

'What kind of games do you like to play?' Cloud asked her.

Journey's ears twitched and she dropped into a play-bow again. 'She's not talking yet,' I said to Cloud. 'But she seems to really enjoy being chased.'

'You do?' Cloud made her eyes wide as she put her face down close to Journey. 'What a coincidence! I love chasing!' She bowed low, tails in the air, rump wiggling, and Journey squeaked in delight and ran away. Cloud bounced after her, much slower than I'd ever seen her move, swiping at the air behind Journey with her claws sheathed. Suddenly, she turned and leapt toward me. 'Don't think you're getting out of this!' she said.

I snorted and skipped away from her lightning-fast swipe. Her eyes glittered with mirth. She growled and sprung at me with such ferocity and distance that I was utterly unprepared. I baaed a laugh as she bowled me over. She landed with her paws braced on my chest, her mis-matched eyes aglow and pupils expanded, her tails lashing the air behind her.

'You're beautiful,' I said without thinking, then immediately blushed all the way through my starfire. Cloud's eyes wavered, and I saw her flame pink too, but she didn't cringe.

Journey beeped triumphantly and bounced over to brace her hooves against me the same way Cloud did. I laughed and touched my nose to hers. 'You got me!' I told her.

Cloud said, 'Ah, but can you catch me?' and leapt away, with Journey cackling and chasing after her on her stilty fawn legs.

'Friend of yours?' a voice at my shoulder asked. I turned to face Nova. She watched Cloud and Journey race around with a gently flickering flame, and I could read nothing in the set of her wings or the stance of her tail.

'Yeah,' I said. 'That's Cloud.'

My other mother slithered up on my other side, claws digging into the dirt. 'Good to see you're finally meeting people other than your siblings,' said

Teera. Her tongue tasted the air thoughtfully. 'I knew if you only applied yourself, you'd manage.'

I considered my mothers as their words started to weigh me down. I knew they thought they were being complimentary, just as well as I knew that nothing I could do would stop them heaping judgement on me. And normally that would make me *so angry* and yet right now...in Lost Circle, surrounded by friends and friendly folk, I found it didn't strike me the same way. It just made me tired. 'It is good,' I agreed evenly, and left it at that.

'Hey, Avari?' Mers approached, three of their heads smiling at me while one stared at Teera with unblinking draconic focus. 'Want to join us? We're thinking of getting a game going. Keera got hold of some kind of human bluffing game.'

'Sounds great,' I said, glad of the excuse. 'I'll see you later,' I told my mothers. 'Make sure you say hi to Jenna.'

As I followed Mers away, they said, 'You okay? We overheard your mothers and didn't want to just leave you there. They were very rude!'

My ears flicked forward hopefully. Mers was normally so calm, but all of them seemed absolutely indignant. 'I'm okay,' I reassured them. 'So there's no game?'

'Oh, there's a game,' said Mers. 'I'll have Keera explain it to you. It sounds awful; Cloud will probably love it.'

And so the afternoon passed comfortably. I settled among my friends and didn't feel much urge to go elsewhere. We played one game after another and even attracted some curious others.

'It's almost like we're not the outsiders,' said Shade, puffing up their feathers comfortably.

'There are too many of us to be outsiders,' said Keera, sensibly.

And I supposed it was true, that although we were all odd in our own ways, we all had each other so it didn't matter.

Cloud spent most of the day bouncing between us and keeping the buffet in order. My siblings joined us by turn and Lur seemed shyly taken by the group. Mers gave Journey rides around the area. Jenna had too many friends here to spend the whole time with us, but she did join us for a few games, and whenever she did, I checked in.

'Okay?' I asked her.

She smiled nervously. 'Okay,' she assured me.

I resisted the urge to trail her when she went.

When Jenna finally climbed up on a root to make her announcement, I held my breath.

'So,' she said. 'Most of you know the Starfire Ancient summoned me after my traveller status was confirmed.' Her voice shook and I saw her lock her hands in front of her. 'What most of you don't know is that the Ancient gave me a gift. And...and I value all of your friendship so much. You have all been so kind and welcoming to me. So I want you to be the first to know. I'm still coming to terms with it myself.'

She talked on. About how she had always felt incomplete, or ill-fitting. About how transitioning had only alleviated some of that feeling. And returning constantly to how grateful she was to everyone, with words that shook so much I could *hear* the plea in them.

And then she transformed into that shining golden smilodon-shape, met first with gasps and then with cheers and questions. She was a human and a cosmoran both.

As she started to do the rounds in her smilodon-shape, I saw that although some were wary or confused, most were simply excited for her. She had chosen her friends well, and we would be there for her no matter what.

And so had I. My friends lounged around me on our broad picnic blanket, some excitedly speculating about what Jenna's transformation might mean, others continuing their card game as if humans shapeshifted into cats every day. My siblings talked amongst each other nearby while my mothers preened a sleepy Journey's feathers, and I found that, for once, I was at peace with them.

Cloud leaned her head against my shoulder and, much though I abhorred touch, I found I didn't want to move away.

'Things are pretty different than they were a year ago,' she said.

'Better different,' I said.

'Oh, definitely.' She paused. 'I wonder how I can honour Jenna's gift at the café? Some kind of colour-changing smoothie, maybe?'

I snorted.

Jenna had changed and she had changed things for the world. The Geminus Galactic Council had tried to declare that humans and cosmorans were different, but The Starfire Ancient itself had used Jenna to put that lie to rest.

I had always known that cosmorans were shapeshifters at their core, but perhaps humans were too. And Jenna, she was the link between us. Neither human nor cosmoran, but both at the same time, and something unique in the process. All of us contained multitudes: all the shapes that all the stars could make us. And all of us could change for the better.

And as good as things were, I wasn't done changing yet.

Acknowledgements

I swear I'm trying to write things with mainstream appeal...and yet here we are again, this time with a queer slice-of-life space fantasy where the protagonist is a magic goat.

And I won't lie...I love it. It's exactly the sort of story I always wanted to read. I wrote it to be a big warm hug, but magical. I hope that's something you've taken away from it.

As ever, I couldn't have published this book without help. Thank you first and always to my partner Joh, who is sounding board, first reader, and most helpful critic. Nothing I have written would ever have made it out of the idea stage without you.

Thanks also to my early readers Gwenfar, L Rowyn, and Azaliz. Gwenfar, your feedback told me I was on the right path. Rowyn, your insightful comments were a huge help and your cheerleading kept me going. Azaliz, you highlighted some important issues I'm pleased to have resolved.

This was the first book I worked on with a sensitivity reader. Sarah Washington, you are the best sensitivity reader anyone could have asked for. This book is so much stronger for your help. Thank you.

Thanks to Meg James, the cover illustrator. Meg, you were so pleasant to work with and your art is incredible. This cover is perfect. Not all authors get to say that!

And finally, I couldn't do this whole writer thing without the folk who support me financially. Thanks to Gwenfar, Lara, L Rowyn, Sophie Jane, StoryDragon, and Tak! as well as others not named here. You have all decided to support a small, weird writer and see what they make. Well, this is it! I hope you enjoy it. I'm sure the next one will be even weirder, despite my best efforts.

Special Thanks

The Old Goat and the Alien was crowdfunded on Kickstarter because I could not have afforded the costs of publishing without help. And a whole load of generous folk came forward and pledged to turn it from a bunch of text on my hard drive into a real book with cover art and everything. This will never stop being magical to me and I am deeply grateful.

With that in mind, I'd like to thank the following people:

Aily Enne, Alana Post, aletheridae, Alex Burka, Alex Q, Alex T. Dragonson, Alexis W., Algot Runeman, Alzbeta, Anke Wehner, Anna Balade, Annie Herrmann, Anonymous, Azaliz, Bas van Haastregt, Ben Hamill, Ben Kramer, Brooks Moses, Brynn Willows, Caleb, Captain Packrat, chimerical girls, Chris Walker, Cyberfossil, D. Moonfire, dana garner, Dominika Zgud, E, Eko Punataival, Elizabeth Somervell, and Erik DeBill.

Thanks also to Fallenaltair, Femke Schelvis, Flo Songweaver, fluffyfied, Fool's Moon Entertainment, Inc., Francesco Tehrani, FRAUD, Gabriel Birke, gim, Gwenfar, Hannes Deeken, James 'Jubal' Baillie, Jamie Turnock, Jay Vivian, Jessa Frost, Jon Kelly Hays, josh giesbrecht, Kas Stark, katre, L. Rowyn, L.J. Lee, Leifi, Leonora Tindall, LilFluff, Liliana, Lilith Blackthorn, Lirleni / Vik-Thor Rose, Louzie, maloki, Max Turner, Michael Warren Lucas, Mistress Rose, MKN, neeneko, Neil Hart, Neo, nethope, and Noam Bergman.

And thank you to Olivia Montoya, Paige Kimble, Paul Whittaker, pawsies, Rebecca Södergren, Ri Guijt, Rob & Jenny Haines, Robin Swift, S Arrowsmith, S. J. Schuchart Jr., Sage Sharp, Sanguine Kitty, Sarah Russell, Sario, Sasha Fox, Sean Manning, Shea Alberson, Sophie Jane, Stephen with a ph, Tak!, tastytea, Terrana, Terri Oda, The Selkie Delegation, Violet Holland, VKNask, Vorindi, WildSolcte, Willard Goosey, Yncke, Zatty, Zeta Mercy Syanthis, and others who have chosen to go unnamed.

VEO CORVA

This book would not have been published without your support.

Sign Up For Publishing Updates!

If you'd like to receive an email every time I announce or publish a new book, and not at any other time, please do sign up for my newsletter! As an indie author, this is the best and most reliable way to hear about new releases.

Go to https://veocorva.xyz/publishing-updates/ to sign up now.

Thank you!

About the Author

Veo Corva writes things and reads things and reads things out loud, and sometimes they get paid for that, which is nice because it means they can feed their cat.

They live in Wiltshire with their partner and their furry familiar and as many books as they could fit in their small flat.

They are anxious and autistic and doing just fine.

Read more at https://veocorva.xyz.

www.ingramcontent.com/pod-product-compliance
Lightning Source LLC
Chambersburg PA
CBHW020052030726
47498CB00006B/1747